VENDETTA

VENDETTA

ROBERT WANGARD

AMP&RSAND, INC.

Chicago • New Orleans

Copyright © 2018 Robert Wangard

ISBN 978-0-9985222-9-6

Design
David Robson, Robson Design

Published by
AMPERSAND, INC.
515 Madison Street
New Orleans, Louisiana 70116

719 Clinton Place
River Forest, Illinois 60305

www.ampersandworks.com

———

www.rwangard.com

Printed in U.S.A.

PROLOGUE: THE FUNERAL

On a steamy mid-August morning when the temperature had already crept into the low nineties, the Sears & Whitney partners and former partners gathered at Our Lady of the Faith Catholic Church on Chicago's west side to celebrate the life of Angela Frances DeMarco, the law firm's first woman managing partner. They filed into the church in pairs according to seniority in the firm. Like all proper mourners, they wore navy blue or charcoal gray in spite of the suffocating heat.

Pete Thorsen took his seat in a pew near the head of the reserved section. The partner on one side of him was a man who'd started with the firm on the same day he had and now was a department head. On the other side was a woman who'd arrived a bit later, but left three years after becoming a partner to join the legal department of one of the firm's largest clients. She was now its general counsel.

He chatted with each of them briefly and then immersed himself in the single-fold program with Angie's color portrait on the cover. She gazed back at him with her bright, impish smile. The inside chronicled her life, something he already knew well: B.A. from DePaul University;

J.D. from the Northwestern University School of Law; nine years with the Cook County State's Attorney's Office and then a partner in Sears & Whitney; membership in the Woman's Athletic Club where she served on its board of directors; Chicago Economic Club; and a host of other professional and civic associations.

The past twenty-four hours were little more than a blur in his mind — the call advising him of Angie's death; his shock over the news; the disappointment at not being able to make her wake because of a twenty-seven-car pileup on the Interstate that choked off traffic into Chicago for nearly three hours.

After checking into his hotel, he'd walked aimlessly through the streets, alone with his thoughts, stopping in front of the steel and glass tower where Sears & Whitney had its offices, trying to identify the floor where he'd spent twenty years of his life, and then visiting Gibsons Bar & Steakhouse, the site of so many power dinners over the years, many with Angie.

Murmurs rippled through the gathered mourners. Pete shook off his reverie and watched Angie's family file into the first pew. Women in somber dresses and an array of broad-brimmed hats, several school-age children, a scattering of men including a silver-haired gentleman in a wheelchair with a blanket across his lap in spite of the torrid weather outside. Pete stared at the procession and wondered who each of them was. As long as he'd known Angie, he'd never met any of her family.

Since entering the church, he'd tried to avoid staring at the casket draped with the white pall, but there was something magnetic that made it difficult to ignore. His eyes settled on it for a while until he willed them to look elsewhere. Inadvertently, he made eye contact with the former partner seated next to him. She tightened her lips and her expression conveyed her sadness. He nodded slightly and gazed around the church some more.

Everything grew hushed as a priest rose to his feet and made some introductory comments, then segued into the funeral Mass. Whenever he uttered Angie's name, it rang in his ears like a faraway echo: *Angela*

Frances DeMarco, Angela Frances DeMarco. . . . The strains of Johann Sebastian Bach's "Ave Maria" seemed otherworldly, too.

Then it was over and Pete waited his turn to file out. When he reached the sidewalk, he found himself elbow-to-elbow with other mourners who were milling around or talking in subdued voices. Men tugged at their collars or loosened their ties, and women fanned themselves with their programs. On the street, the attendants had just closed the rear door of the hearse and he watched it pull away from the curb for the final journey.

The Sears & Whitney partners congregated together in small groups and chatted animatedly, like they'd just come from Wrigley Field and were rehashing the Cub's victory over some historic foe. He knew many of them, but didn't join any of the groups. While he had fond memories of the firm and it had been his life for a long time, he didn't feel part of it anymore.

He sized up the crowd and plotted a route he could take to depart gracefully without the awkward goodbyes and the handshakes and the lame jokes about how great it must be to have nothing to do every day except hit the links and then spend time in the nineteenth hole.

Steve Johnson, the law firm's administrative partner, tugged at his sleeve. "Sad day, huh?" he said.

Pete nodded. "Any more details about how the car fire started?"

"Not that I've heard. I talked to one of our litigation partners who does product liability work and he told me the SUV model Angie drove had some recall notices because of a gadget associated with the fuel line. He thinks it could have been that."

Pete processed what Johnson said. "Has anyone from Angie's family called and asked the firm to look into it?"

Johnson shook his head.

"Maybe you should check in with them."

He seemed to consider it. "That's an idea. I think I'll wait a couple of weeks, though. The last thing a family wants at a time like this is to have a bunch of lawyers crawling all over them."

Pete nodded again.

Then Johnson got a wistful look in his eyes. "This is sort of a watershed for me. Remember when the three of us used to have our war councils, trying to decide whether some move would advance the firm's interests and calculating the amount of political capital we'd have to expend to pull it off? Now you're up north doing your thing and Angie is gone. I feel like the last trout in the pond."

Pete gazed at him sympathetically. Steve Johnson was a good man, but he and Angie had provided the real leadership when they were together. He tried to pump him up. "You'll be fine, Steve. It may take a while to get a new team in place, but you'll be fine."

They chatted a while longer, then said their goodbyes and promised to stay in touch.

Pete saw an opening and slipped out of the crowd and walked to his Range Rover. He tossed his suitcoat on the back seat, stripped off his tie, and slid behind the wheel. He'd have plenty of time to reminisce on the drive home. Too much, probably.

TWO MONTHS LATER

ONE

While the intrusion annoyed Pete, at least the unfamiliar car that had just rolled into his driveway was a plain vanilla sedan and not another flashy vintage convertible with Batmobile-style tail fins, a vehicle he couldn't help but associate with trouble.

He saved his document and moved his laptop to a nearby table and continued to watch the sedan with out-of-state license plates. From the vantage point of his screened porch, he could see a figure behind the steering wheel, but couldn't make out whether it was male or female. Or what the person was doing. Nothing had happened since the sedan arrived five minutes ago.

Finally, the driver's side door swung open and a woman got out. She began stretching, and with the October sun low in the sky, the rays struck the screen in front of him at an angle that created a gauzy effect and made her look almost ethereal. Pete leaned forward in his wicker chair for a clearer look and his eyes widened.

The woman continued to go through her stretching routine, tilting her upper body to one side, then tilting it to the other, and finally bending over several times to touch her toes. She arched her back twice before she reached into her car for her handbag and slung it over her shoulder. Then she adjusted her oversized sunglasses and glanced toward his house briefly before she walked to the narrow beach and gazed out at the lake. She stood with her hands in her jacket pockets and occasionally tugged at the scarf that dangled from her neck as if tightening it against the autumn chill.

Pete's mind was in overtime mode. *The hair,* he thought, *the face.* His mind flashed back to that suffocating day in August and the church and his conversations with his former law partners. *What's going on?* he wondered. It was like he'd been dropped into a make-believe land where diabolical forces were manipulating strings and playing with his mind.

His eyes remained glued on the woman. She strolled along the beach, occasionally kicking at some object in the sand, then gazed out at the water again, like she'd just returned to the summer home of her child-hood years after decades away and was reliving her youth. He knew that wasn't it, however. If the woman was who he thought she was, she'd been at the lake exactly once in her life.

Pete couldn't figure out why she didn't come to the house and thought maybe he should call to her. Memories of the service washed over him again, and he heard the music and the intonations of the priests and the hushed whispers of those who'd come to pay their last respects. And he thought about his conversation with Steve Johnson outside the church.

The woman retraced her steps, head bowed slightly. His thoughts were muddled as he heard her feet on the steps. Then her head appeared at the bottom of the porch screen and she looked at him and said in that throaty voice he'd heard hundreds of times, "Hi, Pete, mind if I come in?"

Still feeling he was in the middle of a bad dream, he got up from his chair and went to meet her. When he opened the inner door and peered through the screen, the woman he thought was dead smiled at him awkwardly.

"You seem surprised to see me," she said.

TWO

"Angie," he blurted out.

Her eyes met his briefly before she looked away. "I'm supposed to be dead, right?"

"I was at your funeral, for crissakes."

She sighed. "Can I come in?"

He held the screen door for her and she stepped past him and went to the porch where she gazed out at the lake. "It's so beautiful up here," she said. Then she dropped into a chair and leaned back and closed her eyes. "I'm really tired. I've been driving all day."

He stared at her for a few moments until his senses reengaged. A thousand questions fought to get out, but he held them in check and said, "Can I get you something? Water? Iced tea?"

"A glass of wine would be wonderful," she said, not opening her eyes.

He shot her a look and went to the kitchen and checked his refrigerator. Finding no wine, he grabbed a handful of ice cubes and dumped them into a water glass, took a stemmed glass from the cabinet, and walked to his wine rack where he selected a bottle of Pinot Grigio and opened it. He carried everything to the porch and moved a small table close to Angie's chair and set the bottle and glasses on it. He poured some wine and took a chair across from her and waited for an explanation that would make sense.

Angie opened her eyes and wiped them with a tissue. She took a sip of wine and swallowed, then dropped an ice cube into her glass and swirled it around with her finger. She gazed out at the lake again. His frustration built and he wanted to go over and shake the words from her mouth.

She looked at her glass and sipped more wine. Finally she said, "That wasn't me in the casket."

Expecting more, Pete couldn't avoid rolling his eyes. "Gee, that's a real revelation since you're sitting ten feet away from me."

She didn't say anything, but he saw the tear roll down her cheek and dialed back on his sarcasm. "Who was in the casket, then?" he asked. "Or was it empty?"

"My friend." She grabbed a tissue and wiped her eyes and blew her nose.

"Your friend."

"Kate Jeffers, a college friend. She . . ." Angie choked over the words and tears began to gush.

As he waited for her to compose herself, the lawyer in him started to take over, seeking logic in a situation that, on its surface at least, seemed wildly illogical.

Angie breathed in deeply and continued. "Kate was staying with me for a couple of days. One afternoon, she borrowed one of our cars to run down to Walgreens. A few minutes after she left the house, I heard this big explosion . . ." Tears flowed again.

Pete frowned.

"I went outside and saw flames at the end of our block. It looked like our SUV was on fire."

He stared at her, still not understanding.

"I was in shock. All these people were coming out of their houses to watch. Someone must have called the fire department because two fire trucks arrived. The firefighters tried to put out the flames, but I guess they were afraid of getting too close to the car. They probably thought the gas tank might explode, if it hadn't already, so they worked from a distance."

"What caused the explosion?"

"I pretended to be one of the street gawkers and asked a firefighter. He wasn't sure, but he thought a bomb might have been rigged in the car."

"You're kidding."

Angie continued to sob and blow her nose and dab at her eyes. "Poor Kate . . ."

"If it was a bomb, who do you think it was intended for?"

She sniffled some more. "Not Kate, that's for sure. No one even knew she was at my house. Except me, obviously."

Pete processed what Angie had just said. "That leaves your husband or you. Or both of you. Where was he when all of this happened?"

"The creep?" she asked, her voice taking on an edge that hadn't been there. "He was at our second home in Lake Geneva, supposedly on a golf outing with some of his scumbag pals. Since the explosion occurred in late afternoon, it's a safe bet that they were hanging out at that strip club up there, watching some skin show instead of putting for quadruple bogies on the sixteenth green."

Pete was aware of the DeMarco's tumultuous marriage because every time he had dinner with her and she had a couple glasses of wine, the flavor of their relationship would come out. He skirted the issue and said, "What did the police say when you talked to them?"

She gazed out at the lake again, and without looking at him, said, "I never talked to the police."

Pete's eyebrows raised. "Didn't they investigate? I thought the first thing they'd do once they identified the car would be to come to your house and question you and your husband. Or you if your husband wasn't home."

"Maybe they *did* come to my house, I don't know. I left before anyone came."

"You left."

"Don't you understand? I was scared."

The picture was finally taking shape in his mind. "So when the fire-fighters got the blaze under control, and they'd salvaged Kate's corpse from the vehicle, you let them believe the remains were yours, which explains the funeral. Then you took off."

Angie nodded and filled her glass again, added an ice cube, swirled it around, and took a sip. She seemed more composed.

He read the tea leaves and said, "Your husband thinks you're dead, too, right?"

"The creep? He's the reason the whole thing happened."

"Explain."

She poked her finger in the wine again and gave the ice cube another swirl. "Remember a few years ago when we were having dinner at Gibsons and I told you my husband associated with some really bad people? I'm no fool, and even before that, I believed he was involved with the mob because of the people he associated with. We both came from the same Italian neighborhood and I knew—or at least knew of—a lot of those people."

Angie poured some more wine and added another ice cube. "One night I overheard a conversation he was having with someone. He was angry—hardly unusual for him—and it was clear that he and one of his rivals within the organization were at odds. I heard the same thing another time, too. When the explosion occurred and I saw our SUV, I knew immediately what had happened. Those guys are all homicidal maniacs. If they didn't get him the first time, I knew they wouldn't stop trying. If I'd been in that SUV instead of Kate, I'd be dead. That's why I knew I had to get out of there."

"I can understand why you were spooked. But you have a law enforcement background. You could have gone to the police, told them your story and found a way out. Filed for divorce or something."

She laughed sarcastically and drank more wine. "You make it sound so simple. I would have actually *increased* my risk by filing for a divorce. How many mob wives have you heard about who've gotten divorced? They know better than to even try. I would have been compounding my problems."

Pete wasn't sure how to respond. "Are you *positive* Carmen's a member of the mob?" he asked.

"Oh yes, I'm positive."

He thought about that for a few moments again, then said, "I still don't see how you solved anything by running and letting a lie about your death stand. Haven't Kate's family or friends been looking for her? It seems to me your whole plan will fall apart at some point."

"Kate hasn't seen her family in years. As for her friends ... she moves around quite a bit. I'm the only one she was in regular contact with. We were sorority sisters in college and have remained close."

Pete stared at her for a while. "In a word, you're banking on the likelihood that no one will come looking for Kate and discover what really happened."

She didn't say anything, only gazed out at the lake again with a weary expression.

"Where have you been for the past two months?" Pete asked.

"In northern Wisconsin. A cabin on a small lake there. It's a family cabin, but Kate's the only one who ever used it. I'd been up there a couple of times before to visit her when I needed to get away."

"Why didn't you stay there?"

Angie shrugged. "I thought you'd be happy to see me." She sipped more wine.

"I *am* happy to see you. And also a little shocked. But is there another reason?"

She cradled the wine glass in her hands and looked down at it. "I was concerned that someone from Kate's family might come by and find me in their cabin."

Pete frowned. "Didn't you just tell me that Kate was the only one who used it?"

"I feel like I'm being interrogated."

"Sorry, I don't mean to interrogate you. But you show up here like Lazarus and tell me this wild story . . . I'm just trying to understand."

Angie took another sip of her wine. "I remember Kate telling me that her uncle visited the cabin once in a while to check on it. Maybe to winterize it or something, I don't recall exactly. It's October, so . . ."

Pete stared at her for a few moments. "Getting back to your main concern, if I understand what you said, you're afraid of getting caught between Carmen and the mob faction he's at odds with."

"Or even becoming a target as a way for them to get at my creepy husband."

"Why is becoming a target a concern if the entire world believes you're dead?"

Before she could answer, Pete's cell phone burred.

THREE

It was his stepdaughter, Julie, calling from Philadelphia.

"Hi, Sweetie," he said, shifting gears and trying to sound natural. "Work out on the Rocky steps today?" He was referring to the steps at the Philadelphia Museum of Art that were immortalized by Sylvester Stallone in the *Rocky* movies.

"Boy, that day really made an impression on you didn't it?"

Pete chuckled. "I thought I did a pretty good job of mimicking Rocky Balboa, though."

"Ahem, Rocky went up and down the steps like a gazillion times. I made *three* trips and could have gone for a lot more. You did it *once*."

"Hey, I've got to stay alive until I get you through college."

A pause, then, "Don't joke about things like that, Dad."

"Sorry. What's your workout regime these days?"

"Running mostly."

"Is that what colleges do in their offseason programs? Or is it more comprehensive?"

Another pause, longer this time. "That was sneaky, Dad, and I know where you're going. We've been through this ten times before. The admissions office knows about my decision and is holding my spot for next year. The soccer coach knows about it, too, and has confirmed that I'll not only be a walk-on next fall, but a *preferred* walk-on because I'll be stronger and more developed. It's all settled."

Angie must have picked up on the friction. She signaled that she could disappear for a while if Pete would like some privacy for the remainder of his conversation, but he motioned for her to stay.

"On another subject, how's your search for Leslie going?" Leslie was Leslie Lehr, a young woman who'd lost her job at a Philadelphia investment banking firm named Harrison Stryker as a result of the financial shenanigans of a man who'd been shot in what came to be known around the lake as the jet ski murder.

Julie's voice turned upbeat again. "No luck so far, but I think we might be onto something. Effie and I have been in contact with a guy at Harrison Stryker who went out with Leslie a few times. We're meeting him after work tomorrow to find out what he knows."

"Effie Zepp is involved in your search, too?"

"Well, yeah, Dad, I'm living with Effie and Aaron now. Effie knew Leslie really well and she's part of the team now."

"I wasn't aware you'd moved."

"It just happened. They have an extra bedroom even with the room they're using as a nursery for the baby. I'm paying them the same rent I was paying the old woman I was staying with, so its win-win for both sides. I have a place to stay where I'm comfortable, and they get some extra money which they really need."

"Okay."

"You sound upset."

"I'm not upset. I just didn't know."

"What's the big deal? How much snail mail do you send me these days? Like practically *none*. You call or email, just like other normal human beings."

Pete suppressed a sigh. It was just another of a string of things where Julie got her dander up recently whenever she thought he was infringing on her independence.

"Anyway," she said, "this guy stays in contact with Effie and a ton of other former employees. Dating your fellow worker is a no-no at Harrison Stryker, and he doesn't want word to get around that he violated the rules and took Leslie out. According to Effie, he's a real 'climber' and doesn't want to hurt his chances for promotion."

"Is he still dating Leslie?"

"We don't know. That's one of the things we hope to find out. Maybe they're even *living* together. Wouldn't *that* be something?"

Pete rolled his eyes. Another touchy subject where his old-school views collided with changing norms.

They talked about other things for a few minutes. Then Julie said, "You wouldn't be interested in coming to Philadelphia for a couple of days to see your favorite daughter, would you? We could see some sights and have a few, ah, *good* meals together." She lowered her voice. "Most of the time I eat with Effie and Aaron and I'm getting real sick of Hamburger Helper recipes."

Pete promised to get back to her. He ended the call and eyed Angie and smiled and shook his head a couple of times.

"That was your daughter I gather."

"Stepdaughter, but she's really like my daughter."

"I couldn't hear her end of the conversation, but it sounded like you handled things about right."

"You mean I wussed out every time she got worked up over something I said?"

"Backing off occasionally doesn't mean you've wussed out."

He shot her a look.

"Besides," she said, "I've known you for what, fifteen years give or take? In all that time, I think those of us who were close to you had to restrain you a lot more times than we had to encourage you to stop being Mr. Milquetoast."

"Dealing with your only daughter is trickier, and it's made more so by the fact that her biological father doesn't like my being part of her life. And," Pete added smugly, "that she calls me Dad and him Wayne."

Angie shook her head.

"Want to go for a walk along the beach while the sun's still out?" he asked. "Or was your stroll when you got here enough?"

"More exercise would be good. It'll help me work off the wine I drank, too."

After donning warmer clothes, they headed out. Angie stopped at her car to get a floppy hat and clamped it on her head. She stared at her car for a moment. "I'm blocking you, aren't I?"

He shrugged. "Just pull it alongside my Range Rover."

She glanced around the area. "Is there somewhere else I can park? You don't have a garage."

"Side-by-side is the best option. I don't know how long you plan on staying, but when the snow starts to fly, we might want to figure out something else."

She seemed to be grappling with the issue.

Pete noticed and said, "When a friend of mine came during the off-season last year, he parked behind the neighbor's house. I suppose we could do that again."

Angie went over and inspected the neighbor's property. She waved at him, then trotted out to the highway and looked back at it. After she returned, she said, "That'll work."

"When we get back from our walk," Pete said, "we'll unload the things you need and move your car. The neighbor won't be back until spring, so there shouldn't be a problem."

Angie pulled her hat lower and looped her arm through Pete's as they headed down to the beach. She appeared more relaxed.

"When was I here that time?" she asked, looking out at the lake and taking another deep breath.

He thought back. "Ten years ago, maybe? My wife Doris was still alive."

"And I was a struggling young woman trying to work her way up in that male-oriented jungle known as the Cook County State's Attorney's office."

"And about to become engaged as I recall."

She cringed. "You should have stopped me."

He looked at her. "What was I supposed to do? Buy you a couple of drinks some night, and when the moment was right, murmur in your ear that I hadn't met the man you planned to marry, but just knew he was all wrong for you?"

She squeezed his arm. "I like the murmuring part."

Pete suppressed a smile. Angie's flirtatious manner seemed to find a way to surface regardless of the circumstances.

"Kate *did* warn me, though. I just didn't listen."

Pete shot her a sly grin and said, "I don't recall being invited to your wedding. Was it because I wasn't a 'made' man?"

She either missed his innuendo or chose to ignore it. "Carmen and I were from the same Italian neighborhood on Chicago's west side," she said. "I'd already moved on and gone to college and law school and everything. He was still tethered to the hood, but he was dreamy-looking and I fell for his line about starting a tech firm that he'd take public as soon as it caught fire. Maybe we'd even move to Silicon Valley."

She laughed bitterly as she reminisced. "Tech firm, what a joke. The only thing technical about what the creep's doing is using a pair of pliers to operate on some poor bastard's fingernails if he doesn't make his juice loan payments on time."

"When did he get involved with the mob?"

She shrugged. "Who knows?"

They walked a little farther and Angie asked, "Did you talk to anyone at my funeral?"

"Steve Johnson, a few others."

"I assume Steve has been elevated to replace me," she said, sounding wistful.

"He has. I don't get much in the way of official firm information these days, but everyone including former partners got a copy of a press release the firm sent out saying that Steve has been appointed to fill the remainder of your term."

Angie nodded and her lips tightened.

They loafed along and she continued to hold onto his arm. He tried to steer the conversation back to her situation. "You've had two months to think about it. What's your plan going forward?"

Out of the corner of his eye, he noticed her jaw muscle twitch.

She didn't say anything for a while, then, "I'm too tired to get into it right now. Should we go back?"

They retraced their steps in silence. When they got to his house, they unloaded her car and moved her things into the second-floor guest bedroom, and parked her car on the neighbor's property. Pete tried to lighten the mood by telling her how Jimmy Ray Evans had piled brush on his Caddy convertible to further conceal it. Angie didn't seem to see much humor in his story and laid a few branches with dry leaves on top of her Toyota Corolla.

Inside, Pete built a fire in the fireplace. Angie stood close to absorb the warmth and looked at the framed photographs on the mantle. She took down one of Doris standing in a stream in waders, fly-fishing, and studied it for a few moments. "Lovely woman," she said. "How long ago did she pass away?"

Pete poked at a log with his fireplace tool and said without glancing up, "Nine years."

She nodded and brushed at the glass with her sleeve as though wiping away specks of dust. Then she returned the photograph to the mantle.

"You wouldn't have some food in your fridge, would you?" she asked. "I haven't eaten anything since breakfast."

Pete went to the refrigerator and surveyed the contents. "What I have," he called, "you probably wouldn't want to eat." He closed the refrigerator door. "I'll tell you what, though. We can go to The Manitou, which is a stone's throw away, and I'll buy you dinner. It's not Gibsons, but very passable."

Her face changed to a mask again. "I really don't want to fight the crowds."

"There shouldn't *be* any crowds on a weeknight at this time of the year. This isn't Chicago or New York."

She seemed ambivalent.

He noticed and said, "And if you're concerned that someone will see you and report that you've come back from the grave, I don't think you have to worry about that, either. I'd be shocked if there's anyone there except locals."

She seemed to struggle with his suggestion and finally said, "Okay."

"Let me call Harry McTigue and beg off my dinner date with him."

"I don't want to interfere with your plans."

"No problem. Harry will grumble about what a jerk I am for standing him up at the last moment, but he'll get over it."

"Are you sure?"

"Of course, I'm sure. Provided, obviously, that I salve his feelings by promising to have lunch or dinner with him tomorrow. And pick up the tab."

FOUR

The hostess with a sheaf of oversized menus clutched to her bosom asked, "Dining room or bar?"

Angie's eyes flicked toward the bar area where many of the booths along the window line were occupied and a half-dozen men in assorted camo attire and plaid shirts had laid claim to space near the mahogany bar and were boisterously rehashing their day and arguing about sports. She looked at Pete from beneath her floppy hat.

He read her body language and said, "Dining room, please. Is the back open tonight?"

The hostess put on a sad face and shook her head and said, "Sorry, not tonight. We're not expecting a big crowd."

Pete nodded.

They followed her into the main dining room where only a handful of tables were occupied. She was about to seat them when Angie said, "Do you mind if we take that table?" She pointed to one in the corner.

The hostess led them to the table without saying anything and gave each of them a menu. When she left, Angie adjusted her scarf and hung her hat on the back of her chair. She looked around and said, "Nice place. Kind of . . . woodsy."

Pete smiled. "Decent food, too."

He flipped over his menu and scanned the wine list. "If you didn't have enough wine this afternoon, there's a list on the back."

Angie studied it for a minute, then looked up and asked, "Are Michigan wines any good?"

"Some yes, some so-so."

"So if we wanted a bottle of our favorite Pinot Noir to celebrate the old days, would you suggest local? Or should we travel west to Willamette Valley?"

"I don't know anything about that particular Michigan vineyard," he said after checking the list again. "I'd go Willamette."

She nodded her agreement, and he ordered a bottle.

They went back to perusing their menus. The waitress came with their wine, and after witnessing the uncorking and going through the usual tasting ritual, Pete clinked Angie's glass and took a sip.

"I'd say happy reunion, but in the circumstances . . ."

Their eyes met briefly before she looked away again.

They discussed weighty subjects like the design and construction of old snowshoes and how to tell the difference between small-mouth and large-mouth bass.

Then Pete said, "When my stepdaughter called, we were talking about your concern about getting caught in the crossfire between mob factions or even becoming the target of the faction warring with Carmen. Explain that."

"What do you mean?"

"I'm hardly an expert on these things, but from what I've heard and read, mob wives usually aren't targets. Rivals for position or power might go after each other, or their underlings, but not the other guy's wife. Unless she's a snitch or something."

"You don't know those people. It's not like the Godfather movies where the little woman asks her fat husband not to forget the cannoli as he's going off to butcher some poor slob. Those guys use every weapon available to them."

Pete studied her. "Okay, I can accept that, but they'd still have to know you're alive, wouldn't they? How would they know that? Or even think to try to find out?"

She rolled her eyes. "When you're in my position, you don't assume *anything* in terms of what they know or don't know. You slip up once and run the risk of something jumping out and biting you."

Changing the subject, Pete said, "How did you like northern Wisconsin? I grew up seventy-five miles from where you were."

"I didn't see much of it, to tell you the truth. I sat by the lake a few times and listened to the loons. I made food shopping runs once a week attired in my lovely hat and frumpy pants."

"Mmm."

Angie took another sip of wine and said, "I can't tell you how good it feels to have someone to talk to again. The only human dialogue I've had in the past two months is with checkout ladies who asked if I wanted paper or plastic."

He smiled and didn't say anything.

Her eyes flicked around the room before they settled on him again. "You think I made a stupid decision, don't you?" she said.

"I never said that."

"You didn't have to *say* it. It's written all over you. The questions you asked, everything. Reading you is like reading a large-print book."

He raised his eyebrows and shook his head.

"It's easy to be a second-guesser if you're not in my position. I had to make a decision, and I made it, okay?"

"Trust me, Angie, I'm not second-guessing your decision. I know it was a traumatic situation and you didn't have days to consider options. I can't say I wouldn't have made the same decision if I'd been in your shoes."

She refilled her glass and sipped more wine and gazed around the room.

Their waitress came and they got their dinner orders in. While they were waiting for their food, they talked about their time together at Sears & Whitney. "Those were good days, weren't they?" she said nostalgically.

"A lot of fun," Pete agreed, preferring not to dwell on the negative things that had driven his decision to end his tenure with the firm.

When their food came, they talked some more about Sears & Whitney and people they both knew and some of their clients.

Afterward, Angie held up their wine bottle and squinted at it against the light. She dangled it in front of Pete, and said, "Do you think we've had enough? Or should we order another bottle?"

"No more for me. I'm driving, remember?"

Angie ordered a glass of the house Pinot Noir. "You know," she said with a mischievous glint in her eyes, "a lot of people in the firm thought we might be having an affair because you kept pushing me for plumb spots on firm committees and taking me out for lunches and dinners."

"I like to think I pushed you for committee assignments because of your ability and promise as a firm leader," he said defensively. "As for the lunches and dinners—other partners were there a lot of times, too. Steve Johnson, others."

"Not all the time."

"No," he agreed, "not all the time."

She put her hand over his. "Having an affair with me wouldn't have been such a bad thing, would it?"

"You are a married woman. I don't have affairs with married women."

She took a swallow of her fresh glass of wine. "You're blushing."

"It's the light from the candle."

"Uh huh."

Their waitress came and asked whether they wanted dessert or if she should bring their check. They agreed to split a piece of key lime pie, and the prospect of her favorite food course got her off the awkward subject.

❖ ❖ ❖

When they got back to his lake house, he didn't offer to uncork another bottle of wine, thinking they'd *both* had enough. Instead, he worked at rekindling the fire in his fireplace while Angie closed the drapes and started to browse through his music collection. He glanced up occasionally when he heard her snicker, anticipating some wisecrack.

"Well, at least you're consistent, Mr. Thorsen. Most of the classical music in your collection was composed a century or more ago and the same is true of your pop selections."

Pete had heard that comment before, usually from his stepdaughter, who like most younger people favored the incoherent mumbo-jumbo produced by "artists" he'd never heard of, or from Harry McTigue when he was trying to yank his chain, which was nearly every time they got together. He'd gotten used to it. He liked what he liked and had no interest in changing.

Pete poked at the fire again and called over his shoulder, "Good music endures, lady. Twenty-five years from now, do you think anyone will even remember Jay-Z's name much less the stuff he spews out?"

Angie ignored his defense of oldies and went on. "The classical music I can understand, millions of people appreciate that, but the rest of it? Jeez, some of this stuff was recorded before you were born."

Pete told her more about Jimmy Ray Evans, his army friend whose parking spot she'd coopted before they went to dinner. He explained that Jimmy Ray had his heart set on becoming a disc jockey specializing in early rock and roll and played the music in their squad room nonstop. He got hooked on the genre, he said, and stayed with it.

"So, did Mr. Jimmy Ray realize his dream of becoming a DJ?"

"He did. If even half of his stories are true, he's also done pretty well for himself."

"It sounds like you stay in contact with him."

"I've seen him exactly twice since we left the army. Five years ago, he called and basically invited himself up for a long weekend. A year ago he just showed up without calling."

"Like me, huh?"

Pete laughed. "Not exactly like you. After he'd been here for a week, I discovered that he was on the lam from a sheriff in North Carolina who was trying to frame him for murder and drug-dealing because he was bedding his wife."

"Wow, I'm impressed. You *do* have colorful friends. You should write a book. Is Jimmy Ray still in North Carolina?"

"I have no idea. When he left here—and I'll admit I was happy to see him go—he was headed for Mobile, Alabama to take a job at a radio station that's owned by another lady he logged sack-time with."

Angie shook her head. She put on a Patsy Cline CD and turned up the sound. She made her way around the room, hips swaying gracefully to the sounds of "Walkin' After Midnight." Between dips and an occasional swirl, she said, "This music makes me feel like I'm in a time warp, but it's kind of nice. Soothing."

Pete rose from his knees and stood with his back to the fire and watched her with an amused expression. She seemed, for the moment at least, back to the spirited woman he'd known for years.

As she got close to him, she asked, "Can you still dance? Or do you need your cane?"

"I never *could* dance."

"Oh, c'mon," she said, as she grabbed his arm and clasped her hands around his neck and began to sway again. He could feel her body against his as they moved around the room to the lyrics. The temptations he'd felt those nights at Gibsons, when the conversation shifted away from business and the wine flowed and her leg would casually press against his, surged again.

The Patsy Cline CD ran its course and Angie stopped dancing long enough to go back to the music collection and scan the CDs again. Without looking up, she said, "Are any of these people peppier than your friend Patsy?"

"Lots of them. Remember, these were the men and women who started the rock and roll genre."

"Such as . . ."

"Such as Buddy Holly, Little Richard, Jerry Lee Lewis . . ."

Angie ran her fingers along the rack for a while, then turned to look at him with an impish smile. "No one except a corporate lawyer would arrange two hundred CDs alphabetically by artist." She selected one and slid it in the player and the rhythmic sounds of Buddy Holly's "That'll be the Day" came blasting out. Her eyes widened and she squealed, "Wow!"

She pranced over to him and grabbed his hand again and went into an energetic jitterbug. Pete tried to keep up, but after five minutes, his stamina was flagging. He backed away and raised his hands in mock surrender and said "I'm going to take a break."

He went back to the fireplace and poked at the logs. Angie kept dipping and gyrating and turning, and he watched her in amazement. It must have something to do with gender wiring, he thought. Women who couldn't run a hundred yards without looking like they needed an oxygen pump seemed to be able to dance for hours without noticeable signs of fatigue.

Angie wound down and plopped into a chair next to him. "That was fun, huh?"

"It was."

She gazed at the fireplace mantle for a while. "Do you suppose Doris would approve?"

"Of what? Our dancing?"

"Yes, that's what we were doing, wasn't it?"

"I'm sure she would. But first she'd probably want to know who my stand-in was. She used to kid me all the time that I couldn't dance for more than thirty seconds without taking a break."

"Speaking of breaks, I'm bushed. I was dead on my feet when I got here, but you plied me with enough wine and food to bring me back to life for a while. Now I'm back to feeling like a zombie who wants to crawl back in the tomb."

Pete feigned surprise. "Bushed? I was about to suggest that we put on Little Richard and dance some more." He got out of his chair and did his best to gyrate around the room.

She laughed. "Now I know why you call yourself the Stud of the North."

"Umm, who started calling me that? Could it have been my law partner, Angela Frances DeMarco?"

She laughed again, said goodnight, and went up to her room.

He doused the fire and tidied up and then headed upstairs as well. After going through his nightly routine, he rolled into bed and turned out the light. Lying there, he realized how tired he was himself. He stared into the darkness and watched the shifting patterns on the ceiling as the moon moved across the sky, wondering about the story Angie had told him. And whether he'd have a visitor that night.

FIVE

ngie was still sleeping when he got up the next morning. He shaved and showered and used a brush on his unruly mop of sandy blond hair. He stepped on the scale and grimaced when he saw the readout. No need to measure himself, he thought cynically. According to what he'd read, his six-two height wouldn't begin to shrink until the onset of his senior years. He squirted some drops into his blue eyes and headed downstairs.

He made a pot of coffee and limited himself to one toasted bagel in view of what the scale had just told him. He left the remaining bagels and a selection of jams on the counter along with a note saying he'd gone to his office and would be back later that morning.

He took the scenic route to town. South Shore Drive hugged the water, and as he drove along, he marveled at the beauty of another splendid October day. The trunks of the birch trees that populated the sandy soil, once part of the lakebed before a nineteenth century entrepreneur unwittingly lowered the lake level, gleamed in the sunshine, their muted yellow leaves adding a touch of gentleness to the vibrant reds and oranges of the season. He breathed in deeply and expelled the air. On days like this, it was easy to forget about how he sometimes missed the action of his former law practice.

He found a parking spot in front of *The Northern Sentinel*'s offices. When he walked in, Harry was hunched over his computer pecking away at the keyboard with two fingers in his inimitable style. The tan sheepskin vest over a bright plaid shirt made his elliptical body look even more roly-poly than usual. He peered over his half-glasses and gave Pete the once-over.

"You missed a great dinner last night," he said. "Line-caught brook trout, *au gratin* potatoes, fresh green beans. It might have been the best meal I've had all year."

"Sorry I couldn't make it. Something came up."

Harry continued to scrutinize him, as though searching for some flaw in his dress. "That Jimmy Bob guy didn't show up again, did he? The one who's always on the run from the law?"

Pete laughed. "No, it wasn't Jimmy Ray," he said, indirectly correcting his name. "Besides, if it had been him, he would have insisted on having dinner with you."

Harry's face grew pensive. "You know, I kind of liked Jimmy Bob. Snazzy dresser, great sense of humor, showed a lot of pizzazz with the way his disc jockey equipment was decorated. And that hat. He played the same kind of dated music you like, but nobody's perfect."

"That 'dated music,' as you call it, is his trademark. To be a successful in the music business, you have to establish a brand. And you need to know your audience. Jimmy Ray scores on both accounts."

"The thing that got me," Harry said, "was when he started a fight at The Fish House and then we found out about those warrants for his arrest in North Carolina."

"All bogus. He was being set up. Framed."

"So you told me. I never saw any proof of it, though."

Pete rolled his eyes. "Changing subjects, do you remember the funeral I went to in Chicago in August?"

"Sure, your old law partner. Angie something or other. I met her when you had her up here a while back, remember? A real looker. Too bad about what happened. Her car caught fire or something."

Pete let Harry's characterization go and said, "I was talking to another of my former partners a few days ago. He tells me there's an ongoing investigation into Angie's death. I haven't seen anything about it in the newspapers up here, though."

"You don't know much about the news business, do you? An incident like that is local news along with fires and zoning disputes and elections for county clerk. It wouldn't be covered outside the Chicago area. Unless of course the deceased was someone like Princess Diana. Or maybe Michael Jackson."

"You wouldn't have a few minutes to —"

"Oh, God, here we go again. I can tell what you're going to ask even before you say a word. You want me to use my proprietary resources to see what I can find about this woman and the police investigation. I should start charging you for my services."

"Would you mind? As a fee, I'll spring for dinner at the place of your choice."

Harry took off his half-glasses and rubbed the bridge of his nose. Pete looked at him and waited, thinking he looked like the spitting image of Lou Grant, the newsman character in the hit television series from the nineteen seventies. Bald head except for a fringe of gray hair, broad face with bushy dark eyebrows, the half-glasses.

"With no right of cancellation on your part?" Harry demanded.

Pete nodded. "With no right of cancellation. Provided, of course, we agree on a date in advance."

Harry peered at him over his glasses and continued to eye him suspiciously. "You willing to put that in writing?"

Pete rolled his eyes again and waited.

"Okay, okay, forget the writing part. What's the woman's full name again?"

"Angela Frances DeMarco. The incident occurred mid-August."

"Any other information?"

"She's five-six, a lawyer, dynamite dresser . . ."

"No wise-guy, I mean any *important* information."

Pete shrugged. "With the Cook County State's Attorney's office before she joined Sears & Whitney, lived in the near west suburbs. Riverside I think."

Harry shot him a disgusted look. "You're damn lucky I'm so skilled at using the databases." He began pecking away at his keyboard.

Pete waited patiently until Harry muttered without looking up, "I think I've got something. Come around and have a look."

The two-column story from the *Chicago Sun Times* detailed how a woman named Angela DeMarco had been killed and her body incinerated when her car mysteriously caught fire and exploded. According to the story, the cause of the explosion was unknown, but it went on to speculate that it might have been due to a faulty fuel line. Harry found a story from the *Chicago Tribune* that said essentially the same thing.

Harry searched some more and found a raft of follow-on stories, including several that quoted an undisclosed source within the Chicago Police Department, which had been brought into the case, as saying that the mob might have had something to do with the incident because a second bomb had been found in another car in the DeMarco garage. The source also speculated that the bombs might have been intended for Carmen DeMarco, the deceased's husband, who was suspected of having ties to reputed mob kingpin, Vinnie Zahn.

Pete was stunned when he saw Zahn's name. He'd encountered Zahn some years earlier when he was representing the widow of slain real estate developer Les Brimley in financial matters related to her husband's estate. The mob secretly had been financing Brimley's golf course project, and when Pete unwittingly gave the widow advice they didn't like, his stepdaughter started being harassed and he was pressured to change his advice. He had to meet with Zahn to broker a truce.

He must have looked distracted because Harry waved his hands in the air and said, "Earth to Pete. Earth to Pete. You want copies of this stuff?"

Pete was about to nod when he remembered something else. "I do, but first, could you see if you can find anything on Carmen DeMarco?"

Harry scowled at him, but returned to his keyboard and extended his search.

As Pete waited again, he wondered if Angie knew about her husband's rumored connection to Zahn. It certainly corroborated her belief that Carmen had mob ties.

Harry finally found some information about DeMarco. The stories repeated the rumors about his alleged involvement with the mob, but besides that, the only new information was that he owned a string of dry cleaning shops on Chicago's west side.

"*Now* can I print?"

Pete nodded.

When the printer stopped grinding, Harry grabbed the sheaf of paper, and holding it away from Pete, said, "Now, about that dinner ..."

Pete knew he was going to have to do a soft-shoe because of Angie. He said, "I'll get back to you on a date. It might be a couple of days."

Harry threw up his hands and said, "I knew it. The old bait and switch routine. I find the information he's looking for, and once he has it, he reneges on his end of the deal. Disgusting."

"I'm not reneging on anything. I just told you it would be a couple of days."

Harry peered at him again and his eyes narrowed. "Your sudden unavailability has something to do with the incident mentioned in those news stories, doesn't it? That's why you cancelled out on me last night and why now you're telling me you can't stick to our bargain."

Pete shook his head. "It's something else. Julie's in Philadelphia trying to find that woman, Leslie Lehr, as I believe you know. I might have to go out there."

"Some problem?"

"Not yet, but I'm worried about her. I just found out that she's moved into an apartment with two people who knew and worked with Leslie at the Philadelphia investment banking firm Bud Stephanopoulis was associated with. I don't like the way things have been trending."

"Why don't you just tell her to come home?"

Pete laughed sarcastically. "It's not that simple these days. Remember when we had dinner at Rona's that night and you preached about the college years being the time young people should break away from their families? She's taken your sermon to heart."

"She's not *in* college. She's taking a gap year."

"Tell *her* that. She's eighteen and is convinced it's time she sprouted her own set of wings."

Harry looked thoughtful. "Maybe I should go out there with you. I have a good relationship with her."

"Let's let it play out for a few days. I'm hoping she'll come to her senses by herself."

"The offer stands. I just need a day's notice to get things organized at the newspaper."

SIX

When Pete got back to his lake house, the drapes were pulled and the blinds were closed and the door was locked. He frowned and used his key to gain entry. Angie watched from the couch and took her hand away from her purse when she saw him. She had an open book on her lap and a cup of coffee was within easy reach. His replica Viking longbow lay on the coffee table in front of her instead of in its usual place in the corner.

He didn't say anything about the drapes or the door, but eyed the bow and said, "Thinking about taking up hunting?"

She smiled weakly. "No, just admiring your weapon."

"That bow was hand-carved for me by an old Norwegian craftsman named Ulf. In case you don't know, that means wolf."

She picked it up and pretended to aim at him. "Can I try it?"

"If you promise to aim at the targets and not at me."

Pete got his arrows and they went outside to where he'd set up three army surplus silhouette targets in the bushes at various distances. Pete strung the bow and showed Angie the basics of form. Then he stepped back and watched. She tried to pull the bow string back without an arrow first and her arm began to quiver after six inches.

She looked at him and said, "Is there some way to adjust this thing so you don't have to be a Cro-Magnon Man to use it?"

Pete shook his head. "Sorry."

Angie made a few more dry runs with the same result. She shook her head and nocked an arrow and pointed in the direction of the closest target. She let the arrow fly. It arced upward before falling to earth twenty feet away where it stuck in the ground. She looked at him defiantly, daring him to laugh.

"Try again," Pete said encouragingly, "it takes practice to get the hang of it."

She nocked another arrow, drew the string back as far as she could, and let it go. The arrow skittered sideways and clanged off a birch tree.

"Keep your eye on the target," Pete counseled soberly.

Angie attempted a half-dozen more shots. The arrow either started up and then fell weakly to the ground or was wildly off target and wound up in the trees. She handed the bow to him in frustration and said, "Show me how it's done, Mr. Viking."

He pulled the bowstring back to his jaw a couple of times, then nocked an arrow and eyed the intermediate-range target. He swiveled his head in Angie's direction and said, "You remember Marty Kral, right?" He was referring to a former Sears & Whitney partner, now gone from the firm, who'd been a perpetual thorn in management's side.

She rolled her eyes. "How could I forget."

"For me, archery is about motivation. Visualizing the face of someone like Marty on the target helps concentrate your senses and gets the juices flowing."

He took his stance again, imagining Kral's sneering countenance on the target, and pulled the arrow back to his cheek and let it fly. *Thunk!*

Pete made no effort to conceal his smugness when he glanced Angie's way. He raised his eyebrows innocently and shook his head a couple of times and shrugged his shoulders, like an NBA star who had just sunk a three-pointer over the outstretched hands of the incompetent guarding him.

She waved her hand dismissively and said, "I could have done that, too, if I'd known about the Marty Kral trick."

He assumed his stance again and went through the same visualization routine. *Thunk!* He repeated the process. *Thunk!* Then he nocked another arrow and took aim at the far target and let it go. It deflected off the shoulder of the silhouette target and skittered into the bushes.

"*Damn,*" he muttered.

Sucking in air, he eyed the far target again and this time was more methodical in his pre-shot routine. *Thunk!* He nodded a couple of times and reached for another arrow.

When he'd exhausted his supply, Angie said, "Impressive," and helped him locate and gather his arrows.

Relieved that he'd performed well under pressure, he said to her on their way back to his house, "Before you coaxed me out to exhibit my archery skills, I was going to suggest we tour the area and then find a place for lunch. Sound like a plan?"

It took a few moments, but she finally nodded.

Pete slowed to turn into the entrance for Sleeping Bear Dunes National Lakeshore, and after showing his pass to the guard at the station, followed the winding road through the dense stand of trees until they came to the small parking lot near the scenic overlook. Before they got out of his Range Rover, he saw Angie staring at the crowd on the observation deck.

"Ready?" he asked when she didn't move.

"I think I'll stay in the car and admire the scenery from here. I've got a cranky hip that's been acting up since our archery outing."

He frowned. "You'll have a better view from the deck. Put on your hat and sunglasses."

She shook her head. "This is fine. I can see."

He avoided sighing and said, "Okay, I'll be back."

Pete crossed the wooden bridge to the deck that offered a commanding view of the famous sand dune and the nearby lake and absorbed the splendor. The viewers were three-deep, but when a young family with the man carrying their baby papoose-style left, he slid into the spot they'd vacated and enjoyed the unobstructed view.

His eyes flicked toward his Range Rover and he wondered if Angie would become more comfortable after a few days. Or whether she'd been permanently spooked. He also wondered what more he could do to check out her story.

After ten minutes, he walked across the bridge again to his Range Rover. When he got in, he saw that Angie had on her floppy hat and sunglasses. Thinking of nothing else to say, he said as cheerfully as he could, "Lovely day." He fired up the engine and backed out.

They made another stop before they left the national park, but observed the autumn splendor from inside his vehicle. Then they headed for Traverse City, and when they came to Apache Trout Grill, the peak lunch period was over so they had no problem finding a parking spot. On the drive from Sleeping Bear, Pete had wondered whether Angie might balk at going into a restaurant, but she didn't.

They were seated at a prime table next to the window that overlooked the marina. Even though it was past mid-October, the harbor was still more than half full with sailboats and powerboats of various stripes. Most were anchored at their moorings, but a few came or went.

Angie glanced around the room, then removed her hat and fluffed her hair, but left her sunglasses on and gazed out at the marina. Pete kept an eye on her, trying not to be obvious.

Their waiter came and they both ordered iced tea. They made small talk for fifteen minutes, discussing the weather, when snow began to fall in northern Michigan, and what they enjoyed doing during the winter months. Pete wanted to get back to what her plans were going forward, but held off, hoping she'd eventually raise the issue.

He doctored up his iced tea and took a swallow. The waiter returned and took their lunch orders. When he left again, Pete said, "By the way, our conversation about the mob yesterday got me thinking about something. Did I ever mention a guy named Les Brimley? It would have been a couple of years after I moved up here."

"Possible. It doesn't ring a bell."

"Brimley was murdered on a golf course he was developing. Shortly after his death, his widow came to me and I represented her on financial matters for a while."

"Okay," she said, seemingly puzzled about where he was going.

"During the course of trying to sort out Brimley's finances, I uncovered what appeared to be a juice loan from the mob and thought it might have had something to with his murder. I raised it with the widow and she claimed she knew nothing about it, although it turned out she was lying.

"Then one day she asked me if she could be personally liable for a loan like that. It was a casual question, almost like an afterthought. I told her I didn't think so, but that the mob might have a claim against her husband's estate, although it seemed unlikely they would assert it for obvious reasons. Not long after that, some goons began to harass my daughter at her boarding school to intimidate me into backing off my advice to Mrs. Brimley."

"This is an entertaining story, Pete," Angie said, frowning, "but what's the punch line?"

"To get out of the mess, I was forced to broker a deal with a mob kingpin named Vinnie Zahn. Which leads me to my question. Have you ever heard of Zahn?"

Angie played with the straw from her iced tea. "I don't think so."

Pete looked at her. "Do you know if Carmen knows him?"

She seemed annoyed. "It's possible, I suppose. I told you, I tried to stay as far away from his scumbag mob friends as possible."

Pete nodded. "Do you know what Carmen does for a living? From what I understand, most mob guys have a job or business they use as a front."

"My God, Pete, you're completely obsessed with this! Can't we talk about something else for a change?"

"Sorry, just curious."

"Okay, for your information, the creep claims he runs a string of dry cleaning shops. I know nothing about it other than that. Once I figured out he was connected, I insisted on filing separate income tax returns instead of joint. I convinced him that our total tax would be less that way. What I really wanted to avoid was signing returns on which he reported—or more likely underreported—income I knew nothing about."

"Smart move."

She didn't say anything, and because of her sunglasses, Pete couldn't see her eyes. She turned and stared out at the harbor like she was checking the boats to make sure they were all accounted for.

Pete backed off his questions. He'd have another run at her about Zahn when she was more receptive.

Their lunch came, and while they ate, their conversation veered in other directions, including the political scene in Washington, D.C. and Pete's concerns about Julie and her quixotic search in Philadelphia.

When they finished eating, he drove through downtown Traverse City to show her the business district. He wanted to stop at Horizon Books, but predictably, the area was clogged with traffic and there weren't any open parking places close by so he abandoned that idea. On the way out of town, they stopped at a seafood store and picked up crab legs, whitefish dip and a loaf of French bread for dinner.

Driving back to the lake, Angie grew quiet again, and when Pete glanced her way, he saw that her eyes were closed and her upper body was tilted toward the passenger-side door. He still had questions.

SEVEN

They got back to his house shortly after five just as the shadows were lengthening along the lake. Pete put the food away and placed the bottle of Sauvignon Blanc that Angie had slipped into their shopping cart in the freezer for a quick chill. He joined her on the porch.

She stood gazing out with her arms wrapped around her upper body because of the crisp weather. "I'm surprised it's still this light," she said.

"Different time zone than Chicago, remember? We're on the western edge of the eastern zone."

She nodded absently. After staring out a while longer, she said, "I think I'll check on my car and then take a shower. I need hot water."

Pete reviewed his voicemail messages while Angie was gone. He was just returning a call from Joe Tessler, the detective in the sheriff's department, when she returned and went straight upstairs. Tessler didn't answer and Pete left a message that he'd returned his call.

He heard the water running and busied himself being a good host. He built a fire in the fireplace and moved two wing chairs in front of it so they faced each other. Then he positioned a coffee table between the chairs and popped the cork on the bottle of Sauvignon Blanc and put it in a wine cooler. He found a couple of stemmed glasses, and after inspecting them for cleanliness, added them to the table arrangement along with a stack of cocktail napkins. As the final touch, he emptied a box of wheat crackers into a glass bowl and placed it and the dip on the table.

He was admiring his handiwork when Angie came down again. It was a new her. Gone were the floppy hat and frumpy khakis. In their place was a red sweater with silver threads running through it and a pair of snug-fitting black slacks. Her hair looked freshly shampooed.

She looked at the fire and the rest of the setup and said, "Very impressive. You've been a busy boy."

Pete nodded several times as though in wonderment of himself. "Talents as yet undiscovered by mere mortals."

They settled in and Pete poured wine in their glasses. Angie stared at the fire and said, "When we were doing our archery thing this morning, you mentioned Marty Kral. I've been thinking about our law firm ever since."

"Umm."

"Don't get me wrong," she said. "Marty is the *last* guy I miss. There are a lot of others I do, though. Steve Johnson and people like that. I wonder if I'll ever see them again."

"Now you're getting maudlin."

"Easy for you to say. You can go back and visit anytime you want. But I'm dead, remember?"

Sensing an opening, Pete said, "That's the reason you need to come up with a plan going forward. Hiding isn't the way to spend a life."

Angie's eyes flicked toward him and then away again. "You make it sound so simple."

"I'm sure it's not, but it's reality."

"Maybe you should start offering ideas instead of just interrogating me every chance you get."

"Asking a few questions is hardly interrogation."

She didn't say anything right away, then mused, "I wonder what the firm did with the personal things in my office?"

"Packed them up and put them in storage, I imagine. Or maybe shipped them to your house."

"I hope not," she said, sipping some wine. "The thought of that creep pawing through my things . . . The pictures of my mother and everything."

"Don't make yourself crazy thinking about it."

"I can't help it. The law firm was everything to me."

"It was everything to me, too, but I managed to adjust."

"Ah, in slightly different circumstances?"

"Yes, in different circumstances."

They made small talk for a while and sipped their wine and nibbled on crackers and sampled the dip. During a lull in the conversation, Angie glanced around the room and then asked, "Do you mind if I close the drapes? I feel exposed."

Pete shook his head and watched as she went around the room and pulled the drawstrings and closed the blinds on the kitchen windows. She sat down again and took another sip of her wine and stared at the fire some more. Without looking at him she said, "You think I've lost it, don't you?"

He frowned. "What makes you say that?"

"The way you've been looking at me. Like I'm a paranoid nutjob."

"C'mon, Angie, you know that's not true."

"I get the feeling you're analyzing every move I make, looking for signs."

He frowned again and shook his head and turned away.

She didn't say anything for a while, just drank wine and nibbled on crackers and ate dip. Then she shifted gears and said in a pensive voice, "I wonder if my second car had a bomb in it?"

"It did," Pete said.

Her eyes immediately fixed on his. "And you know that how?"

"It was reported in the newspapers."

"You saw it in the papers when you came to Chicago for my funeral?"

Pete didn't want to tell her an outright lie so he said, "No, later."

Her eyes bored in on him like twin lasers now. "How much later?"

He knew he'd boxed himself in and tried to put the best spin on it he could. "I stopped at Harry McTigue's office this morning to talk to him about something, and while I was there, I asked him to check his databases about the bombing incident. The stories reported that the second car had a bomb in it as well."

Her eyes widened. "You told Harry I'm here?"

"No, I didn't *tell* him you're here. He knows nothing about any of this other than that I attended your funeral and was curious about the press accounts."

She finished her wine and stared at her empty glass. Without looking up, she said, "One more sign you don't believe my story."

"Angie, I'm beginning to think you *might* be paranoid. All I've been doing is trying to get my arms around your situation. And as far as the press accounts are concerned, I'd think you'd be interested, too."

"I see."

"Remember, I didn't *have* to tell you I asked Harry to see what had been reported by the press. I could have made up some story, but I didn't. I was honest. And as I said, Harry doesn't have the foggiest notion that you're not dead and are staying at my house."

She didn't say anything.

"And while we're on the subject, I'm getting a little tired of feeling I have to apologize every time you go off on me because of some little thing I say or because you take my words in the worst light."

Angie set her glass on the table and got to her feet. "I'm a mite tired, as you country folk like to say. I think I'll turn in. I have to be fresh for the morning so I can run into town and get a copy of the local paper and read all about the fugitive who's staying in Pete Thorsen's house."

Pete rolled his eyes.

She feigned going into a thinking mode. "Maybe I can buy all the copies so one doesn't fall into the hands of someone in Chicago."

Pete clenched his teeth as he watched her climb the stairs. "Aren't you going to wait until I break out the crab legs and bread?" he called. "Crackers and whitefish dip isn't exactly dinner."

"Enjoy your crustaceans."

He listened to her rummage around in the upstairs hall bathroom and then heard her bedroom door close. So much for honesty, he thought, sighing. Or at least semi-honesty. He dribbled the last of the wine into his glass and propped up his feet on the edge of the table and stared at the empty chair across from him. He considered trying to talk her into coming back down, but promptly forgot about that. He'd learned from experience that once Angie DeMarco's temper was ignited, it took a while for it to cool.

Pete watched the flames flicker in the fireplace and tried to think of other things: his stepdaughter, Julie, and her quixotic quest in Philadelphia; Harry's proposal for a three-day fishing trip, their last of the season; the writer's conference he'd been thinking about attending.

Angie's situation crowded out everything, though. He thought about the inconsistencies in her story and how she professed not to know of Vinnie Zahn even though that seemed improbable. And he thought about Julie some more. He wanted her home, but also knew it was better if she remained in Philadelphia until things shook out with Angie.

He put on an Eagles CD and kept the volume low so he wouldn't disturb Angie if she were trying to sleep. Then he opened a bottle of Pinot Grigio, and after getting a supply of ice cubes from the refrigerator, threw a couple of fresh logs on the fire and settled into his chair again. He filled his glass, added a cube, and took a sip. The logs crackled and sent showers of sparks up the chimney.

Pete swiped a cracker through the dip and munched on it, then did the same with another cracker. As he ate, he considered getting the crab legs out, but the thought of melting butter and going through the hassle of cracking the shells didn't appeal to him. He grabbed another cracker and poured more wine.

When the Eagles CD ran its course, he replaced it with a collection of Johnny Cash's greatest hits. He turned up the sound a bit and went back to his chair and settled in again and watched the flames lick at the wood. "Ring of Fire" came on, which somehow seemed appropriate, and he hummed along with the lyrics. "Folsom Prison Blues," one of his favorites, followed and he was tempted to turn up the volume a little more, but restrained himself. He refilled his glass and took another long sip of wine and leaned back in his chair and rested his eyes.

He opened them after a while and glanced at his watch; it was nearly 11:00 p.m. He used more crackers to finish off the dip and checked the wine bottle. It was maybe a quarter full, and he refilled his glass and leaned back again. Jumbled thoughts bounced around his head. The weekend coming up is when he'd planned to make his first visit to Cornell to attend parent's weekend. *So much for plans,* he thought.

Pete finished off the wine and surveyed the room from his chair. It was a mess. Furniture out of place, empty wine bottles and glasses standing around, cracker crumbs on the table. Even on a night when he'd over-served himself, the neatnik in him took over and he spent ten minutes tidying up.

The fire was down to a bed of glowing coals. After making sure the protective screen was tight against the fireplace stones, he made his way up the stairs, keeping a hand on the wall to maintain his balance. He passed Angie's room and didn't see light under the door. After finishing in the bathroom, he stripped off his clothes and crawled into bed.

The knock on his door and muffled voice roused him. He blinked in the darkness, then closed his eyes again and adjusted his pillow and rolled over and pulled the blanket tighter around his neck. He heard the sounds again and sat up in bed this time, feeling disoriented, and stared into the darkness. The door inched open and a voice, clearer now, said, "Are you awake?"

He groaned and fell back. Seconds later, the bed sagged when a figure climbed in and snuggled close and wrapped an arm around him. His eyes were wide open now. "Angie?"

"I thought you might want some company," she murmured.

He groaned again.

"It's cold in here. Do you mind if I get under the blankets?"

He rolled over, freeing the covers on one side, and she slipped under them and moved close.

"What time is it?" he asked, still feeling disoriented.

"I don't know. Nighttime." She brushed his neck with her lips and snuggled closer. Then he felt one of her legs slide over his. Her face moved closer and her lips found his and she kissed him. "This is nice, isn't it?"

He wrapped his free arm around her and squeezed, pressing their bodies together. She had nothing on under her short nightgown. He ran his hand up and down her back and felt her warm flesh under the silken fabric.

"I'm sorry I spoiled dinner," she said. "I thought I'd make it up to you."

She rolled on her side and took his hand and rubbed it slowly back and forth over her breasts. Then she slipped her nightgown down on one side and put his hand on her again. He massaged her and felt her nipple harden. She moaned and whispered, "I've been wanting to do this for so long."

He kissed her, longer this time, more hungrily. She got on top of him and undulated her hips and reached back and stroked his legs. He wanted to move her to the side and pull his pajama bottoms off, but she had him pinned to the bed and continued with the undulating movement.

Finally, he couldn't stand it any longer and he rolled her to the side and slipped the nightgown over her head. With a hand on one of her breasts, he used the other to stroke the insides of her legs. Then he felt her hands fumbling with his pajama bottom tie.

EIGHT

The sun streaming through the window blinds woke Pete the next morning. He rubbed his eyes and raised up on an elbow to see the alarm clock on his nightstand. It read 8:10 a.m. He groaned and fell back on the bed and pulled the blanket over his head, trying to shut out the light. His head throbbed and his back felt stiff and his mouth was like used flannel. He lay there, trying not to do anything that might aggravate the throbbing. Angie's midnight visit flashed in his mind.

Finally, he mustered the will to slide out of bed and stumble to his bathroom. He checked his reflection in the mirror and saw that he looked as bad as he felt. His eyes were crisscrossed with red roadmaps, and his hair stood up in places like a fright wig. The stubble on his face made him look like he hadn't shaved in days even though it had only been twenty-four hours. He splashed water on his face and toweled off, then brushed his teeth and ran a brush through his hair and squeezed drops into his eyes.

He eyed his bed and was tempted to crawl back in, but he knew from experience a better tonic was a run to purge his body. He put on a pair of running shorts and a moth-eaten gray sweatshirt and laced up his Nikes and headed for the stairs. Angie's room was quiet when he passed her door. He went down, grateful he could put off facing her, and left a note saying he'd be back in an hour. He washed down two Tylenol gels with a glass of orange juice and thought of his bed again. Then he clamped his "Save the Boat" cap on his head and grabbed a pair of sunglasses and headed out.

The morning was windless, but his bare legs still felt cold because the temperature was forty degrees at most. He wished he'd had the foresight to wear sweatpants and another layer on top. His body heat was revving up by the time he reached the junction where South Shore Drive branched off the highway, and he was grateful for his cap and sunglasses because of the sun's glare. He loped along and tried to ignore the drummer at work in his head.

To take his mind off how he felt, he forced himself to concentrate on the boat docks that were stored along the road for the winter, their pipe footings pointing at the sky, which was always a sign of changing seasons. A pickup truck with a ladder protruding from its rear box and country music blaring through a window that had been cracked a few inches rattled past.

The Tylenol gels had yet to do their job. Every time one of his feet landed on the asphalt, a burst of pain surged through his head and he made a conscious effort to land on the balls of his feet. His cell phone burred just as he passed the public beach. He slowed to a walk, grateful for a reprieve, and fished his phone from his pocket. It was an unknown caller. He was tempted to ignore it like he usually did with such calls, but since it was from his local area code, he answered with the intention of cutting off the caller at the first indication it was a telemarketer.

"Pete, it's Joe Tessler. Am I catching you in the middle of something?"

"Just out for a run. What's up?"

"Sorry I didn't get back to you last night. I had a date with Kelene."

He didn't want to encourage a conversation about Joe's love life so he just said, "No problem."

"Are you free for lunch today?" Tessler asked. "Tomorrow would be a distant second choice if you can't make it today."

Pete thought about his busy schedule, which like most days, was free from pressing engagements. The prospect of getting away from Angie for a couple of hours also appealed to him. "Today would be fine," he said.

"Great. Usual menu and dining room?"

"Sure," Pete said, knowing that meant picking up sandwiches at Ebba's Bakery and then going to the bluff in Elberta that overlooked the Lake Michigan beach. "Are you driving?" Pete asked.

A pause, then, "I can, if you promise not to complain about odors."

"Does that mean you're smoking again?"

"Kelene smokes, as I think you know. I might have one now and then to, you know, be social when we're together. I crack my car windows whenever one of us smokes, but tobacco odor lingers."

"Okay," Pete said, "you spring for the sandwiches — the usual for me — and I'll pick you up in front of Ebba's at noon."

"I kind of thought that's what you might want to do."

"Did you get a new phone?"

"I'm calling on one of those prepaid things from Target. I'll explain at lunch."

Pete put his phone away and began to run again, wondering what Tessler wanted to talk about other than Kelene Brill. He reversed directions after another half-mile and was grateful to have the sun at his back for a change.

He thought some more about how he was going to handle things when he walked into his house. Hopefully, Angie would make it easy for him and throw out her patented one-liners rather than wanting to talk about their "relationship." He'd also resolved not to repeat the experience of the previous night whatever the temptation. Until her situation was cleared up, at least.

When he reached his driveway, he slowed to a walk to cool down a little and gather himself. He walked up his front steps, rehearsing in his mind some lines he might use. He pushed open the door and saw Angie standing at the breakfast bar with a cup of coffee in one hand, a half-eaten bagel in the other, and her purse close by.

"Well," she said, eyeing his cap, "Save any boats?"

He forced a grin. "A whole fleet."

"Uh huh. How was the run?"

"Chilly at first, but as soon as the old body generated some heat, it was great. You been out?"

She shook her head. "I peeked out the window. Mostly I've been gorging myself on bagels and cherry preserves."

"A well-fed person is a happy person." As soon as the words came out of his mouth, he saw the impish smile cross her face and he feared he'd opened the door to a subject he wanted to avoid.

"Chock full of homilies today," she said.

Pete headed upstairs with hot water foremost in his thoughts. He lingered in the shower longer than usual, enjoying its soothing effects and feeling grateful that the drummer at work in his head had toned down his act a bit. He shaved and brushed his hair and squeezed more drops into his eyes. After he got dressed, he glanced at his reflection in the full-length mirror. He didn't feel at the top of his game yet, but he looked a hell of a lot better.

"Wow," Angie said when he came down, "you clean up pretty good."

Pete forced another grin.

Angie watched him eat, and as he munched on a bagel, he thought she might be edging toward a "conversation." Then he remembered his promise to call Julie and punched in her number before Angie could initiate anything. He was used to his calls to Julie going to voicemail and was pleasantly surprised when she answered.

"Hi, Dad."

"Good morning. What's happening?"

Her voice sounded excited. "We might have a breakthrough in our investigation. Effie and I talked to a guy who used to work in the Harrison Stryker mailroom. We believe he might have some idea where Leslie is."

"Is this the person you mentioned the last time we talked?"

"That didn't go anywhere. This is a different guy. He used to work in the mailroom like I said. You know how those people are. They soak up information about co-workers like a Hoover sucks dirt."

"Huh."

"Do you like that expression? I got it from a *Seinfeld* rerun."

"Nice to see you're expanding your cultural awareness."

"Anyway, after the mailroom guy lost his job at Harrison Stryker, he got another job, but now he's lost that one, too. I guess his cell phone provider shut off his service so he has to communicate by email from places that have WiFi."

"Okay."

"Effie and I are meeting him at a Starbucks to see what he knows."

"If you have his email address, why don't you just email him?"

"Email isn't the same as talking to somebody in person, Dad. There isn't the same give and take and you can't read the other person's body language. That's why we're meeting him."

"Okay—"

"Dad, Effie is waiting for me. I've got to go. I'll call you later."

His phone went silent. He stared at it, feeling like he'd just been flattened by a blitzkrieg.

"That was fast," Angie said.

Pete shook his head. "Adults just don't understand the time pressure teenagers are under, particularly if they aren't in college and don't have jobs."

She giggled. "So, what's our plan for today?"

"*My* plan is to meet Joe Tessler for lunch. He needs to talk to me about something."

"And who may I ask is Joe Tessler?"

"I mentioned him before. He's the detective in the local sheriff's office."

"Right. And the sheriff is the guy you always butt heads with."

"I don't know if *always* is the right term. Two percent of the time we get along just fine."

Angie smiled this time. "You do have a way with words."

Pete resisted making a quip.

After a pause, she said, "Is Detective Tessler the guy who used to be with the Chicago PD?"

"He is."

She didn't look at him, but her eyes seemed to move around. Finally she said, "This isn't more of your double-checking of my story about the bombing, is it?"

Oh God, he thought, *not that again.*

"Angie," he said, "I doubt if Joe even *knows* about the bombing so relax."

She didn't look convinced.

He glanced at his watch and saw that he was due to meet Tessler in twenty minutes. He headed upstairs to get his wallet and car keys and hurried back down. "See you in a couple of hours," he said.

As he was halfway out the door, she said, "When you get back, maybe you'll be a little more relaxed yourself. You don't have to feel awkward about what happened last night. I'm a big girl."

NINE

"Now this is more like it," Tessler said, when they pulled into the lot on the bluff and found it deserted. He brushed the lock of black hair away from his forehead and gazed around with a satisfied expression.

Tessler spread a napkin across his knees to catch the crumbs and tore off a corner of his potato chip bag and crammed some chips into his mouth. He crunched on them as he glanced around again. Light cloud cover had moved in since the morning and the wind had kicked up a bit. Farther out, the water was cobalt blue, but it had a brownish cast near the beach and inside the breakwater where waves churned up the sand. A bald eagle circling in front of them caught the draft and hovered in mid-air for a few seconds before it swooped down with deadly speed toward some hapless prey on the ground.

The detective bit into his sandwich and said with his mouth full, "This is the way it should have been the day I had the picnic lunch planned with Kelene. Not the weather, but the serenity if that's the right word. No tourists in their minivans and friggin' pickups, all feeding their faces and taking a bunch of pictures. No idiot motorcyclists."

Pete suppressed a smile as he ate.

"I'm not a resident of Elberta," Tessler said, taking another bite of his sandwich, "so I can't do this myself, but I'm going to see if I can get some of the locals stirred up about the issue and have them present the village elders with a proposal to require special vehicle stickers as a condition of parking up here. I'm thinking maybe a sticker will entitle the holder to park here five times a year. Does a hundred bucks a year sound about right? It's got to be high enough to keep the riff-raff out."

"A hundred seems right. So what's on your mind?"

Tessler looked at his watch. "Jesus, look at the time. You let me get sidetracked with this other stuff." He stared at Pete's bag of potato chips. "You going to eat those?"

"Help yourself," Pete said. He couldn't figure out why Tessler didn't weigh three hundred pounds the way he ate, but he remained skinny as a rail.

Tessler crunched on a handful of his new supply of chips and said, "Frank is launching an internal investigation in our office to ferret out who's been pilfering drugs and other stuff from our evidence room." Frank was Sheriff Franklin Richter, Tessler's boss.

Pete raised his eyebrows. "When did you find out about this?"

"Two days ago."

"Does Frank have a suspect? Or does he just know that stuff is missing."

"That's what I wanted to talk to you about. I can't get anything out of him. If I raise the subject, he always finds a reason not to discuss it. Frank is spearheading the investigation with Connie in reserve. They're playing things real close to their vests."

Connie was Connie Chapman, the county attorney, and Pete knew her reasonably well.

"What exactly has been happening?"

"We have an evidence room, see, like all law enforcement agencies. Everything germane to our cases is kept there. Guns, knives, other pieces of material evidence like confiscated illegal substances, everything."

"Illegal substances, meaning drugs."

"Right. So many of our cases these days involve drugs of one kind or another. Weed, meth are big ones. When a case is opened, everything that's considered evidence is placed in bags and tagged, cataloged, and kept in a secure room that's locked except when an authorized person goes in or out. I've seen the way things are handled by the big law enforcement departments around the country, including the Chicago PD, and I got to tell you, the way we do it is on a par with most of them."

"And drugs are mainly what's missing?"

"Mainly, I guess. But a knife is missing, too, and a partial box of ammunition, and some other stuff."

"Who has access to the evidence room?"

"In our office?"

"Yeah."

Tessler's lips tightened. "Frank and me."

"Do you have keys?"

He shook his head. "Not keys. We use electronic cards like the hotels use. That's one area where we're behind some departments. They've gone to some kind of recognition system — voice, fingerprints, eyeballs, things like that. But our county can't afford to install that kind of system."

"Can the cards you and Frank have be duplicated?"

Tessler appeared to think. "I suppose so, I don't know the technology."

"Where do you keep your card?"

"In my wallet." He pulled it out and showed Pete. The card was plain with no indication of where it came from or what it was for.

"Your earlier answer suggested that someone outside the department might also have an access card."

Tessler nodded. "Connie has one."

"Is that it?"

"As far as I know."

"You have a good relationship with Frank. Why do you think he's being so close-mouthed with you?"

"Don't know, that's what has me worried. Then yesterday a deputy in the office who I'm tight with told me he heard that *everyone* in the office is considered a suspect until the investigation is concluded."

"Who's conducting the investigation?"

"An outside guy named Bernard Nichols. Everybody got an email from Frank saying that he'd been hired as a special investigator and will be in our office interviewing people. Have you ever heard of him?"

After thinking for a few moments, Pete shook his head.

"That deputy I just mentioned? He says he heard Nichols is ex-FBI. I guess he works as a private dick in Detroit these days. Do you know anybody down there who might be able to give us a reading on him?"

Rae Acton immediately came to mind. Pete said, "I might."

"Could you call him? I mean like right away? This thing is driving me nuts."

"It's a her. And yes, I'll call. No guarantees she knows Nichols, though."

"As soon as you talk to this woman, will you call me on this phone? I'll give you the number." He pulled out his pocket notebook and wrote down the number. He tore out the page and handed it to Pete.

"You were going to tell me why you got a new phone."

"It's an *additional* phone, not a new one, and nobody knows about it except you and me. I don't want you to think I've gone all paranoid or anything, but I'm also no fool. If you're in law enforcement, you know how the forensics people can reconstruct just about everything from your friggin' phone. I don't want some innocent thing I say to be misconstrued and used against me. That's why I got this burner. It's for private conversations. If things go south in this investigation, this baby," he said, tapping the burner, "goes bye-bye."

Pete nodded. He didn't remember seeing Tessler so spooked. He thought about his own problem with Angie and saw a chance to trade favors.

"Joe, speaking of calls, you still have contacts in the Chicago PD, right?"

"Yeah, we don't communicate on a regular basis, but we're all still pretty tight. We went through a lot of crap together."

"If I give you the background, are you willing to contact one of them about a case?"

"That's fair, I guess. You help me and I help you, huh?"

Pete gave him a copy of the *Sun Times* story and a couple of the follow-on pieces. "What I'm looking for is information that the press hasn't picked up on yet."

"Which department is investigating, do you know?"

"No idea. Maybe the one charged with mob investigations. Or maybe the bomb investigators. I can't say."

"I'll make some calls, see what I can find out. And you'll call that woman in Detroit, right?"

TEN

Carmen DeMarco sat at his desk in one corner of his den, a large windowless room that provided privacy from prying eyes outside the house, sorting through a stack of mail. Occasionally he swore under his breath when he saw a bill or something else he didn't like.

Across the room, the *Judge Judy* show played on a jumbo flat screen television. All the shouts and arguments and gavel-banging were annoying DeMarco. His right-hand man, Joey Lebo, was sprawled on a couch with the remote in one hand and a can of Miller Lite in the other watching the show like it were about to divulge the secret of life.

DeMarco turned away in disgust and tried to concentrate on finishing the mail. Subconsciously, he passed a hand over his short black hair that was graying at the temples and looked like it had been razor trimmed an hour earlier. Then he touched the small gold earring in one ear and smoothed his closely-clipped mustache and beard that circled his chin. His hand returned to his hair.

Lebo leaned forward on the couch and worked the remote to turn up the sound and took another gulp of his Miller Lite. He shook the can to make sure it was empty, then crushed it in one of his big hands and tossed it on an end table where two other mangled cans lay. He listened intently as a character made his argument.

"Friggin' idiot!" he screamed in his high-pitched, scratchy voice. "That's a stupid argument! That's not what you should say!" Then he settled back as the parties made their closing arguments. When Judge Judy rendered her judgment, Lebo jumped to his feet and pointed at the television screen and screamed, "Told you so, asshole, told you so!"

"For crissakes, Leebs," DeMarco said, "control yourself! And turn the damn sound down. Or better, turn that moronic program off. You're driving me crazy. Clean up your garbage, too. Every time you're here, you turn this place into a pigsty."

Lebo seemed chastened and lowered the sound a couple of clicks. He picked up the crushed beer cans in one hand and walked over to a wastebasket and dropped them in. "This program is great, Carm," he said when he was back on the couch. "You should take a break from the junk mail and grab yourself a beer and come over and watch."

He'd been a valued lieutenant for a long time, but right now, everything about him irritated DeMarco—his cone-shaped head that hadn't seen a hair in years, his lanky frame with the stooped shoulders, those freakishly-large hands that made him look like a monster out of some twisted fairy tale. And his addiction to that idiotic *Judge Judy* television show. DeMarco flipped a piece of junk mail in the direction of the wastebasket and missed it by a foot.

"Just keep the friggin' sound down, okay?" he said.

Looking unhappy, Lebo slumped on the couch and occasionally shot a sullen look DeMarco's way.

A minute later, DeMarco pounded his desk and screamed, "I said turn the friggin' sound down!"

Lebo scowled and looked his way again. "Jeez, Carm, I *did* turn it down. If I turn it down more, I won't be able to hear the arguments."

DeMarco scrambled to his feet, knocking over his desk chair, and pointed his letter opener at Lebo and jabbed the air.

Lebo hurriedly manipulated the remote to lower the volume even more. He pouted as he threw sofa cushions on the floor and moved closer to the television screen.

DeMarco righted his chair and sat down again and continued to go through the dwindling pile of mail, slicing open bills or letters that looked important and tossing junk mail toward the wastebasket without barely a glance. *Amazing how much crap accumulates in just ten days*, he thought.

He picked up a letter from First Chicago Trust and saw that it was addressed to Angela DeMarco with a prominent notice on the envelope that read, "Statement Enclosed." He stared at it for a moment, then flung it toward the wastebasket, muttering, "You can bet your ass I'm not paying *that*."

He disposed of several more items and then came to a catalog from Victoria's Secret. He flipped through it, staring at the various lingerie items that were modeled seductively by buxom women.

"Hey, Leebs," he called, holding up the catalog, "look what the bitch was subscribing to." He fanned the pages so Lebo could see.

Lebo glanced in DeMarco's direction briefly and quickly returned to his show.

"Are you listening?" DeMarco called.

"I heard you, Carm, and I agree. Only porno flick stars get their stuff from places like that."

DeMarco tossed the catalog in the direction of the wastebasket and went back to finishing the mail. Then his eyes fixed on the statement from First Chicago Trust laying on the floor again. He stared at it for a few moments before he went over and picked it up and returned to his desk. He sliced open the envelope and began going through the statement. It showed itemized charges totaling $2,156.20 for the billing period ended October 5. He scanned the charges, all of which had September dates, and frowned, wondering how that could be. Then he thought about the late August charges that had appeared on the prior statement. "Goddamnit!" he muttered to himself.

Lebo glanced up from the cushions on the floor, but didn't say anything.

DeMarco was going over the September charges a second time. "Come here, Leebs," he said.

"One minute. The Judge is hearing her last case."

"Screw the Judge! Get over here!"

Lebo got up and walked over and peered over DeMarco's shoulder while at the same time keeping an eye on the *Judge Judy* program. "What?" he asked.

"Look at these charges."

Lebo leaned over and squinted for a moment. "So?" he said. "The card companies always give you a list of the charges you made." He pointed the remote at the television and the volume increased.

DeMarco snatched it from his hand, hit the off button, and threw the remote across the room. It skittered off a coffee table and banged against the wall.

Lebo stood motionless, staring at the remote that lay on the floor. "Jesus, you might have broken it."

"I don't give a crap if I broke it or not! Look at these friggin' dates!" He shoved the statement in front of Lebo's face.

Lebo chafed at DeMarco's language and demands, but peered at the statement again. "All I see is a bunch of dates in September and where the charges were made."

"When did little wifey die, huh, answer that?"

Lebo thought about it and said, "The middle of August sometime. I don't remember the exact date."

"August 17. If she died on August 17, how is she making charges on her credit card on those dates in September, explain that to me?"

Lebo appeared confused.

"Remember when the last statement came and there were a couple of charges for late in August that we concluded must be carryovers from when she was alive? Remember that?"

Lebo nodded.

"How I got to thinking and called the credit card company, but they wouldn't talk to me because I wasn't on the account?"

Lebo nodded again.

"After the first call, I called the company again a few days later and was more forceful, saying I had to know about the charges because I was co-executor of wifey's estate—I didn't use that term, of course, I tried to play nice and all of that bullshit—but they still wouldn't talk to me. They kept saying I had to show them an order from the probate court."

"I didn't know you were the co-executor."

"I'm not, for crissakes! I just told them that to try to get information. After the calls, I put the thing out of my mind and convinced myself that the dates on the statement must just be a screwup. Now this statement shows up with all these other charges in September . . ."

Lebo appeared to think, then his eyes lit up as though he'd had a revelation. "I bet I know what happened," he said. "Someone stole her credit card and has been using it to charge things."

DeMarco rolled his eyes and looked away in disgust. "Nobody *stole* her credit card. If someone had stolen her card, she was so damn anal that she would have been sitting in the credit card company's offices five minutes later, demanding that they cancel her card on the spot and issue a new one. No, that's not what happened. I bet anything little wifey is still alive."

Lebo frowned and shook his head several times. "Impossible. I drove past the SUV a half-hour after the explosion and saw what was left of it. Uh, uh, I don't believe it. Nobody could have survived that."

DeMarco continued as though he hadn't heard him. "I'll tell you what happened. Someone else was driving that car and met up with good old St. Peter. I don't know who or why, but that's what must have happened. If wifey dear had been driving, she would have had her purse with her because of her driver's license. Everything would have melted when the car went up in flames, the license, credit cards, everything. And if everything melted—or was eviscerated or whatever the hell the word is—the credit cards couldn't have been used by *anybody* in September. They'd be a blob of goo."

Lebo looked confused and didn't say anything.

"She's out there somewhere, hiding, that's what she's doing."

"I still don't think—"

"That's the problem with you, Leebs, you don't think! She's alive! This is proof, goddamnit!" He waved the credit card statement.

Neither of them said anything for a minute, then DeMarco said, "We got to find her and finish the job."

Concern showed on Lebo's face. "Don't we need to clear this with Vinnie first? He was mad as hell that you'd put a hit on your wife without clearing it with him first."

"It wasn't a *hit*. Taking care of someone who's lying and cheating who you just happened to be married to ain't a *hit*. That's personal business, and the way a man takes care of personal stuff is up to him and nobody else."

"That's not the way Vinnie sees it," Lebo said defensively. "He regards anything that might bring investigators down on the organization as organization business, not personal. That's what happened here. Those Chicago detectives who interviewed you a month ago . . ."

DeMarco waved a hand, dismissing Lebo's comment. "And that didn't go anywhere, did it? I put on the grieving husband bullshit and they bought it. Haven't heard a word from them since."

"Still . . ."

"You know what the problem is these days? Guys like Vinnie want to control everything, but they've gotten soft. Not too many years ago, maybe even when Vinnie was a few years younger, things were different. In those days, if a man found out that his wife had been screwing every guy in town and he took care of her, why crap, he'd be treated like a friggin' man among men and everyone would be slapping him on the back and maybe putting on a dinner where they served Dom Perignon and those little fish eggs."

"Remember, Vinnie's not only the boss, he's your uncle."

"*Kind* of my uncle. I was adopted, remember?"

"I don't know, Carm, you've treated him as your uncle all your life."

DeMarco glared at him for a long time, and when he was calmer, said, "So what are you suggesting?"

"Follow protocol or whatever the word is. Talk to Vinnie, explain what we think happened, get his go-ahead to correct the situation if it needs correcting."

DeMarco didn't look happy. He said, "You can't even call the old man anymore," he groused. "Or go to see him. He's up in Michigan on some damned grape farm these days, pretending he's the emperor of Sicily."

"We know how to reach him. We just have to do it through procedure. Security, that's the important thing."

DeMarco didn't look pleased. "Okay, set it up." Then his scowl darkened and he muttered, "Friggin' guy's afraid of his own shadow."

ELEVEN

The Betsie Valley Trail to Beulah was almost void of other cyclists so Pete and Angie biked along riding side-by-side and talking without concern about impeding the progress of others. Angie had on nondescript clothes topped by a helmet and goggles instead of her customary floppy hat.

"You never did tell me what your summit meeting with Detective Tessler was all about," she said.

"Really high-level stuff. We started off talking about his girlfriend, Kelene Brill. Then we segued into his beef about the way tourists take over the Elberta overlook and mess up his plans for a romantic picnic lunch with her. Finally we got to the minor stuff about an investigation the sheriff has just launched to find out who's been pilfering from the department evidence room."

"Wow, exciting! Tell me about the investigation."

He told her what Tessler had told him. "I'm trying to get some background on the investigator the sheriff has brought in."

"Pilfering in law enforcement agencies isn't uncommon, you know."

"I didn't know, but I'm not surprised. I'm sure there are plenty of temptations."

"Does the missing evidence relate to open cases or cold ones?"

"No idea. What does that have to do with anything?"

"There are generally two motives in these cases. Three, actually. If the missing items are drugs, the pilferer might be a user who's feeding his habit. Related to that is the officer who's making bucks on the side by peddling the stuff. Then there are pilferers who want evidence to disappear, which is germane to my question about the kind of case."

"Speaking of 'wow,' maybe I should introduce you to Sheriff Richter. After you've explained to him that you're dead but not *really* dead, maybe he'll hire you as special counsel to the outside investigator. You'll probably have to reduce your hourly billing rate to take into account this is northern Michigan and not Chicago or New York, but it'll give you something to occupy your time until you've resurrected your body."

As soon as the words came out, he saw the hurt look on Angie's face and regretted his irreverent stab at humor. After an awkward silence, she said, "You thought my body had been resurrected pretty well the other night."

"That was a stupid attempt on my part to be funny and I apologize. But as for the other, maybe we're better off keeping things professional until this is sorted out."

"Right," she said without turning around. She began to pedal faster.

He tried to catch up, and when he did, said, "Angie . . ."

"Don't get too close. I might molest you again."

He stayed behind her and they rode for another mile without speaking. Then she swiveled her head and said, "Sorry, I've been under a lot of stress lately. I'm always taking it out on you."

"No apologies necessary."

She stopped and backed up her bike so they were parallel and said in a low voice, "Don't look now, and you'll probably think my paranoia is on display again, but do you suppose that guy back there is following us?"

"What's he doing?"

"He's a hundred yards or so behind, dressed in a Lycra biker's outfit and a helmet. We've been poking along, but he hasn't gained on us. Now we've stopped and he's stopped, too."

"Just a minute." Pete wheeled his bike around so he was facing the rear. He leaned to the side and reached down by Angie's rear wheel, as if he were adjusting something, and said, "He's taking pictures."

"Why did he stop when we stopped if he's just taking pictures?"

"No idea. Let's move again and see what he does."

They started pedaling, and after they'd gone a half-mile, Pete glanced back. "I don't see him," he said.

Twice during the next hour, they caught a glimpse of the cyclist. He wasn't in sight when they reached the small town of Beulah on the east end of the lake.

"Ready for lunch?" Pete asked as they coasted down the main drag. She nodded.

"We have limited choices," he said. "I'd suggest Ursa Major Bistro where we can sit inside or out." He pointed to the restaurant coming up.

They locked their bikes in a rack and Angie pressed for the inside dining option. Only a couple of tables were occupied and they took an open one next to the floor-to-ceiling tinted glass window that looked out on the street. Pete doffed his helmet and goggles and ran a hand through his hair. Angie only removed her goggles.

They both ordered iced tea and spent a few minutes perusing the menu. After they got their orders in, Pete tried to ease Angie's concerns by saying, "I really think the guy behind us was a bird watcher or photographer. Or maybe both."

"Why did he act the way he did, then?"

Pete shrugged. "Maybe he was enjoying the day the same as us."

Angie took a swallow of her iced tea and didn't say anything.

"Look," he said, "I understand why you're nervous, but think about it. The only way that guy could have been following us is if someone saw you after the bombing, or you talked to someone, and word got around you were alive and you were followed to northern Wisconsin and then over here. That's too many 'ifs.'"

She drank more iced tea.

"So I really don't think—"

Angie grabbed his hand. "There he is," she whispered, jerking her head toward the window.

The cyclist with a camera dangling from a strap around his neck pedaled slowly past the restaurant and glanced around the quaint village. Seconds later, he disappeared again.

"He's gone," Pete announced.

Their food came and they ate in silence and drank more iced tea. When he finished, Pete scrubbed his hands with a napkin. "Picking up on our conversation, I know you've been careful, and I don't want to come across as interrogating you again, but can you think of anyone—anyone at all—who knows you and might have seen you after the bombing?"

She shook her head.

"And you didn't call anyone, right?"

"There he is again!" she hissed. "At the takeout counter."

Pete shifted positions as though he were stretching his legs and glanced at the counter. The cyclist was lanky with a tight-fitting Lycra suit and a black helmet with yellow lightning bolts along the sides.

"He's just getting something to go," Pete said in a low voice.

Angie shook her head. "That's a ruse. He's looking for us."

Pete glanced at her and frowned. "Let's see what he does," he said.

A few minutes later, the man had a tall cup in his gloved hand, and before going out to the patio, surveyed the restaurant. Because of his dark glasses, Pete couldn't tell whether it was a natural move or he was looking for them. He sat down at one of the wrought iron tables and propped his foot on a nearby chair.

Angie turned so she faced the restaurant's interior.

Pete kept an eye on the man as he sipped from his straw and gazed around.

"Now that you've had a closer look at him," Pete said, "does he look familiar?"

"I don't know. Something . . . With that helmet and dark glasses . . ."

The man got up and fastened his chin strap, tossed his Styrofoam cup into a trash receptacle, and pedaled down the street.

"He's gone," Pete said quietly.

Angie turned back to face him and chewed on her inner lip.

Pete didn't believe the man was following them, but to ease Angie's anxiety, said, "I know we might be retracing old ground, but maybe we should go through the bombing again. When you heard the explosion and went outside to see what happened, did you bump into anyone you knew?"

She thought for a moment, then shook her head. "The crowd was farther down the street watching the fire. I didn't go down there."

"And you didn't know the firefighter you talked to, right?"

She shook her head again.

"When you went back into your house, do you think anyone noticed?"

An irritated expression appeared on her face. "Pete, you're asking questions no one can answer. Someone *might* have noticed me go in, I don't know. I don't think so, but so what if they did? No one knew it was our SUV burning at that point, and I don't think people were standing on the street taking notes so they could later report that a live person or a dead one came or went from a particular house at a particular time."

"Point taken," he said. "When you left your house with the suitcase, did you see anyone? Wheeling a suitcase down the street might have been more noticeable than just stepping out to watch a fire."

"I went out the side door and cut through the back alley. The only human beings I encountered until I caught the taxi were a few kids playing on the sidewalk."

"And from the bus station until you reached the cabin, you didn't run into anyone you knew and only did your business. Bought a ticket or whatever."

She nodded. "Oh, on the bus, I had this really important conversation with an older lady who kept pestering me about why I was going to Appleton. I made up a story about visiting an elderly aunt. Then she wanted to know whether I planned to visit the Green Bay Packers Hall of Fame when I was in the area. I told her I was a Bears fan, which shut her up for the rest of the trip."

Pete smiled. As a life-long Packers fan, he'd had a few semi-civil conversations with Angie over the years about the football rivalry."

"You rented your car in Appleton. I assume it's in your name."

"Of course. What choice did I have? I prepaid three months with my debit card and gave the manager my credit card number for security."

"And you didn't know the agent."

She shook her head again.

"I pretty much know what you did at the cabin. You went out to buy food once in a while, bought some clothes. But you never ran into anyone you knew, right?"

She shook her head once more.

"How about on the way over here?"

She smiled for the first time in hours. "I had a very sweet conversation with a pimply-faced teenager about whether to order a Big Mac or the Chicken McNuggets."

Pete smiled himself. "Well," he said, "based on what you've told me, I don't see any way someone would know you're alive and up here."

Angie's expression reverted to worry.

"Should we head back?" he asked. "Unless you'd like a little diversion first, in which case we can go across the street to Crystal Crate & Cargo. It's a marvelous store owned by a friend of mine, Sally Berlin, and has all kinds of trendy cookware and household items, some great books written by an author who summers up here, jewelry, other gift items."

"Sounds great, but I'd like to go back."

TWELVE

They didn't see the cyclist on their return ride, and when they got back to his house, he checked his messages and found that Rae Acton had called him back. The other three calls were from Joe Tessler wanting to know if he'd talked to "that woman in Detroit" about Bernard Nichols. The calls had been made from his burner cell phone and each sounded more anxious than the one preceding it. He called Acton back first.

"Pete," she said when she answered, "it's been awhile. You're calling to hire me for a juicy new case, right? One with a little sex, but without any danger of getting your private parts shot off?" Her cackle came from her belly and lasted half a minute.

Pete couldn't help but chuckle. "If I come up with a case like that, you're number one on my list."

"How's that perky daughter of yours doing? She must be halfway through her first semester by now."

"She's not in college. She decided to take a *gap* year, if you know what that is."

"Gap. That's like a gulch, right?"

"A gap year seems to be the in thing with young people these days. They put off college for a year to find themselves."

Acton didn't say anything for a few moments and Pete imagined her shaking her head in disgust, which is kind of the way he felt about it. Then she said, "Shoot, when I was eighteen, if I wanted to find myself, all I had to do was reach for my behind." She cut loose with another cackle.

"I'm with you, Rae. The reason I called is—"

"So where is Miss Julie trying to find herself? In your basement?" More cackles.

"She's in Philadelphia looking for a woman whose life was ruined by the guy who was killed while jet skiing on my lake last summer."

"Oh, that must make you *real* happy. You had her life all planned for her. A neurosurgeon at the Cleveland Clinic, or maybe managing partner at one of those snooty Wall Street law firms. A lot can go wrong in your head when you take time off."

"You're partly to blame, you know. On the way home after our last visit with you, she told me she'd added private investigator to her list of possible career choices."

"Oh, God. Okay, we both live by the billing clock, Pete. What can I do you for?"

"Have you heard of a guy named Bernard Nichols? I'm told he's a private investigator in Detroit. Ex-FBI."

A pause. "You're not thinking about hiring him, are you?"

"No." He explained how Nichols had been brought in to conduct an internal investigation at his local sheriff's department.

Acton grunted.

"I gather from your reaction that you know him."

"I've bumped into Bernie a few times. Ex-FBI like you said, some-thing he manages to work into just about every conversation. And that he uses in his marketing activities to an extent that makes you want to puke. I happen to know, however, that he didn't leave the Bureau entirely of his own volition. He's apparently something of a cowboy with a penchant for cutting corners and was eased out by the boys above him."

"Really."

"Personally, he's a bear of a man, maybe six-six and two-fifty or two-sixty. Views himself as slick as that old movie star, Clarke Gable. The one who used a tub of axle grease on his hair? But you don't have to be around Nichols long to know where he's coming from. Oily at first, but then closes the trap when he thinks he's got a guy by the you-know-what."

"You said he cuts corners. Any ethics charges against him?"

"Not that I know of, but he probably should have some. Oh, and nothing is ever his fault. If a case goes south, he finds a way to blame it on the lawyers for screwing things up."

When Pete got off the phone, he had a hunch that Tessler wasn't going to be thrilled with what Acton had to say about Nichols. Angie was napping on the couch. He grabbed his car keys, locked the door, and headed for town. He hoped Tessler had talked to his old pals in the Chicago PD and didn't want Angie eavesdropping on his conversation.

Tessler must have been sitting somewhere with the burner phone in his hand, because he answered a second after Pete punched in the number. "Christ, I thought you'd been kidnapped by aliens or something. Where've you been?"

"Personal stuff," he lied. "I talked to Rae Acton about Bernie Nichols. She doesn't know him well, but gave me a pretty good reading on him." He summarized his conversation with Acton.

Tessler was silent when he finished and Pete could imagine him sitting there with a scowl on his face, brooding. "That doesn't sound good," he finally said. "I hate people like that. Pretend you're buddies, but the whole time they're looking for a way to screw you over."

"To be forewarned is to be forearmed."

"I suppose, but I still don't like it."

"Relax. You don't even know if you're on Nichols' interview list."

"*Everyone* in the department's on his list according to the email," Tessler grumbled.

"Tell you what. If Nichols contacts you and says he wants to talk to you, put him off for a while so you and I can talk about it. Don't try to buy too much time, though. That'll only raise suspicions."

"Like if he wants to meet in the afternoon, give him some bull about the things I've got to do on a case, but offer to meet with him the next morning?"

"Something like that. From what Acton said, he's likely to low-key it at first so just act casual and unconcerned when you talk to him."

Tessler didn't say anything for a few moments. Then, "If he wants to meet, do you think you should go with me? You know, as my lawyer?"

"We can talk about that, too. It'll come down to a tactical draw. But understand, Joe, I consider you a friend and I'll do what I can to help you."

"Thanks, I appreciate it." He paused again. "With this friggin' thing hanging over my head, it's hard to sleep or concentrate on my work."

"I understand. Have you had a chance to talk to your friends at the Chicago PD?"

"I have. You know, it's been a year since I talked to them, and I realized how much I miss those friggin' guys. Working cases together, getting scumbags off the streets, enjoying a few beers at Muldoon's in the evenings and telling war stories or maybe sharing insights about the lady species. A ton of memories."

"Sounds like your heart's in Chicago."

Tessler sighed audibly. "That ship has sailed, I'm afraid. But I struck gold on your matter. One of my oldest pals, a guy named Paulie Rozinski, is actually working the bombing case and filled me in on what he knows. He doesn't have it all nailed down yet, but he senses the bombing is part of some power struggle that's going on within the mob. He just doesn't know whether the target is Mr. Big himself, Vinnie Zahn, or if it's one lower level faction against another. Either way, the techs they brought in from the Bureau of Alcohol, Tobacco, Firearms and Explosives to analyze the bomb they found in the second car said it was a pretty sophisticated piece of work. And—get this—your friend, the dame who got blown to smithereens, was the wife of Carmen DeMarco, Zahn's nephew."

Pete was stunned. The newspaper accounts mentioned a possible connection between DeMarco and Zahn's organization, but said nothing about a family relationship. How could Angie not know that?

"The working premise they're operating on right now," Tessler continued, "is that the bomb was intended for Carmen. I guess he was out of town somewhere, but his wife was home, and when she got in the vehicle to go somewhere, *kaboom!*"

"What's the rationale for concluding the bomb was intended for Carmen?"

"Logic I guess. The mob, even rogue factions, doesn't usually go after family members unless special circumstances are involved. An unwritten code or something. Like soldiers aren't supposed to kill civilians."

Ah, he thought. That's what he'd heard from other sources and now it had been confirmed by someone who should know. It was the part of Angie's story that bothered him the most.

"Here's where they are now," Tessler said. "I guess Paulie's team has a snitch inside the organization who feeds them information. He's trying to find out which faction might be behind the bombing, but these things take time. The snitch can't appear too eager or push too hard. It's got to appear casual, you know?"

"Right."

"Here's something else that'll blow your mind. Zahn, who's been running mob operations in the Chicago area for years, apparently spends a lot of time up here in our neck of the woods these days. He has this humongous yacht, see, and likes to cruise up this way. During one of his trips, he found out about a vineyard that was for sale, looked at the place and fell in love with it. Now he likes to think of himself as a wine bigshot. The feds picked up on this, too, and are trying to figure out how he can afford his life style on the income he reports for federal income tax purposes. I guess they're hoping to pull an Al Capone on him. That's the way they got Big Al, you know, on tax evasion charges."

"Interesting."

Tessler was quiet for a few moments. "Jesus, Pete, if I'd stayed in Chicago, I could have been working cases like this. Maybe even written a book when it was all over and made a fortune. You would have seen me interviewed on all the cable stations, and if I had the right publicity guy, maybe even on the big-three networks."

"That would have been something. But it's water over the dam as you just said."

He sighed again. "A guy can dream, can't he?"

"Joe, I owe you. Thanks."

"You'll have a chance to repay me if this Nichols guy comes kicking my door down and I scream for help."

Driving back to his lake house, Pete wondered why Angie was playing coy about Vinnie Zahn.

THIRTEEN

"Carm, wake up," Joey Lebo said, flicking DeMarco's shoulder with the back of his hand. "You're not going to believe this friggin' place."

DeMarco opened his eyes and tried to shake off the grogginess from his nap. He worked the controls on the side of his seat to return it to an upright position and gazed around. On both sides of the tree-lined driveway, he saw neat rows of grapevines, now brownish because of the changing seasons, and straight ahead, a massive slate gray manor house perched on the crest of the gentle hill.

Lebo guided the black Cadillac Escalade toward the manor house and gawked around. "Jeez," he said, "I bet you can see the whole damn countryside from that house."

At the top of the hill, the drive widened into a broad cobblestone piazza with a gargoyle fountain anchoring the center. The fountain had been shut down for the season.

"And that fountain . . . That's something you see in the old country in front of some humongous castle."

DeMarco seemed unimpressed and glanced around with a sullen expression.

Lebo circled the fountain and said, "Where do you think I should park? By that smaller house with the visitor's sign? Or closer to the front door?"

"For crissakes, Leebs, stop acting like a tourist who's never been out of the neighborhood. Just park. This ain't the Vatican."

Lebo looped around the fountain again and parked in front of the manor house, but discreetly away from the front door. He shut off the engine and gazed around, both hands clutching the steering wheel. "You ever been here before?" he asked.

"No, I've never *been* here before."

"I heard about it from some of the crew," Lebo said. "Leave it to Vinnie to find a place where he can live like a friggin' emperor."

"Yeah," DeMarco said in a sour tone, "and tell us how to run our personal lives."

"I guess this place has a real colorful history," Lebo continued. "The guy who built it, name of Conti I believe, was in the hospital with some kind of ailment, and this other guy who worked for him came to visit one day. Only it wasn't a visit, you know? The guy had come to feed Conti some lead poison and, you know, take over the business. But I guess Conti didn't get where he was by being a fool and had a gun of his own under a blanket. They wound up plugging each other. Even with all the medical dudes around, both of them still croaked. That's something, huh? Right out of a Godfather movie or something."

DeMarco just grunted.

"I guess Vinnie didn't buy the place from the stiff, though," Lebo continued. "Some other guy bought it first, but he had this fantasy of making Michigan wines better than the stuff the Froggies make and poured a ton of coin into the place. The business went belly up and he had to file bankruptcy, you know? Vinnie swept in like a friggin' white knight and scooped up the place for next to nothing."

"Figures," DeMarco muttered.

"Think we should go in?" Lebo asked nervously. "We're still a half-hour early."

"Tough shit that we're early. We're the ones who had to drive a thousand miles to get to this place. We could have handled everything on the phone. What's there to talk about anyway?"

"I guess Vinnie has something else he wants to discuss. Besides your thing, I mean, and he's careful about not talking business on the phone because phones can be tapped."

DeMarco rolled his eyes and got out and walked toward the front door. Lebo seemed anxious and glanced at his watch again, but hurried to catch up.

Seeing no doorbell, DeMarco used the ornate gargoyle-shaped knocker to herald their arrival. When no one answered in ten seconds, he was about to bang the knocker a second time, but the planked wooden door swung open a couple of feet and a black-clad man of medium height with a square jaw and bristly salt-and-pepper hair stared at them through the opening. "You're early," Freddy Pole, Zahn's caporegime, said. He wasn't smiling.

"We just drove a thousand miles to get here, Freddy. Sorry if we couldn't time our arrival to the second."

Pole fixed him with an icy stare. "It's three hundred miles, sunshine, not a thousand."

DeMarco's jaunty grin morphed into a scowl. "Just tell Vinnie we're here."

"The boss ain't too happy with you. You might want to show more respect."

"Tell him we're here, okay? And say we apologize for being," he glanced at his watch, "twenty-three minutes early."

Pole closed the door.

DeMarco stared at the door, then glanced Lebo's way. "Do you believe that dickhead?"

"Don't make a stink about it, Carm," Lebo said, trying to calm the waters. "Let's sit and have a conversation with the gargoyles and enjoy the scenery. It's a beautiful day."

"Goddamn jerk," DeMarco muttered. "The day's coming . . ."

They sat on the edge of the inactive fountain and made small talk until Pole opened the manor house door again and beckoned them inside. When they walked through the door, they saw two other men they didn't know standing about ten feet apart behind the arch. "You have pieces with you?" Pole asked.

"Of course," DeMarco said.

"Leave them on the table and pass through security."

DeMarco started to object, but Pole cut him off and motioned for them to do as he'd asked. After hesitating for a moment, DeMarco complied and Lebo followed his lead. A minute later, Vinnie Zahn appeared in a motorized wheelchair. He was a heavyset man with hair turned silver that was slicked straight back, and even though it was October, he had a deep tan. A colorful blanket was folded neatly over his lap and lower torso.

"Carmen," he said, extending his arms. DeMarco stepped forward to embrace him and kissed him on both sides of his face. Zahn nodded at Lebo and said, "Good to see you, Joey."

With the formalities out of the way, Zahn said to DeMarco, "It's a beautiful day. We won't have many more like this. Let's talk on the patio. I'm not getting out enough these days."

Zahn reversed directions with his wheelchair and headed down a hallway with DeMarco following. When Lebo started after them, Pole blocked his way and shook his head. "Family business, Joey."

Pole held the door for Zahn and he coasted down a ramp to the cobblestone patio. He stopped in a patch of sunshine and motioned for DeMarco to sit in one of the chairs. Opera music began to drift from the outdoor speakers.

Zahn gazed around at the sea of grapevines on the rolling hills and his pride was evident. "You've never been here before, have you, Carmen?" he said.

DeMarco shook his head.

"I love this place. After we're finished talking, I'll have Freddy give you a tour if you want. Maybe I'm getting old, but more and more, I appreciate the beauty of nature. You don't get this in Chicago."

"Very nice," DeMarco said, nodding.

"There's another reason I thought we should talk outside. Our friends the feds are lurking everywhere these days. I believe the house is secure, but you can never be sure. This is better."

"Can't be too careful."

"What's this I hear about you thinking Angela might still be alive?"

"Not long after the funeral," DeMarco said, "I think it was early in September, I was opening the mail and came across a credit card statement addressed to the bitch. I —"

Zahn raised a hand. "We don't call women who've been members of our family that name, Carmen. It's not respectful."

"But that's exactly what she was. She —"

"You still need to speak of her in respectful terms."

"I —"

Zahn shook his head.

DeMarco took a deep breath and continued. "Anyway, I looked at the credit card statement and saw a couple of charges that were after the date of the funeral. I called the bank that issued the credit card, but of course the jerks wouldn't talk to me. Gave me some bull about me not being on the account. I thought about it some more and decided that the charges must have been made before the funeral, but were just late being posted."

Zahn gazed at him solemnly.

"Then a few days ago, I was opening the mail that had built up while I was playing golf at Lake Geneva and found this new statement. It showed nine new charges, all with dates in September and all made at stores in places in northern Wisconsin. I called the bank again and explained the situation, but like before, they wouldn't give me any information."

"Maybe Angela lost her credit card before she died and someone has been using it," Zahn volunteered.

DeMarco shook his head. "I thought of that, but if little wifey had lost her card, she would have been on the phone to the bank ten seconds later, cancelling it and demanding a new one. That's how she was. And if she'd died when the car went up, all of her credit cards and everything else would have been melted into a hunk of goo the size of a dime and nothing would have been left to use."

Zahn continued to listen, obviously waiting for some kind of conclusion to DeMarco's rambling story.

"And then there's something else," DeMarco said. "I got to thinking and I called Angie's cell phone number. It rang and rang, but no one answered. That collaborated everything else I told you. If she'd been in that car, her cell phone would have been incinerated along with everything else. It's not in the house, either. I tell you, Vinnie, she's still alive."

"Who was driving the car then?"

"I don't *know* who was driving the car. I just know she's not dead."

Zahn appeared to think over what DeMarco had just said. "I've been thinking while you've been talking, Carmen. It might not be the worst thing in the world if Angela *isn't* dead. If she shows up, the investigation into her death goes away and you could divorce her. If she doesn't show again, she's as good as dead whether she is or not. It's win-win either way."

DeMarco's face darkened. "I don't see how it would be win-win. She was whoring around with every shithead in Cook County. I deserve justice."

Zahn's voice took on a sterner tone. "I don't like to lecture you, Carmen, but you didn't have my blessing to begin with and it's created problems for us. This isn't the old days anymore, when if someone disrespected us, we'd go after them. We're businessmen now. We're smarter and have lowered our profile. We do better if we approach things in a quiet way. We use muscle only when necessary."

DeMarco clenched his teeth and tried to remain calm.

"Bombings attract attention," Zahn continued. "The Chicago PD is involved and, we're pretty sure, the feds. You've been questioned. Others may be, too. Maybe even me."

DeMarco shook his head and waved a hand. "Their bullshit investigation is going absolutely nowhere. I set it up so I was seventy-five miles away playing golf at the time the car went up. Three witnesses will testify to that if they have to. They haven't questioned anyone else in the organization, not Leebs, not anyone."

"But they know you're my nephew."

DeMarco shrugged.

"They know, Carmen, you can ask Freddy. It was in the papers a few years ago. Cops can read. At this point in my life, I want to attend to business and enjoy what time I have left rather than deal with a problem my nephew created."

DeMarco shook his head again. "There ain't gonna be a problem, trust me."

"There *could* be, though. That's why you can't just go around whacking people. We have rules for a reason."

"I didn't whack her. I just took care of a personal problem because she disrespected me in a way no man should have to tolerate. It wasn't like I hit some guy without getting permission. This was personal. Me and her."

Zahn gazed out over his vineyard for a few moments, then turned to DeMarco and said, "Carmen, you're my sister's only child, God rest her soul." He crossed himself. "My nephew. I always treated you as blood even though you came to us in a different way. What do you want from me?"

"Let me use some of our resources to find her."

"And then?"

DeMarco fidgeted with his hands. "Finish the job. It'll be quiet, but I need to finish it."

Zahn just looked at him.

"I promise I won't do anything without clearing it with you first."

Zahn thought about it. "Do you have the names of any of the men you believe Angela was being unfaithful with?"

"Nothing specific, but believe me, I know."

Zahn nodded. "Let's approach this like businessmen and confirm whether Angela is dead or not. If she's not, we can talk about it some more."

"How am I supposed to confirm it beyond what I just told you?"

"Maybe you and Leebs should pay a visit to her gravesite some night." Zahn crossed himself again.

"You mean . . ."

"Is there a better way to find out for sure?"

A shudder rippled through DeMarco's body. "This isn't like she had a heart attack or something. Her body . . ."

"I'm told DNA testing still might be possible. We have a man in Gary, Indiana who owes me. Freddy will give you his name when we finish. He'll tell you what he needs—a body sample, things to test against. A swab of the inside of her mouth would be best, but you can't get that obviously."

DeMarco considered his suggestion, only with Vinnie, it was more of an order.

"You can borrow a couple of soldiers from Dino's crew to help with the excavation."

DeMarco looked at Vinnie. A graveyard expedition hadn't occurred to him, but it made sense. The old shit's best days might be behind him, but he could still get to the heart of the matter.

"Let's ask Freddy and Leebs to join us," Zahn said. "I need the two of you to stop at a place called Venus on your way back to Chicago and talk to the owner. Man named Simon Frei. Venus is just outside a small burg south of here called Thompsonville. It's an adult entertainment place and fits with our other business ventures. We thought we had an agreement with Mr. Frei, but now he's being difficult."

FOURTEEN

The next morning, Joe Tessler called on his burner cell phone and told Pete that Bernie Nichols, the outside investigator, had just contacted him and asked to meet at 4:00 p.m. that afternoon. Tessler said he was forced to agree because he couldn't come up with a credible reason to put him off.

They hashed it over a few moments and agreed to meet in Pete's office in an hour to discuss strategy in more detail. Pete could tell he'd have some hand-holding to do because his detective friend sounded like a basket case already. He decided to stop feeling like he had to explain to Angie every time he twitched and just told her he was running into town.

The block where Pete's office was located was free of vehicles when he got there and he parked right in front. Tessler was already leaning against the wall with hands in his pockets and his jacket collar turned up to ward off the morning chill.

"Where's your Acura?" Pete asked.

"On a side street. I didn't want someone to come by and see my car parked in front of your office."

Pete nodded and unlocked his office door and they went inside. Tessler rubbed his hands together to warm up while Pete made coffee. When they were seated, Pete asked, "How was Nichols on the telephone?"

"Like a slick French diplomat calling to set up an appointment with the Queen of England. He kept saying things like, 'I know you're busy' and 'I want to make this convenient for you' and all kinds of bull like that. I'm glad you told me about him being oily. I had to wipe the phone after we finished to get rid of the grease."

Pete chuckled. He opened his wallet and took out a dollar bill and slid it across the desk towards Tessler. "Now give it back to me and tell me you want me to be your lawyer for purposes of the investigation."

Tessler looked puzzled. "Of *course* I want you to be my lawyer. That's why I'm here."

"The dollar is consideration for the relationship we're establishing. If anyone asks about our conversations, I want to be able to plead attorney-client privilege."

Tessler rolled his eyes and did as Pete asked.

"Does Frank know you're meeting with Nichols?"

"Yeah, he knows. After I finished with Oilcan, which is what I call the guy now, I went down to his office to talk to him, kind of casual-like, about one of my cases. When we finished, I mentioned the meeting and asked Frank if he knew what Oilcan wanted to talk about, not using that term of course. He just shrugged and referred to the email he'd sent around earlier."

"So you think Frank knew Nichols had called you before you mentioned it."

"I'm damn near positive he knew. He was slick as hell himself, like he'd rehearsed ahead of time what he was going to say in case I raised the subject. I think he was expecting it, you know?"

Pete nodded. "Okay, let's start with the background."

Tessler scowled. "If you're going to ask me if I did it, no, I had absolutely nothing to do with it."

"My questions are more specific than that."

Tessler eyed him warily. "Okay, shoot."

"Have you ever used drugs?"

Tessler shifted around in his chair. "Just so I understand this privilege thing, is it like a man giving confession to a priest and the priest can't tell anybody?"

Pete didn't think it was necessary to get into the nuances of attorney-client privilege so he just said, "Yes, very similar."

"I smoked weed once in a while when I was with Taty," he said, referring to his estranged wife who still lived in Chicago. "Sometimes she got a bag of the stuff and I—"

"You only used it when you were with her?"

Tessler stared at the desk top a moment. "Maybe a few other times when I was with some lady and was trying to be polite. To tell you the truth, I really don't like the crap."

"Were any of those 'other times' up here?"

Tessler appeared to think. "None I can think of offhand." He laughed derisively. "It would be a hell of a lot cheaper if Kelene used weed instead of drinking those damn Pink Silk Panties martinis she likes. Every time she takes a swallow, all I hear is cha ching, cha ching."

"How about other drugs? Heroin, coke, meth, things like that."

"Never. That stuff's poison and I hate it. Over the years, I helped put away a lot of dealers and wholesalers. All the lives they ruin . . ."

"So only marijuana and then only on occasion with a lady friend."

"Yeah, that's right. But Pete, this has to stay between you and me and can't get out. On my applications for jobs with law enforcement agencies, including when I was hired by our department, I always answered 'no' to questions about drug use. If it ever got out that I've used weed now and then . . . it might jeopardize my career, you know? Smoking dope, falsifying employment applications."

"I understand."

"I'm glad you raised this, though. If the Oilcan asks, how should I answer?"

"You won't be under oath this afternoon, and Nichols isn't regular law enforcement, so you won't be guilty of perjury or some other offense if you answer incorrectly and the doo-doo later hits the fan. But I still think you need to be careful. If Nichols asks if you've ever used drugs, you might want to come back with a question of your own, like 'You mean heroin, coke, things like that?' Chances are he'll nod or say 'yes,' and you can honestly answer that you haven't. If he asks about marijuana specifically, you're going to have to make a decision."

"Now I'm more nervous than I was. If I admit I used weed a few times, Oilcan is going to tell Frank and then I'll have problems even if he's satisfied I had nothing to do with the evidence room bull."

"Well, I can't advise you to lie, but I certainly understand the potential consequences if you were to admit to marijuana use. You'll have to make your own draw if the issue comes up directly. Next question, and I know what you said a few minutes ago, but I also know you feel you're underpaid for what you do. Have you ever supplemented your income either by removing a controlled substance of some kind from the evidence room and selling it directly to users or indirectly to a street distributor, or by—"

"Jesus Christ, Pete, I *told* you I had nothing to do with that."

"Or by holding back some of the product seized when you made a drug bust, rather than turning it all in as evidence."

"Never. Maybe I smoked weed once in a while because of some lady friend or other, and I told you how that happened, but I damn sure never did any of those other things."

"Good."

Tessler scowled at him again.

"Next question. Is there a procedure for signing in and out of your evidence room?"

"Sure, there's a sign-in book outside the door to the room. You have to be an authorized person to enter and then you have to sign before you actually go in and again when you leave."

"And the authorized persons are you, Sheriff Richter and Connie Chapman, right?"

"That's what I said."

"Does anyone else ever go in the evidence room."

"Occasionally. We're a small office, remember, and we can't have overly rigid procedures. One of the deputies may have to go in sometimes. When I'm not around and Frank isn't around, maybe, or when we're both busy and can't take the time to accompany him."

"How does the deputy get in in those circumstances? You need a key card, right?"

"The desk officer lets him in if necessary. He has a card he keeps locked up in a drawer."

"So there actually are *four* access cards: the ones you and Frank and Connie have, plus the one in the desk."

Tessler appeared to think about it. "Yeah, that's right, I guess there are four. I never thought about it before."

"So, in reality, everyone in the department goes in the evidence room at one time or another."

"I don't know if *everyone* goes in, but most of our people do."

"How about at night?"

"At night, the deputy manning the desk is the only one in the building the entire time. Others may come in from time-to-time."

"So theoretically, at least, the desk officer could use the card to get in the evidence room. Or he could let another deputy in."

Tessler considered it. "Yeah, he could I suppose."

"How about Frank, does he ever go in the evidence room after hours?"

Tessler shrugged. "I assume so, I really don't know."

"Have you ever gone in after hours?"

Tessler appeared to think again. "A couple of times. Six or seven months ago, I was working on an affidavit for a case where the perp had stabbed the victim and I needed to make sure my description of the knife was accurate so I went in and examined it. Another time, we busted a meth lab one night, and when we got back to the station, I went into the evidence room to log in the stuff we confiscated. Those are the two times I remember offhand."

"Was anyone with you either time?"

More thinking, then, "Not with the knife, I'm sure of that. With the meth, I'm not sure."

"Okay, when you meet with Nichols, stick with the answers you just gave me if the issues come up. If he doesn't mention the fourth key card, see if you can work it into the conversation somehow to demonstrate that a lot of people had access to the evidence room, not just those of you who permanently carry cards. That should widen the universe of suspects, so to speak. The marijuana issue, you'll just have to play that by ear and do what you think is best."

"If Oilcan asks me about weed, I'm going to give him an answer that's consistent with what I put on my employment application. I don't have any other choice."

Pete nodded. "I didn't hear that. However you answer, just be careful you don't put it in a way that lets Nichols trip you up later."

Tessler looked around the room before he asked, "Have you decided if you're coming with me to the meeting?"

"I thought about it, but concluded it's not a good idea. It would elevate the importance of your meeting with Nichols, and I don't think we want to do that at this stage. You're better off treating the whole thing casually, like you're not concerned. Plus, if I show up, Frank would know about it in a nanosecond, and given our past relationship, he'd not only think you have something to hide, but I'd probably become a distraction as well."

Tessler nodded and didn't say anything for a while. "I'd be lying if I said I wasn't concerned about the investigation. I know I'm repeating myself, but I feel my career is on the line."

"You wouldn't be normal if you weren't concerned."

Tessler didn't say anything.

"I know you said you feel that Frank dodged your questions, but do you have any reason to believe he suspects you?" Pete asked.

Tessler got up and refilled his coffee mug. After he sat down again, he took a sip of his fresh coffee and wiped his mouth with a sleeve. "You think that hasn't been on my mind? When something like this happens, all of a sudden you replay every conversation you've had with the guy in the past year. You begin imagining things, you know? Reading things into this comment he made, or that action."

"Has your relationship with Frank changed in any way?"

"I didn't *think* our relationship has changed. Until this investigation crap popped up and now I have all these thoughts . . ."

FIFTEEN

On the way back to his lake house, Pete changed his radio setting to a Sirius channel that featured old time rock and roll just in time to hear that an icon of the genre, Fats Domino, had died. Sadness swept over him. He'd never seen the "Fat Man" in person, but he had about ten CDs of his music, including several that featured his lesser known songs. He turned up the volume as one of his big hits, "Walkin' to New Orleans," came on.

The music soothed him, and as he listened, his mind drifted back to his meeting with Tessler. Learning of his occasional marijuana use didn't shock him, particularly in the circumstances he described, but the economic thing stuck in his mind because of what Angie had mentioned. He turned up the sound some more when another Fats Domino song came on.

The drapes were closed again and the door was locked. When he walked in, Angie was sprawled on the couch, reading, as she often was.

"How was town?"

"Quiet." He decided not to say anything about his prep session with Joe Tessler.

She went back to her book.

"By the way," Pete said, "did you hear that Fats Domino died?"

She looked his way again and frowned.

"The old rock and roll icon? 'Blueberry Hill' and those songs?"

"Oh, another of your octogenarian music heroes."

"Fats was one of the original inductees into the Rock & Roll Hall of Fame, you know. He set the standard for a lot of stars to come. He was also synonymous with New Orleans. President Clinton even awarded him the National Medal of Arts. When Hurricane Katrina came along, Fats' house was flooded along with hundreds of others and the medal was lost. President Bush flew to New Orleans to meet him and replace the medal."

"You're a walking music historian."

Pete's cell phone burred. It was Julie. "Hi, Sweetie," he said.

"How's the weather at the lake?"

"Glorious. Sunny, lots of color. Cool, obviously. How's your investigation coming?"

"Have I talked to you after Effie and I met that guy at Starbucks?"

"I don't think so."

"He turned out to be real squirrelly. You know the type I'm talking about. Likes to give you the impression he knows everybody and everything. It turns out that he hadn't seen or talked to Leslie since she left Harrison Stryker. It was still a useful meeting, though. He gave us the names of a couple of people who know her and we're following up with them. That's the lifeblood of investigations, you know. You talk to one person who mentions someone else and you talk to them and so on. All of a sudden, you're onto something. I think that could happen here."

Pete enjoyed the lecture on investigative technique by a gap-year teenager and said, "Sounds like you're on the right track."

Julie didn't say anything for a few moments, then, "Dad, do you suppose you could put two thousand dollars in my account? I have a bill I need to pay."

The number got his attention. "Yeah, what?"

"I told you I've moved in with Effie and Aaron and the baby. The other day, Aaron got into an argument with the owner of the shoe store where he's been working and lost his job. He's looking for something else. Bad timing, because things have also been slow with Effie and her part-time accounting work. Our rent is due in a few days and—"

Pete rolled his eyes. "And someone has to come up with the cash, right?"

"Well, yeah. Effie and Aaron are going to reimburse me for their share as soon as their financial situation straightens out, so it's not like I'd be paying their bills *permanently* or anything."

"Julie, a lesson I learned early on in life is to keep my friendships separate from my financial affairs. You start lending money to friends and usually it doesn't end up well."

"Oh, for God's sake, Dad! That's what friends are for, you help each other out. You've always had a good job and never had to worry about things like money. Not everyone is that lucky."

Pete's blood pressure rose as he thought about the days in college and law school when he couldn't afford a Big Mac for dinner.

He kept calm and said, "I'll tell you what, I'll put the money in your account, but you need to have a talk with Effie and Aaron and let them know it's a one-shot thing. If you can't work out an arrangement whereby you're comfortable they can meet their obligations, you need to move out and get your own accommodations again."

"That's why we have disagreements sometimes, Dad. You never seem able to see things from the other person's point of view. People have financial problems when they're just starting out in life, particularly these days. Besides, your friend Bud Stephanopoulis? That big buddy of yours? It's *his* fault that Effie and Aaron are in this mess. They wouldn't have lost their jobs but for him. I'd think you would be more *understanding!*"

Pete didn't say anything for a long moment, then trying not to sound annoyed, he said, "Sorry, Julie, someone's at my door and I have to go. I'll put the money in your account, but you need to have that conversation with your roommates. I love you and I'm always here if you want to talk."

He put his cell phone down and noticed Angie's smile. He used it as an opportunity to vent.

"You probably heard enough of that to get the drift," he said. "Julie has moved into an apartment with two other people she claims are helping her search for Leslie Lehr. Now they can't pay the rent and want Julie to pay. Just this month, you understand," he said sarcastically. "Next month, everything will be hunky-dory. Get it?" He shook his head.

Angie looked at him sympathetically.

Before he could go off some more on deadbeat roommates, his cell phone burred again and Tessler said, "I just got out of my meeting with Oilcan."

"Did it go okay?"

"I think so. No questions about whether I used drugs, but a ton about the evidence room and procedures and my access to it and what I did and didn't do. I managed to work in the fourth key card. That session in your office was really helpful because it refreshed my memory about a lot of things."

"But, no real problems, huh?"

"No real problems, but he asked questions about a place called Venus. Ever hear of it?"

"Nope."

"It's in an unincorporated area outside Thompsonville. We've been trying to close it down for two years because we suspect it's nothing but a sex club with prostitution and drug dealing and other bad stuff going on. It's organized as a private club, but we believe that's only to get around some technicalities I'm not completely up on."

"Okay."

"Oilcan asked me if I was familiar with the place and I said I was. We have an undercover guy who works the joint for us, trying to see if he can ferret out something we can use. One night he had a conflict and I went out there and moped around myself. Another night, I staked out the parking lot to see if I could spot someone I recognized coming or going."

"What's the connection between Venus and his investigation?"

"Drugs, I suppose. That's mostly the stuff missing from the evidence room and Venus may be an outlet."

"But he didn't accuse you of anything."

"No, but he's a sneaky sonofabitch and I could see where he might be going."

"How did he leave it?"

"He said he was just getting started with his investigation and would be back to me if he had any more questions."

"That's it?"

"That's it."

"Should I send you my invoice for the balance due for my services?"

"Hey, buddy, you've been paid." Tessler paused for a few moments before he added, "I've got to tell you, though, I'm a bit of an expert on intimidation myself, but this guy . . . Maybe I should stop calling him Oilcan and start calling him The Hulk. He's an absolute moose of a guy. You're been in our interview rooms enough to know how tight they are. With him on one side of the table and me on the other, Jesus, you couldn't have wedged a chihuahua into the room with us. I kept trying to move my chair back to create more separation between us, but it was impossible. I got the feeling the guy was deliberately leaning across the table to get closer to me. I tell you, when I walked out of the room, my pits were dripping. And facing down bad guys is what I do for a living."

"Well, hang in there."

"I'm gonna try. Maybe I'll make a date with Kelene tonight to take my mind off things."

SIXTEEN

"Jeez, it's not even nighttime and look at all of these friggin' vehicles," Lebo said as he eyed the array of pickups, vans, SUVs and sedans and looked for a parking spot. "The place is packed already."

DeMarco had been silent on the ride south from the vineyard, still seething over his private conversation with Vinnie Zahn. He glanced around, his expression surly, and said, "Stop complaining and park, will you? We need to find that asshole Frei and make sure he gets the message, then get out of here." His mind was on the cemetery back home.

Lebo found a spot under a tree, away from the other vehicles and they got out and walked toward the door. Lebo pulled his stocking cap lower on his head and grinned when he glanced DeMarco's way. He'd known the guy since they were kids, but had never seen him with headgear no matter the weather. There were advantages to not needing to worry about messing your hair.

The Venus building was a boxy industrial-style structure laid out in an architecturally unimaginative rectangle. It appeared higher than one story, but not quite high enough for two. Like it once had been an assembly plant or warehouse that required extra space to accommodate overhead equipment.

"Looks like a goddamn factory," Lebo grumbled. "I wonder why it's such a big deal."

DeMarco ignored him and picked up his stride toward the polished wooden door flanked by ornate light fixtures. A man in black athletic clothes with white trim down the arms and legs leaned against the outer wall with folded arms and watched them come. When they got close, he said, "Can I help you, gentlemen?"

"We're here to see Simon Frei," DeMarco said.

"Do you have an appointment?"

"No, but he'll want to see us."

"Names?"

"Never mind our names. Where do we find Frei?"

"He's not here."

"This is his place, ain't it? Venus or whatever you call it."

The doorman stared at them with baleful eyes. He still hadn't moved.

DeMarco stared back for a few moments, then started toward the door. "I think we'll wait for him inside."

The doorman finally moved and blocked DeMarco's path. "Members only," he said. "If you don't have a business appointment, you have to be a member to go inside."

"I told you we're just here to see Frei. We ain't here to squeeze boobies or pinch butts."

The doorman shook his head. "Sorry."

Lebo peered over DeMarco's shoulder. "This is bullshit," he muttered.

The doorman continued to block the door.

"What do we have to do to become members?" DeMarco asked, seeing where the conversation was headed and wanting to avoid unnecessary confrontation that might interfere with their mission.

"Pay the initiation fee."

Lebo continued to glare over DeMarco's shoulder at the doorman, his big hands clenching and unclenching.

"How much is the fee?" DeMarco asked.

"Depends. You guys locals?"

DeMarco shook his head. "Chicago. A suburb."

"You got ID?"

"Oh, for crissakes!" Lebo said. DeMarco put his arm out to restrain Lebo and pulled out an Illinois driver's license under a false name.

The doorman looked at it and handed it back. "You qualify for non-resident membership," he said. "Initiation fee is a hundred a head. Cash only, no checks, no credit cards."

"Friggin' ridiculous," Lebo muttered.

DeMarco didn't say anything. He opened his wallet and counted out four fifty-dollar bills and handed them to the doorman. He examined them briefly with a small light, then handed DeMarco two key-like objects. "Welcome to Venus, gentlemen. Cash policy applies inside, too." He opened the heavy door for them.

"Would you tell Mr. Frei we're looking for him?" DeMarco asked.

"If I see him."

When they were inside, Lebo said in a snarly voice, "You should have let me take care of him, Carm. Two hundred bucks. That's friggin' ridiculous. Extortion."

"We're here to deal with Frei, not get into a hassle with an asshole doorman."

They heard disco music blaring from the area straight ahead and pushed through the heavy velvet curtain. The main room was massive, at least a hundred feet long, with strobe lights blinking on and off and psychedelic images floating across the ceiling and the walls and the floor. In one corner, a woman who was naked except for a flimsy thong strutted around a small stage and periodically writhed around a pole.

"Holy crap," Lebo said as his eyes darted around.

DeMarco just pushed through the crowd toward the polished metal bar which, like everything else in the room, seemed to be in perpetual motion with the ever-shifting light patterns.

They both ordered a Miller Lite. The bartender brought the beers and asked for twenty dollars. Lebo started to protest again, but DeMarco handed the man a twenty and an additional ten as a tip. The bartender turned to walk away when DeMarco said, "The doorman told us Simon Frei isn't here yet. Would you let us when he comes in? He's expecting us."

The bartender stared back at them.

DeMarco picked up on the scam and passed him another twenty-dollar bill. The bartender stuffed it in his apron pocket and left without saying anything.

"Ten bucks for a friggin' beer," Lebo groused. "You can buy a six-pack in the lousy grocery store for that. And that's retail."

When DeMarco didn't say anything, Lebo added, "For the membership fee they charge, you'd think that they'd at least give you a couple of beers on the house."

DeMarco took a swallow of his beer.

"What do those membership things look like?" Lebo asked.

DeMarco fished in his pocket and dropped one of the keys on the bar. Lebo examined it. "Hey," he said, "this is cool. It has a naked lady on it." He ran his fingers over the embossment.

DeMarco drank more Miller Lite.

Lebo put the key in his wallet and rolled his beer bottle between his big hands, saying, "And to be held up by that stinking doorman . . . I know you didn't want to start no ruckus, but two minutes with the guy and I would've had him begging us to go in this joint on the house and with free drinks for the whole friggin' night."

DeMarco looked at him. Lebo could come off like a buffoon, but he had a nasty streak that unnerved even him at times. "Vinnie wants this thing low-keyed," he reminded him. "It wouldn't exactly be low-key if you dismantled a dude in public, would it?"

"I just don't like to be jacked around," Lebo said.

DeMarco patted him on the shoulder. A scantily-clad woman who looked like she'd spent time with an enhancement specialist came up to them. She gave DeMarco a squeeze and patted Lebo's arm. "I haven't seen you gentlemen in here before."

"First time," Lebo said, turning into a puppy waiting for a treat.

"My name is Blaze."

"You mean like flames?" Lebo asked. He raised his big hands and flicked his fingers up and down.

"Like *hot*," she said.

"Ohhhhhh, I like it."

"What are your names?"

Lebo moved closer and put an arm around her waist. "I'm Hank Markov and this is Dick Viola," he said, using their aliases.

"Hank and Dick, Dick and Hank. Sounds like a dangerous duo." She batted her heavily made-up eyes. "You two from around here?"

Lebo shook his head and grinned. "Passing through. We're on business."

"I like businessmen," she said, raking her fingernails down his arm. "What kind of business are you in?"

"Oh, a little of this, a little of that. I guess you might say we're with one of those conglomerates." Lebo chuckled at his joke in his high-pitched, scratchy voice.

"That sounds—"

"Look, doll," DeMarco said, "why don't you peddle your cute little fanny somewhere else? Like my friend said, we're here on business and the guy we need to see is coming any minute."

Blaze stuck out her lower lip in a feigned pout and said, "Your friend is a lot more fun than you." She squeezed Lebo's arm and snuggled closer to him.

DeMarco slid off his stool and looked down at her for a few moments, then jerked his thumb away from the bar several times.

She backed away in surprise and said, "Okay, okay, I'm going." She shook her head peevishly. "I thought guys came in here to have fun."

Lebo's eyes followed her as she disappeared among the patrons. "Jeez, Carm, she's just a working girl. It was kind of nice having her around while we're waiting for that Simon guy to show his face."

"Business, Leebs, keep your mind on business. We're here to have a heart-to-heart with Frei, then split. Got it? You want to whore around, do it on your own time."

Lebo sulked and ordered another Miller Lite and drank it in silence.

DeMarco checked his watch every few minutes and looked increasingly agitated. Finally, a man with dark hair slicked back and tied in a short ponytail came up to them. He looked dapper in his black suit over a scarlet-colored mock turtleneck. "Mr. Viola, right?" he said in a voice that sounded like too much cigarette smoke had marinated his vocal chords.

DeMarco slid off his stool, and after sizing him up, said, "Is there somewhere we can talk in private, Simon?"

Frei stared at him, obviously trying to figure out who they were and what they wanted. "I can hear you fine right here."

"We heard you aren't a very cooperative fellow, Simon. We found that hard to believe and decided to see for ourselves." DeMarco caught Lebo's eye and he stepped closer and grabbed Frei's upper arm and squeezed. Frei tried to free himself, but Lebo increased the pressure.

"You must have an office in back, Simon," DeMarco said soothingly. "That would be a lot better than having all these fine people see you start to cry in your own business establishment."

Frei continued to try to break free from Lebo's grasp and the color drained from his face. "Okay, okay, we'll go to my office. But let go of my arm, for crissakes."

DeMarco nodded to Lebo, who eased his grip. Frei wrenched free and rubbed his arm and glared at them.

"But Simon, let's have an understanding," DeMarco said. "Any more bullshit and it won't be your arm Leebs grabs, it'll be your friggin' neck."

Lebo shoved one of his huge hands in front of Frei's face and let him look at it, opening and closing his fingers.

Frei shrank back and rubbed his arm some more. "What the hell do you guys want?"

"Office, Simon."

Frei looked at them a while longer, then turned and led them through the crowd to an unmarked door at the rear of the room. It opened into an outer office suite and DeMarco closed the door behind them and locked it and signaled to Lebo again. He shoved Frei against the wall and began to pat him down and ripped back his suitcoat to expose a shoulder holster. Lebo pulled a handgun from the holster and passed it to DeMarco.

DeMarco examined the piece and smiled. "A Junior Colt, Leebs. Simon must carry this in case a burglar comes around. A real *small* burglar." He chuckled at his joke, then popped the magazine and dropped it in his pocket and tossed the gun on a nearby desk.

"That your office?" he asked Frei, pointing to an inner door.

Frei looked at him sullenly and opened it and walked in. He started toward the high-backed chair behind the desk, but DeMarco grabbed his shoulder and spun him around. "Uh, uh, Simon, that's my seat. You can have one of the guest chairs."

Frei seemed startled. "You can't tell me where to sit in my own friggin' office!"

DeMarco nodded to Lebo again who sprang at him and wrapped a hand around his neck and squeezed. Frei's eyes bulged and his face reddened and both of his hands went to his neck as he tried to break Lebo's grip.

DeMarco propped his feet on the desk and watched Frei struggle. After a few moments, he said sympathetically, "I realize this is a transition period for you, Simon, but I think you'll get used to it. You might even begin to enjoy it. Running a business without a partner can be damn stressful these days."

On DeMarco's signal, Lebo eased up on Frei's neck. It had ugly red marks where Lebo's fingers had dug into his flesh. Frei rubbed his neck and wheezed and gasped for air as he tried to regain his composure. He said in a croaky voice that was barely audible, "I need some water."

DeMarco stared at him balefully. "Water? That comes after we know you'll be a good boy, Simon."

"Tell me what you guys want," Frei said again as he looked up at Lebo with fear showing in his eyes.

"I guess you weren't listening to what I said a minute ago. We understand that a gentleman made you a very fair business proposition last week and he didn't get a very polite response."

Frei's eyes hardened. "You can forget that bullshit offer. No friggin' way."

DeMarco signaled to Lebo again. Frei tried to ward him off, but Lebo grabbed his neck with both of his hands and squeezed. Frei's eyes bulged again and his face turned beet-red and he struggled to free himself from Lebo's vice-like grip. Lebo only loosened his hands when Frei slumped forward.

"I don't think the offer our friend made had a yes or no option attached to it, Simon. The gentleman thought he made an offer you wouldn't be able to refuse, to use the old saying."

Frei's chest heaved and he gasped for breath. Both of his hands were at his neck, massaging it, and he wheezed as he tried to suck in air. Finally he forced out, "Maybe we can work something out if we can agree on the terms."

DeMarco shook his head and looked sad. "I know it's difficult sometimes to think straight when you're under stress, Simon, so let me explain it again. This ain't a choice between A and B. It's a choice between A and A."

"Bullshit—"

Lebo started towards Frei again. He tried to scoot his chair back and it tipped over and he sprawled on the floor. Lebo stood over him, flexing his fingers. Frei held up both of his hands with palms facing out. "Okay," he said. "No more. No more." He continued to gasp and wheeze and pant.

DeMarco gazed at him impassively. "Are you telling us that you and the gentleman have a deal, Simon? On the very fair terms he offered?"

Frei seemed unable to speak and just stared back at him.

DeMarco shook his head again, feigning another sorrowful look. "I'm getting a little tired of your attitude, Simon. You're not being very businesslike."

When Frei didn't respond, DeMarco beckoned to Lebo again. Lebo kicked a chair out of the way and dropped to his knees and reached for Frei's neck again. "No, no," Frei croaked, "we have a deal."

"On all terms, Simon?"

Frei's chest heaved and he gulped for air and squirmed away from Lebo.

"I want to hear it from you, Simon. In front of a witness. You accept this great deal the gentleman offered you, right? All the terms."

Frei nodded weakly. "All terms."

DeMarco still had his feet propped up on Frei's desk. "See, Leebs? Didn't I tell you Simon was a reasonable guy? He just needed to have things presented to him the right way."

Lebo grinned like a wolf about to gorge itself on a fallen lamb.

DeMarco got up and came around the desk and looked down at Frei. "A couple of the gentleman's business associates are planning to visit you again to implement the new arrangement. And you know what, Simon? We'd hate it if word got back to us that you'd reneged on any part of deal you just confirmed. We'd feel very inconvenienced if that happened and we had to come back here and have another heart-to-heart with you. We'd be very upset."

Frei stared up at them.

"And you might want to suggest to that piece of crap doorman you've got working for you that he might want to be more respectful when we visit in the future. My friend here is itching for some exercise."

SEVENTEEN

"Pete, this is Harry McTigue, remember me? I run a newspaper in the northwestern Michigan town of Frankfort. We used to have dinner once in a while."

"Ha, ha."

"Does that mean you *do* remember me? A tall, good-looking guy? Suave and kind of worldly?"

"You're calling to remind me I owe you dinner, right?"

"Lordy, lordy, you don't know what a relief that is. I keep reading that memory loss is a sign of dementia setting in, and I was desperately hoping that hadn't happened to my old buddy. You know, the one I used to enjoy a meal with now and then and go fishing and maybe play some golf?"

Pete shook his head. Harry was on a roll. He eyed Angie across the room and thought, *screw it*. "When do you want to have dinner?"

"If I'm speaking with the man I think I am," Harry continued, sounding thoughtful, "I know I'll probably have to give him a week or two notice because of his extremely busy social calendar. How about—"

"Tonight soon enough?"

"Tonight." A pause and then, "Just a minute, please, I feel unusual palpitations in my chest cavity." Another pause. "They might be getting worse."

"Well," Pete said, tiring of the game, "are you free tonight?"

"Wait, I think the palpitations might be subsiding. Yes, I believe they are. Let me check my calendar for tonight. Mmm," he murmured, "tonight, tonight. Hot dog, it looks like I just had a cancellation! Yes, tonight would work."

Pete rolled his eyes. "Good. Usual time?"

"Usual time would be splendid. You *do* remember you're buying, don't you?"

"Of course. Rona's okay?"

"My very first choice. It'll give you an opportunity to reintroduce yourself to the owner. You remember her, the hot woman I've been carrying on with for years who just can't stay away from me?"

"See you tonight, Harry."

After he ended the call, he looked Angie's way again and said, "That was—"

"I know, Harry. You're having dinner with him."

Angie buried herself in her book again. Pete studied her for a moment and felt a little like the husband who'd just told his wife he planned to enjoy a night out with the boys.

He went to the kitchen for a drink of water and checked the refrigerator. When he came back, he said, "There's fresh ground beef and a carton of vegetable soup in the fridge. And—in the freezer—your very favorite key lime pie."

She glanced up and said, "Thanks."

Pete went upstairs to change clothes and thought that maybe he and Angie were beginning to get on each other's nerves. With any luck, maybe she'd open up about her plans because things were beginning to feel awkward.

When he got downstairs again he said, "I'm off. I need to stop at my office for a few minutes before I meet Harry."

She wiggled her fingers in a goodbye sign without looking at him and said, "Don't say hello for me."

When Pete walked into Rona's Bay Grille, Harry was already there seated at their usual table with a cardboard sign that read, "Welcome Home, Pete." Pete shook his head. Harry could be relentless.

He was about to sit down when Harry hoisted his elliptical body from his chair and stuck out his hand. "Pete Thorsen, right?" he said.

"No, I'm Pete's brother. I'm not as good-looking as Pete, but . . ."

Harry laughed and clapped him on the shoulder and plopped down again. "You don't know how good it is to have things back to normal. We've got some catching up to do."

"Yeah," Pete said dryly, "a lot can happen in a week."

Harry grinned. "What do you hear from that daughter of yours?"

Pete brought him up to date, including on her financial entanglements with Effie Zepp and Aaron Jacobs.

"I had a roommate like that my first year out of J-school. We rented this two-bedroom walkup, see, and this guy whose name I can't even remember grabbed the biggest bedroom before I even stepped foot in the place. He fed me this line about how he was supposed to start this primo job with the Associated Press the following week and asked me to front the first month's rent on our apartment. Trouble is, next week never came and I learned that to him, starting with AP meant sending a blind resume to the attention of the human resources department." He shook his head at the memory.

"I don't know if Effie and Aaron are as bad as your former roommate, but I lectured Julie on the importance of keeping friendships in one corner of your life and financial affairs in another."

"Amen, brother. Do you want me to talk to Julie? I could pass on the lessons I learned the hard way."

"Let's see if what I told her gets through."

Rona Martin, the restaurant owner and Harry's long-time girlfriend, came over and joined them on what was shaping up as a slow night for business. Rona was a tall woman, easily Harry's five-ten height, with thick dark hair and eyes that could stop an army in its tracks. They spent a half-hour discussing local gossip and the situation in Washington, D.C. until she was called to the kitchen to solve some crisis or other.

Her absence gave Harry an opportunity to add an extra dollop of sour cream to his baked potato before he tore into his brook trout and the rest of his meal with the customary gusto, all the time babbling on about happenings around town and on the national scene. He scraped his plate clean and peered at Pete over his half-glasses and said, "Since this is kind of a reunion dinner, I think we should have dessert." Pete's belt was already telling him he'd had enough food, but he agreed to split a piece of key lime pie. Each of them had a double espresso, decaffeinated in Pete's case.

They sipped their espressos, and after more talk about the local scene, Harry said, "I passed by your place a couple of days ago and saw a white sedan parked behind your neighbor's house. I thought he left for Florida just after Labor Day and didn't return until the following spring."

Pete glanced at him, trying to determine whether there was a hidden inference in his comment. "Don't know," he said, choosing his words carefully. "Charlie Cox and I aren't on the most neighborly terms, as I think you know. Maybe he let a friend or relative use his place for a few days."

"Umm," Harry murmured. "The car was still there this afternoon when I happened to pass by again."

"Gee, I didn't know you ran a cottage inspection service on the side. I've never gotten a bill from you."

Harry grinned, and after he'd consumed eighty percent of the pie, looked over his espresso cup and said, "We've gone through a lot over the years, and I think I've gotten to know you pretty well and you've also gotten to know me. You know what my gut tells me? It tells me something is going on in your life that you're not sharing with your best friend."

Pete looked at him and frowned.

"You've seemed to be different recently, like something's bothering you. Your unavailability for dinner lately is another thing."

Pete frowned again. "I thought I explained that."

"You explained it, but isn't it a coincidence that it all started around the time I pulled up those news stories for you?"

Pete saw where Harry was going and wondered how he could squirm out of the box his friend had put him in. He approached it head-on and said, "I'll tell you about it sometime."

"Okay," Harry said. He continued to peer at him over his half-glasses. Their eyes met briefly before Pete glanced around the room.

"If you don't want to talk about it, fine. But I'm here if you change your mind."

The wheels in Pete's head ground away and he felt a need to unburden himself. Finally, he said, "Angie isn't dead."

Harry's bushy eyebrows edged up. "The woman whose funeral you attended?"

Pete nodded.

"So the newspaper stories were 'fake news' as someone likes to say."

"I guess you could say that."

Harry stared at him, clearly not understanding. "I'm all ears if you want to share a few more details."

Pete was almost relieved that Harry had figured out part of it. He sighed and said, "I'll tell you, but it has to stay between just us, okay?"

Harry nodded.

"I assume that's a promise."

"You have my word."

"Angie DeMarco's at my house as we speak."

Harry's eyebrows moved higher.

"She showed up at my house unannounced about a week ago," Pete said. "I thought I was losing my mind, because, as you know, I was one

115

of the people at her funeral." He told Harry the entire story based on what Angie had told him.

Harry was speechless for a full minute. Finally he said, "That's incredible."

Pete nodded.

"You remember I met Angie once. Ten years ago or thereabouts."

"I know."

Harry appeared to think some more. "And she took off after the car explosion because she knew her husband's in the mob and he's in a pissing contest with other mobsters who might be after her, too?"

"That's what she claims."

"Incredible," Harry said, repeating himself. "And for obvious reasons," he continued, "she doesn't want news to get around that her friend died in the car fire and not her."

Pete nodded again. "She's absolutely paranoid. She keeps the drapes closed and the blinds pulled in my house even in the middle of the day and is jittery every time she goes out. When she does venture out, she wears a battered hat she wouldn't have been seen dead in, if you'll excuse the expression, before this happened. She does other things to disguise her appearance, too."

Harry shook his head.

"Then a couple of days ago, I took her for a bike ride to Beulah. There was only one other guy on the trail, but she was absolutely convinced he was following us. Which would have been impossible if no one knows she's alive and up here."

"Do you believe her story?"

Pete shrugged. "Most of it seems to check out, including the news stories you pulled up for me. Without telling him Angie's here, I also had Joe Tessler check with one of his old detective pals in Chicago about the bombing. It turns out one guy he talked to is actually working on the case. He believes the bombing was mob-related which squares with her story."

"Mmm."

"I have a feeling Angie might be holding something back, though. I asked her about Vinnie Zahn, the mob kingpin, and she acted like I'd asked her about a Martian. Then I learned that Zahn is her husband's *uncle*. It doesn't seem possible she wouldn't know that."

"Do you think she just might have been embarrassed?"

He shrugged. "Who knows?"

Harry turned thoughtful. "If she's scared of the mob, have you looked into those witness protection programs?"

"It hasn't come up, and I haven't wanted to ask. She has a law enforcement background and I assume she knows about those programs. From what little I know, though, you have to have something to trade—be a witness to a crime or something—to get in. You can't just have a general fear of the mob."

"Umm," Harry murmured again. "And Angie hasn't told her husband she's still alive, huh?"

"She claims she hasn't. They hate each other. I guess she felt her best option in the circumstance was to disappear after the bombing and let everyone believe she's dead."

Harry shook his head again, then said, "One thing I think you should have her do is move her car. I know it's parked behind your neighbor's house, but I didn't have any trouble seeing it when I drove past."

"On your cottage inspection tour, you mean."

Harry grinned weakly.

"Where would she move it to? The reason we parked it behind Charlie Cox's house is because I know he doesn't come up until spring. Some of the other owners in the area do, though."

Harry looked thoughtful again. "We could do what we did that other time and park the vehicle in my garage."

"Are you missing something, Harry?"

He looked puzzled.

"If I suggest moving her car to your garage, she'll know in a nanosecond I told you she's alive and she'll go off like a NASA rocket."

"Oh yeah."

"Besides, I'm not sure she's in any danger. Unless she's lying to me, that is."

"Getting back to your point, are you planning to tell her that you confided in me?"

"I'll probably have to. I want to pick the time, though."

Harry nodded again.

"Remember what I said, until then, you can't tell anyone else about this. And I mean anyone, including Rona."

Harry looked offended. "You've known Rona almost as long as I have. She doesn't blab things around."

Pete shook his head. "No one, Harry, not a soul."

Harry stared at him a while. "Another idea," he said. "After you *do* tell her, maybe the two of us should meet with her and talk things through. A lot of times, ideas can come out of sessions like that."

"That's a thought. Let's see if I'm still standing."

EIGHTEEN

Joey Lebo clicked his Maglite's switch and flashed the beam on the headstone in front of him and crouched to read the inscription.

"Cut the light, Leebs!" DeMarco hissed.

Lebo switched it off. "I'm having a hard time seeing where I'm going," he whispered over his shoulder.

"I thought you mapped the friggin' scene ahead of time."

"I did, but I need to see my landmarks."

"You knew it was going to be dark for crissakes. You should have picked out landmarks you can see. We can't attract attention by shining a friggin' light all over the place like a bunch of idiot high school kids."

When Lebo's eyes readjusted to the darkness, he resumed picking his way through the headstones, bending down now and then to try to read an inscription. He glanced over his shoulder every twenty feet to be sure the others were still behind him. Everyone was dressed in black, and except for DeMarco, wore knit hats pulled low on their foreheads which made them difficult to see.

Lebo walked forward slowly and tried to remember the landmarks he'd identified earlier. A tall monument loomed in front of him. He took off a glove and pointed to it, hoping his bare hand would be visible to the others. He veered left to skirt the monument and glanced over his shoulder again to be sure the others were following.

He began to count his steps and hoped he was headed in the right direction. When he got to thirty-seven, he took off his glove again and signaled for the others to stop. He dropped to his knees to examine the headstones and felt the letters chiseled into the stone. He found an "A" and stood up again and beckoned for the others to approach.

He whispered in his scratchy voice, "I think this is it, Carm, but I need light to be sure."

"Okay, but make it fast. Two friggin' seconds, no more."

Lebo dropped to his knees again and his Maglite flashed in the night before everything went dark again. He rapped on the headstone and whispered over his shoulder, "This is it."

DeMarco stepped around Lebo and kicked at the headstone with his heavy boot and cursed. The thud resonated in the still night.

Lebo scrambled to the side to avoid DeMarco's wrath. He heard DeMarco's heavy breathing and cautiously placed his hand on DeMarco's arm to move him back from the headstone.

When he thought DeMarco had gained control of himself again, he grabbed the wrist of one of the men in back of him and guided him toward the gravesite. He tapped the headstone with the toe of his boot and whispered, "Start digging."

The quiet sound of shovels digging and earth being dumped disturbed the silence.

Demarco wandered off twenty feet and sat down on a headstone. Lebo remained close to the gravesite, and while DeMarco was a mere hulk in the darkness, Lebo realized what he was doing. He shuddered at the thought of sitting on some stiff's headstone.

DeMarco listened to the sounds of the gravesite being excavated and began to seethe again and wanted to scream at the grunts to dig faster.

When a shovel struck something solid, sort of a scraping noise, he got up and went to where Lebo was peering into the hole.

"I think they've got it," Lebo whispered to him.

More earth flew out of the hole until one of the grunts called up in a muffled voice, "We're going to need some light down here."

DeMarco elbowed Lebo. "Let them use your Mag. Just make sure they keep the beam down."

Lebo dropped to his knees and handed his Maglite to one of the grunts and relayed DeMarco's instructions. DeMarco stepped closer to the grave and looked into the partially-illuminated hole as they continued to scrape dirt from the top of the casket. A hoarse whisper from the hole asked, "What now?"

"Open the friggin thing," DeMarco said impatiently. "Take a good sample of the corpse and put it in your plastic bag."

He could see the grunts exchange glances.

"Get going, goddamnit! We don't have all night!"

One of them pried at the casket's cover, and in minutes, had it open. He used a box cutter to slice open the heavy plastic sheath that contained the remains, and the other grunt began working on it with his mini chain saw. The high-pitched whir split the silence.

Lebo backed away from the grave and crossed himself. "Jesus, I think I'm going to puke."

Demarco continued to stare down at the open casket. When the men in the hole were finished and had the bagged the sample, he said, "Close it up and fill in the dirt and let's get to hell out of here." He spit in the direction of the casket a final time.

Except for a raccoon that bolted from a dumpster when they pulled in, everything was quiet in the parking lot behind the ramshackle apartment building where they'd left the Cadillac Escalade. Everyone piled out of the beat-up Chevy Blazer and DeMarco said to the grunts, "You've got ten minutes to clean yourselves up and take a leak. Then get your butts behind the wheel again and hightail it to Gary, Indiana. Deliver that bag and the other bag I gave you to this man at this address."

He handed one of them a slip of paper with the name and address he'd gotten from Vinnie Zahn. "Call Leebs as soon as the deliveries have been made and assure him it's been done."

One of the grunts snuck a glance at his wristwatch.

DeMarco saw him and said in a snarly voice, "Don't worry about the friggin' time, okay? You can sleep when you get back." Then he added, "And don't get yourselves pulled over by some idiotic cop for speeding or some other nutty offense. This has got to come off without a hitch."

Lebo and DeMarco piled into the Escalade, and when they pulled up in front of DeMarco's house twenty minutes later, Lebo asked, "Can they test DNA from a body that's been fried to crisp in a friggin' fire?"

DeMarco shrugged. "Vinnie seems to think so. The old fart knows everything, doesn't he?"

"What was in the second bag?"

"Wifey's tooth brush, a couple of her hair brushes, some other shit."

"To test against, right?"

"No, Sherlock, for her to *use*."

As DeMarco was getting out of the Escalade, Lebo asked, "What if the tests show that Angie wasn't the broad in the car?"

"What do you think?"

NINETEEN

Tessler walked into Pete's office looking tense and drawn. He helped himself to coffee and dropped into a guest chair.

"Tell me about it," Pete said.

"Like I said on the phone, Oilcan popped into my office first thing this morning and told me we needed to talk. Or *demanded* might be a better way to put it. I tell you, if I thought our first session was a little unnerving, it was nothing compared to this time. My office is half the size of one of our interview rooms, and with this big hulk looming over me, I felt like a bug about to be squashed."

"What did he want?"

Tessler slid a thick manila envelope across the desk to Pete.

Pete opened it and pulled out a sheaf of grainy nine-by-twelve photographs. He flipped through them and looked up at Tessler quizzically.

"Oilcan claims those are stills taken from the Venus security camera tapes."

"So?"

"Remember when I said I'd been out to Venus a couple of times as a stand-in for our undercover guy? I told Oilcan the same thing. When he came into my office this morning, he threw the photographs on my desk and accused me of lying. He said they have evidence I was at Venus on more than twenty occasions. He said the figure circled in white is me and the photos have dates on them."

"Is he right?"

Tessler fidgeted in his seat and said sheepishly, "I admit I've been there a few more times than I said."

"More than twenty times?"

"Maybe. I didn't keep track."

"How about the figure circled on the photographs. Is that you?"

Tessler shrugged. "Could be."

Pete took a deep breath. "Okay, so Nichols caught you in a misstatement. Last time I checked, it wasn't a crime for someone, including an officer of the law during his off hours, to go to a sex club. It might look bad, but it's not an offense."

"But Pete, we've had that place under surveillance for illegal drug activities like I told you. Oilcan didn't come right out and say it, but he implied that the reason I was at Venus all those times was to peddle drugs I'd pilfered from the evidence room."

Pete set his jaw.

"I swear, I had nothing to do with any of that."

"You were just there for the girls."

"Well, yeah, I guess you could say that. A lot of men go to places like Venus to let off steam. *And,* I haven't been there *once* since me and Kelene have been seeing each other. Twenty times spread over three or four years really isn't that much, either."

"Were you ever there on nights your undercover guy was working the joint?"

"Never. I knew his schedule and didn't come close to the place on those nights."

"Did you see anyone you know when you were at Venus?"

Tessler scoffed. "You'd be surprised who I saw. But if I spotted someone I knew, I disappeared in the crowd so he wouldn't see me. Once I actually left the place when I saw three guys I recognized."

"Did Nichols grill you about the evidence room again?"

"Not directly. It was more trying to paint me as a bad guy because I'd been to Venus a few times."

Pete let the "few" comment go and asked, "Why do you think Nichols checked the Venus security tapes? It seems to me that's something the police would do if a crime had been committed and they wanted to see if a suspect had been at the scene."

Tessler's hangdog look vanished and his expression darkened. "Someone is trying to set me up, Pete. Whoever it is has pointed Nichols in my direction."

"Any ideas who it might be?"

Tessler shook his head.

"The first time we met, I asked you about Frank. Have you thought any more about whether he might be behind this?"

Tessler brushed his long dark hair away from his forehead. "I've analyzed this thing ten ways from Sunday. Went back to see if there was something in my relationship with Frank I'd missed, everything. I didn't see a thing. Frank still relies on me a ton. Maybe I'm letting my ego get in the way of my analytical processes, but I think he'd be like a wounded carp on the beach in the July without me."

"Mmm."

He shook his head again. "This thing is driving me nuts. And it's even worse after this morning."

Pete thought it over. "Maybe it's time to go on offense."

"Meaning what?"

"Everything Nichols has done so far has been a free shot. Maybe it's time to fight back."

"Well I agree with that," Tessler said, continuing to look sullen.

"Besides, if I let them railroad you, who am I going to be able to rely on to bail my ass out of trouble now and again?"

Tessler actually grinned.

"If your friend Nichols requests another meeting, or if he pays you another impromptu visit, tell him you won't talk to him without your lawyer present."

TWENTY

"Getting caught in a lie wasn't very smart," Angie said after Pete gave her a capsule of what had happened during the second meeting between Nichols and Joe Tessler.

"I wouldn't exactly call it a lie. It was more of an understatement."

"Yeah," she said sarcastically, "I guess claiming he'd been to Venus twice and then have it turn out to be twenty times qualifies as an understatement."

Pete didn't say anything.

"Your friend Tessler's action were pretty stupid if you want my opinion. As law enforcement, he should have known that places like Venus have security cameras."

Pete shrugged. "We talked about that. He didn't say so, but I got the impression he probably thought the same thing as the rest of us, which is that nobody looked at the tapes unless there was a robbery or something."

"Do you know what I'd do? Get ahold of the tapes and see if you can spot something that might be useful to Mr. Tessler's case. Assuming, obviously, that's what the internal investigation is about."

"And how am I supposed to get ahold of the tapes? As a private citizen, I can't just barge in and demand they turn them over. And since we're not in litigation, I can't get them through discovery."

"You might have to be creative." She smiled coyly.

"Meaning what?"

"As members of the bar, we're also officers of the court, so I'm sure you don't want to do anything illegal. But looking at the situation on a purely hypothetical basis, it occurs to me that if an interested person had something on the Venus owner, he might be able to persuade him to let him look at the tapes. Unofficially, of course. People who run sex clubs often have a lot of baggage so maybe you can zero in on something."

Pete thought about it. "Not a bad idea," he said. "A minute ago, you said something else that was interesting. I don't remember exactly how you phrased it, but it was something like, 'assuming that's what the investigation is about.' What did you mean?"

"Maybe there's a motive behind the investigation other than the missing evidence."

Pete frowned.

"This wouldn't be the first time a superior who wanted to get rid of an underling manufactured incriminating evidence against him."

Pete shook his head. "Tessler and I talked about that, too. He believes someone is trying to set him up, but doesn't think it's Frank."

"The other possibility is that Tessler's lying through his teeth to you."

Pete didn't say anything.

They left the subject and made small talk for a while. Angie's mood seemed more buoyant than it had most days since she arrived and he'd been looking for an opportunity to tell her about his dinner conversation with Harry.

"There's something I'd like to talk to you about," he said. "During my dinner with Harry, he mentioned he saw a white Corolla parked behind the neighbor's house when he happened to drive past one day. He drove past a couple of days later and saw the car again. He didn't know it was yours, of course, but he started asking questions. I—"

Her buoyancy faded and her shoulders slumped. "You told him, didn't you?" she said quietly.

The way she said it made him feel like a complete turd. "Look," he said, "the car was just part of it. He's a smart guy and noticed my behavior pattern had changed and . . ."

Her look of resignation telegraphed her feelings that she wasn't interested in his explanation.

Pete continued anyway. "If I'd denied it," he said, "he probably wouldn't have believed me and would have continued to probe. Maybe he even would have found an excuse to drop in unannounced someday as he's been known to do. What then? Would we pretend no one was home even though my Range Rover was in front?"

She ignored his words and her eyes flicked around the room.

"This is what I've tried to get at a couple of times. Sooner or later someone's going to stumble onto the fact you're here. It's impossible to keep it under wraps forever unless both of us become total recluses."

"Maybe I should leave and go somewhere else," she finally said.

"I can't stop you if you if you're determined to leave, but if you decide to, I really hope you have a plan. Also, while you're probably not going to put a lot of stock in what I say, Harry isn't going to tell anyone you're here. I asked him not to and he agreed. I trust him."

She continued to gaze around with a defeated look.

"While you're still here, Harry knowing the entire story might actually prove to be a benefit. He's already volunteered his garage if you want to get your car out of sight."

From her expression, Pete wasn't sure whether his words had sunk in.

His cell phone burred. It was Joe Tessler.

"Pete, you free? I was thinking about stopping by your house. I need to vent some more about that damn investigation."

Great, he thought. "Just a minute, Joe, my stepdaughter is calling."

He put the phone against his thigh and whispered to Angie that it was Tessler and he wanted to come over. He said he was going to suggest dinner out as an alternative.

"Will you be okay?" he asked.

She nodded.

Pete got on the phone with Tessler again and said, "How about this? It's coming up on the dinner hour so why don't we grab something to eat at The Manitou instead?"

"That place is expensive, isn't it?"

"As your trusted legal counsel, I'll buy."

"Well in that case . . ."

Pete ended the call and looked at Angie with raised eyebrows.

She obviously knew what he was doing and said, "Thanks."

"I've got a half-hour until I have to leave to meet Tessler. There isn't much food in the refrigerator so I'll run into town and pick up some fresh lettuce and other stuff so you can make one of your favorite salads."

A faint smile finally broke through. "Don't forget the red peppers."

TWENTY-ONE

"I haven't been here in years," Tessler said. "I think the last time was when I was seeing that woman Beryl something or other. She drank this pricey wine like it was going out of style and ordered the most expensive entree on the menu to boot." He shook his head. "Dessert, too, I almost forgot about that. The tab was higher than the tax bill on that crappy house I rent."

Pete chuckled. "It's those tony ladies you run around with."

His face turned dark and he muttered, "That's why I'm so ticked about the way those nutty tourists have screwed up the overlook. It used to be a place where you could take a date for a romantic picnic lunch and not feel you had to file for bankruptcy afterward."

"Umm," Pete murmured. He didn't want to say anything that might encourage Tessler to go on another rant about his pet peeve.

Tessler glanced around the room. "Kelene's been bugging me to take her here," he said. "I can't get off work soon enough for the early bird menu, which is only available for about seven minutes anyway, and then there are those damn martinis she drinks that go for twelve bucks a pop.

I can't just drink water myself to hold the bill down because then she'd rag on me for being a dullard."

Pete shook his head sympathetically and watched Tessler attack his jumbo shrimp appetizer. "I've been thinking about what you said about being set up," he said.

"Yeah?" Tessler dunked the remaining half of a shrimp in a bowl of seafood sauce and took another bite.

"We talked about Frank and you don't think it's him. Anyone else in the department who might have it in for you?"

Tessler began working on a fresh shrimp. "Not that I can think of," he mumbled as he chewed. "We've got internal jealousies, sure, but nothing I can think of that would rise to the level of one officer trying to do in his fellow officer."

Pete mulled it over. "Okay," he said, "if you think of anyone, let me know."

Tessler nodded and chewed.

"Stepping back and looking at it," Pete said, "everyone seems to think that the drugs missing from the evidence room and Venus might be connected somehow because the club seems to be one of the centers of drug activities in this area. Any ideas about how we might get ahold of the Venus security camera tapes? We might spot something."

Tessler finished the last shrimp and swiped his mouth with a napkin to wipe off the seafood sauce residue. "That asshole Oilcan got them."

"Right, but Frank might have paved the way for him. We're not in the same position."

Tessler appeared to think. "Have you ever heard the term 'midnight requisition?' Or in our case I guess it would be an early morning requisition."

Pete knew exactly what he was talking about and he'd been forced to make a couple of those in the past. This was different, though. Venus clearly had security cameras and, most likely, an alarm system as well, so it wouldn't be like entering someone's less-protected house.

"I don't think we want to go there, Joe. I don't know about you, but I'm not keen on the idea of spending a year in the lockup."

"Mmm."

Pete thought about Angie's suggestion that if they had something on the Venus owner, they might be able to persuade him to let them see the security camera tapes. He floated this with Tessler in general terms and asked whether he could think of anything.

"Offhand, I'm not sure what it would be. He probably has a lot of skeletons in his closet and some bad things seem to go on at his club, but I'm not sure how we'd come up with information to use against him."

"Let's keep it in mind. Maybe we'll discover something."

Their entrees came—venison tenderloin for Tessler and The Trawler, an assortment of seafood, for Pete—and while they were eating, Tessler said, "You know, I've been thinking about the Venus security camera tapes. I see now what an idiot I was, but the times I went there to relax, I never dreamt they'd be a problem."

"It's water over the dam as they say. We've got to play the hand that's been dealt."

"Umm."

"How about stakeouts?" Pete asked. "You've done that once already. If we gave it a few more tries, maybe we'd get lucky and see someone from your department that might shed light on what's happening."

Tessler snorted. "You wouldn't believe the people I saw the last time I was there. If I were in the blackmail business, I'd have enough material to keep the money rolling in for twenty years."

"But remember, our goal isn't to tarnish the reputations of upstanding citizens of the county, it's to clear your name."

"I know, I know, I'm just saying . . ."

"How about it? What do you think of the stakeout idea?"

"That's a thought," Tessler said as he sawed off another chunk of venison. "In fact, it might improve my romantic life as well. You mention stakeout to a lady and she goes all gaga. For some reason, women think stakeouts are at the top of the food chain as far as law enforcement is concerned. They don't seem to have the foggiest notion how boring those things are."

"I take it that's a yes."

"We can give it a try."

They finished eating, and over coffee, kicked around other ideas, but came back to either finding a way to pressure the Venus owner to let them look at the security camera tapes or staking out the parking lot and hope they'd get lucky that way.

"Do you have to go right home after we finish?" Tessler said. "Or would you like to take a peek at the parking lot for a couple of hours?"

Pete thought about Angie and considered calling her, but abandoned that idea. To his knowledge, she'd never answered the phone since she got there and had no reason to believe it would be any different that night.

He looked at Tessler and said, "I've got to warn you that my billing rate goes up for evening work."

Pete followed another vehicle into the Venus parking lot, but peeled off and parked at the far side in the shadows away from the harsh glare of the light atop a high pole. He backed in so he'd be positioned for a quick exit if necessary. And also so he and Tessler could watch comfortably through the windshield without craning their necks around.

The club's doorman checked in a steady trickle of guests, and so far, hadn't looked their way. Pete tilted his seat back so he'd be less conspicuous and suggested that Tessler do the same.

"I'm going to depend on you to identify anyone who looks interesting," Pete said. "About the only person from your department I'd recognize is Frank."

"Jesus, wouldn't that be something? I mean if Frank showed up here?" Pete grinned.

A couple of times, Tessler spotted someone he thought he recognized, but then decided it wasn't who he initially thought. An older-model pickup pulled in and parked and a man in camo pants and a bulky green jacket got out. Tessler leaned forward in his seat to see better. He chuckled and flicked Pete's shoulder with the back of his hand.

"That's Les Hacker who runs the range where I keep my marksman skills fine-tuned," he said. "Wait until I see the goddamn pervert the next time I'm there. They don't make enough Viagra for that old shit to do anything about it even if he *did* get lucky." He chuckled again.

They continued to watch and it was a refresher course in how boring the staple of law enforcement could be. Pete reminisced and thought about Angie some more and intermittently eyed a man entering Venus. Then someone banged on his window and startled him. He looked through the glass and saw a man standing next to his Range Rover motioning for him to lower his window. A second man appeared on the passenger side and did the same. *Crap*, he thought.

He lowered his window and the man on his side leaned in so close Pete could smell his foul breath. He said, "Care to explain why you yahoos have been sitting out here in the parking lot for two hours?"

So much for whether someone was keeping an eye on the lot. Pete was about to reply when Tessler jumped in and said, "No cash. When we got here, we discovered that neither of us had enough cash for even a Diet Coke. We called a friend who was supposed to come over and help us out, but he hasn't showed."

The man on Pete's side leaned in further to get a better look at Tessler and after studying him for a few moments said, "Are you guys cops."

Tessler snorted. "You've got to be kidding."

"Let's see your driver's licenses," the man demanded.

"Why should we show you anything?" Pete said. "Are *you* cops?"

"Listen wise guy," the man said, grabbing Pete's arm.

Pete wrenched his arm free and the man stared at him. Then he looked across at Tessler again and said, "Haven't I seen you before?"

"Possible. I've been here a couple of times."

He continued to stare at him and then said to Pete, "It doesn't look like your friend is going to show, so if you don't have cash, I think it's time to move on."

"He's right," Tessler said to Pete. "It's getting late and we both have to work tomorrow."

Pete adjusted his seat to an upright position and turned the key in the ignition and put the Range Rover in drive. When they started forward, he hit the window and lock buttons and the glass on both sides started to slide up. The man on Pete's side hastily withdrew his arms and screamed, "Sonofabitch!"

Pete smiled and said, "Nice talking to you, gentlemen" as the windows closed. He eased out of the parking spot.

Tessler giggled. "Jesus, you almost took their friggin' arms off."

Pete looked in his rearview mirror as he drove toward the exit and noticed that one of the men seemed to be writing something. "I think they're taking down my license plate number," he said.

"I wonder where they came from? They popped up out of nowhere."

"I don't know, but it answers our question whether they keep tabs on the parking lot."

"The guy on your side recognized me, too, which really freaks me out. A man can't even go to a sex club without being surveilled. It's getting to be like a goddamn police state."

Pete was feeling more relaxed and said, "You badmouthing the police all of a sudden?"

"I'm not talking about the *police-police*. I'm talking about society in general becoming a police state."

Pete laughed. "Well, at least we know we'll have to use a different vehicle if we stake out Venus again."

"Either that," Tessler said, "or sneak in here on foot."

"I think I'm busy that night."

Driving back to where Tessler's car was parked, Pete said, "I'm not suggesting we give up our stakeouts after one stab at it, but I think we ought to try to come up with some leverage to force the owner to let us look at his security tapes."

"Leverage that doesn't get me in more trouble than I'm in now."

"Right, but every idea that has a payoff also carries *some* risk."

Tessler was quiet for a few minutes. "You know, much as I hate to think about it, I'm wondering more and more if Frank is out to get me."

TWENTY-TWO

eMarco talked on his cell phone as Joey Lebo watched *Judge Judy*. Lebo could tell his boss was in a bad mood so he had the sound so low he could barely hear the characters' voices. That killed him because part of the enjoyment of the show was to become fully engaged and second-guess a character who made a stupid argument or scream at the judge because of a ruling he disagreed with while finishing off a couple of cans of Miller Lite.

On occasion, DeMarco's voice drowned out the already faint voices of the television characters, but Lebo resisted the temptation to increase the sound. He hoped DeMarco's telephone conversation would go on for a while so he could at least *see* the rest of the show even if he wasn't able to follow every argument like he usually did. He'd learned a lot about legal crap by watching *Judge Judy* over the years, and while he knew that going to law school at this stage of his life wasn't in the cards, particularly since he'd never finished high school, he valued the legal knowledge he gleaned from the show. It might come in handy someday given his line of work.

Suddenly DeMarco dropped his cell phone on his desk with a clatter that startled Lebo. "I knew it!" he screamed. "I friggin' knew it!"

Lebo worked the arrow on the remote to lower the volume even more. "Bad news, Carm?" he asked.

"That was the DNA guy. You know what he said? He said, 'I don't know who you sawed that piece of bacon off from, but it damn sure doesn't match the stuff on the hair brush and the toothbrush and the other things you sent me.' Not a friggin' match, he said! Two entirely different people! You know what that means, don't you? It means little wifey is still out there some goddamn place just like I suspected!" He swiped at the golf bag-shaped pencil holder on his desk and sent objects scattering across the room.

"Is he sure?" Lebo asked as he glanced at the soundless television screen.

"What do you mean, is he sure?" DeMarco said as he rubbed the back of his hand. "He said so didn't he? He's supposed to be some expert ain't he? And do you know what he did after he told me this? He laughed, like he thought it was a big friggin' joke or something. Jesus!" DeMarco banged his fist on the desk.

Lebo watched cautiously as DeMarco tilted his head back and stared at the ceiling for a long time, then banged the desktop with his fist again and scattered more papers. He snapped a couple of pencils and flung the pieces across the room. Then he tilted his head back and stared at the ceiling some more.

Just as Lebo thought it might be safe to turn up the sound a click or two, DeMarco got up and went to his credenza and began rifling through a stack of documents. He plucked one out, stared at it for a moment, then searched some more and pulled out another. He took the documents back to his desk and smoothed them with his hand and began studying them, checking each against the calendar on his desk.

It pained him to do it, but Lebo turned off the television and walked to DeMarco's desk and peered over his shoulder. DeMarco had Angie's credit card statements in front of him. He stared at them a few moments longer, then pulled out a road atlas and flipped it open to the Wisconsin page. DeMarco studied the credit card statements again and drew an irregular circle around several small towns in the northeastern part of the state.

"I bet she's up here," he said without looking back at Lebo. He jabbed his finger at the circled area.

Lebo leaned closer. "Jesus, that's really up in the sticks. There's practically nothing there. And look at all of those lakes."

"That's where she's hiding."

"If she's still alive, who do you suppose was driving the car when it exploded?"

"How the hell would I know who was driving? Maybe the cleaning lady or somebody. You know what a princess she is, can't do anything herself. Maybe the cleaning lady used the car to pick up her dry cleaning or something." He swiped at the pencil he'd used to make the circle on the map and sent it flying. "She thinks she's too goddamn good to use one of my shops."

Lebo eyed him cautiously. "So what's the next step? Talk to Vinnie again?"

The scowl on DeMarco's face grew darker. "Screw Vinnie. You saw the old shit when we were up there, needs a wheelchair to get around and everything. I told you before—and I told him—this is personal. It's between me and her."

"I don't know, Carm, he runs a pretty tight organization. Wouldn't it be better to get his go-ahead? He seemed reasonable when we were up there. He suggested the DNA testing and gave us the name of an expert and everything."

DeMarco glared at him for a full minute. "How many times do I have to explain this to you people? This ain't a goddamn hit!"

"Okay, I agree with that, but I think Vinnie is worried that things might get out of hand and attract attention we don't want. You've already been questioned by the locals."

"And like I've said ten times, they haven't been back, have they? That's what I predicted would happen and it's happened."

"I know, but—"

"Who's friggin' side are you on anyway, Leebs?"

"I'm just trying to provide counsel. That's what you pay me for, right?"

DeMarco gave him a surly stare and didn't say anything for a minute. He ran a hand lightly over his hair and smoothed his sideburns. "Anyway, this is a two-part operation. Find her and then decide how to correct what got screwed up the first time."

Lebo exhaled and said, "That's good thinking. Complete mission one and then decide how to execute mission two."

DeMarco stared at the Wisconsin map again. "We know from the credit card charges that she stopped in Appleton, which is here." He jabbed at the map and drew another circle. "That was her first stop. That's where she rented a car."

"How did she get to Appleton?"

DeMarco rolled his eyes. "What difference does it make? Maybe she sprouted wings and flew, I don't know. Witches can fly, can't they? The important thing is that she passed through Appleton on her way up to these other burgs. See the dates?"

Lebo nodded.

"The other charges were on later dates and they're all centered in these smaller towns farther north. See the charges in Rhinelander and Eagle River on dates after she passed through Appleton?"

Lebo studied the dates and nodded again.

"See those charges at the Oak Tree Boutique and Sassi's Aesthetics? I bet those are clothes places. Remember how I found all of her stuff still in her closet? I bet she took off with nothing but her friggin' purse, and when she got to the sticks, she loaded up on new stuff. She always gorged on clothes. I bet she couldn't help herself and did the same thing up in the sticks."

Lebo nodded again.

"We're going on another road trip, Leebs. And take enough artillery."

Lebo looked puzzled.

DeMarco grinned. "It's bear country up there. We might need protection."

TWENTY-THREE

Pete paged through the only two volumes about the Vikings that the local library had on its shelves, looking for material he could use in the article he was writing for *The Fjord Herald* about the body armor used by the storied warriors. He did most of his research these days on the Internet, but had connection problems at his house and used it as an excuse to escape for a few hours.

In one of the books, Pete saw a photo spread showing Viking reenactors in full battle mode facing off against some foe that was defending a castle. He smiled when he saw the cone-shaped leather helmets and remembered the dinner conversation he'd had with Harry who adamantly maintained that Viking helmets had horns. In support, he'd cited the Minnesota Vikings football team mascot and the *Hägar the Horrible* comic strip which unfailingly showed Hägar with a horned helmet even when sick in bed.

Pete went to the copy machine and made copies of the reenactment photographs and slipped them in his briefcase.

He finished going through the books and made notes of a few things he thought might be useful for his article, then plugged in his laptop and began to search the Internet where he found a treasure trove of information. He'd learned from experience which sites he could trust and which he had to treat with a skeptical eye and took that into account. Then he began playing with possible opening sentences that would grab readers' attention.

Two hours later, he glanced up at the clock on the wall and saw that it was past noon. He packed up, and after saying goodbye to the librarians, headed up the street, hoping Harry hadn't gone to lunch yet.

When he walked in, Harry peered over his half-glasses and said, "I've been trying to call you."

Pete patted his briefcase and said, "Research at the library. No cell phone use, remember?"

Harry nodded and said, "I wanted to talk to you about a couple of thoughts I have about that friend staying at your house. You know, protective measures."

"I'm dying to hear them. Want to talk over lunch?"

"God, you're a savior. I've been sitting here with my stomach rumbling for the past two hours. You probably heard it all the way down at the library."

Pete chuckled. Harry never ceased complaining about the diet Rona Martin had him on.

"Before we go," Pete said, "I have something for you." He opened his briefcase and pulled out the reenactment photographs.

Harry studied them for a few moments before he looked up at Pete and squinted. "Are these supposed to mean something? All I see are a bunch of silly guys playing Viking, as if that would be of interest to a pure-blooded Scotsman."

"The helmets, Harry, the helmets. See any horns?"

Harry glanced at the photographs again. He shook his head and said, "I know what you're trying to do. You're trying to relitigate our dinner conversation. But these photographs prove exactly squat. The caption at the bottom of the page says these are a bunch of reenactors pretending they're involved in a criminal assault on a civilized English castle. They're not *real* Vikings. The reason the helmets don't have horns on them is because so many of those reenactors come from working class backgrounds and can't afford authentic garb."

Pete rolled his eyes. "Ready for lunch?"

Harry grinned triumphantly as they headed for Dinghy's. After Pete made his selection, he noticed Harry studying the dinner side of the menu and said, "I don't want to break your concentration, but the lunch selections are on the other side."

Harry's expression grew sullen and he flipped his menu card over. He settled on the fish and chips after the waiter assured him that the standard order included a generous pile of chips.

Harry took a long suck on the straw in his iced tea and leaned forward and said in a hushed voice, "My first idea is the one I mentioned at dinner. That place of yours and the neighbor's place are pretty exposed because they're close to the highway. If we move her car to my garage like I suggested, there won't be any exterior signs she's here in case someone is looking for her."

"I already mentioned your offer when I came clean with her. She said she's thinking about leaving."

"It's no problem, you know. Rona can park in the garage, too, because there's room for two vehicles. I can keep my Explorer outside for a while. That shouldn't be a problem until the snow starts to fly."

"I'll say something to her again."

"Did she say where she's going if she decides to leave?"

Pete shrugged. "She didn't say. I just advised her to have a plan before she takes off again."

"Umm. My second idea is this. I know you're skeptical about how much danger she's actually in, but to be on the safe side, we should consider moving her to a more remote location. Assuming, of course, she stays for a while. The place I have in mind is the camp we always stay at when we fish the Holy Water."

Pete thought about it and said, "I'm not so sure about that one. One of the reasons she said she left Wisconsin was she was going stir crazy. It would be just as bad on the Au Sable. And if something happens, Millie might get caught up in it. I'd feel terrible if that happened."

Harry whispered, "Keep your voice down." Then he turned thoughtful. "You don't think the goons would hurt her, do you?" he asked. "She's an old lady."

Pete tried to conceal his amusement at how Harry's conspiratorial side had taken over, but his concern for Millie Tate was real even if the risk to her were miniscule. He said, "Don't know, but I'd never forgive myself if something happened."

"I see your point. But the car's a go, right?"

Pete shrugged. "Like I said, I'll mention it to her again. I can't see why she'd object. As far as I know, she hasn't used it since she got here."

Harry went into his thoughtful mode again. "Explain to me again why you think your house guest isn't in any real danger?"

"I'll tell you what I told her. Two things would have to happen for her to be at risk. First, someone would have to discover she's alive and that seems highly unlikely if what she told me is true. And second, someone who wants to harm her would have to track her up here which also seems improbable."

"Mmm," Harry murmured. "Why's she so jittery then?"

"All I can think is that the trauma of seeing her best friend blown away by a car bomb lingers and now she senses danger around every corner."

"It sounds like what she *really* needs is a good psychiatrist."

"Maybe. All I know is being around her these days is like walking on eggshells."

They finished their lunch and paid their bill and left. When they got back to *The Northern Sentinel*'s offices, Harry said, "Dinner tonight?"

"I'll have to check with my guest."

"Well, let me know. And about the car."

TWENTY-FOUR

Pete was in his cubbyhole office just down from the living room disconnecting and reconnecting the modem cable for about the tenth time as he tried to get his wireless system up again. Angie stuck her head in and in a concerned voice said, "Someone just drove in. He's next door looking at my car." Pete put a book on the end of the cable to hold it in place and went out to check.

"That's Joe Tessler."

"What's he want? Didn't you just have dinner with him?" Angie asked.

"No idea, but that's what I've been saying. People drop in unannounced. I finessed him last time, but . . ."

Pete watched Tessler walk around her Toyota Corolla like he was inspecting it. After a couple of minutes, he started toward the house.

"I'm going upstairs," Angie said.

Pete heard Tessler clump up the front steps and met him at the door. "What a surprise," he said, "I haven't seen you for twelve hours."

Tessler's jaw muscle was pulsing. "You wouldn't have a bottle of water, would you? My mouth is parched."

Pete went to the kitchen and grabbed two bottles of Evian from the refrigerator and handed one to Tessler. He studied him again. "Something happened, didn't it?"

Tessler looked out the closed French doors toward the lake and licked his lips and took a swallow of water. "I've been suspended," he said.

Pete's eyebrows arched. "When did this happen?"

"An hour ago. Frank came into my office and said he had no option given what the internal investigation had turned up so far. He asked for my gun and badge. And my access card to the evidence room."

Pete studied Tessler's ashen face. "Has more evidence come to light?"

"Frank said that old Oilcan laid out the case against me as he sees it to this point: I was a regular at Venus, which is a bunch of bull; Venus is the center for alleged illegal drug activities in the area; I had unfettered access to the evidence room; and get this, that woman Beryl I mentioned at dinner? She gave an affidavit saying that I'm a druggie and regularly complained about my low salary."

"How did they happen to talk to her?"

"As I understand it, Oilcan claims he's interviewed five different women I've dated in the past few years. I went out with Beryl exactly three times. One night I smoked a little weed with her in her apartment. I didn't even think of her when we talked in your office that day. And it was *her* weed, for crissakes, not mine. She brought out three jars of the stuff, each a different type, and asked which I preferred. Weed is weed to me and I don't even remember what I said. But in her friggin' affidavit, she made it sound like I start smoking the stuff as soon as I get up in the morning and had a supply in the trunk of my car that I brought along to her house. That's bull. *She's* the one who's hooked on the stuff, not me."

"Did you tell Frank that?"

"Yeah, I told him. I got the feeling that he didn't take that part of it seriously because he kind of looked at me like he was trying to hold back a giggle. But it's part of the case they're building against me."

"Do you know if he got affidavits from the other women?"

"Not that Frank told me. He did say that Oilcan mentioned Kelene. I guess she didn't say anything about me using drugs, but made some stupid comment about how it might make me more exciting if I did."

"Mmm."

Tessler gazed out at the lake again. "Exciting," he said shaking his head and spitting out the word like a bitter seed. "When I was with the Chicago PD, I headed up teams that were responsible for putting away thirteen scumbag murderers. *Thirteen*, for crissakes! I've put away a few up here, too. And I'm not trying to build myself up or anything, but I was consistently the top marksman in our unit when we had qualifiers on the pistol range. What does she mean, exciting? I've already had enough real excitement to last *ten* men their entire lives."

He took another gulp of Evian and stared through the French doors again.

Pete watched Tessler and could see he was genuinely distressed.

"The only good thing that came out of my talk with Frank," Tessler said dejectedly, "was that he said I'll continue to receive full pay and benefits pending outcome of the investigation."

Pete nodded. "That's something. Is he going to appoint someone to assume your duties while you're suspended?"

Tessler's face darkened and his expression grew surly. "Cap, do you believe it?"

"Ernie Capwell?"

Tessler shot him a look. "Do you know him?"

"I met him once or twice. He's a friend of Harry's. Or at least he's one of Harry's regular sources within your department."

"He's a friggin' hack is what he is. Do you know how many times he's tried to get me to team up with him and go to Frank with a proposal to expand the detective group to two and help get him promoted to detective? Working under me, of course. He was always careful to emphasize that." Tessler shook his head.

"Did you ever take his proposal to Frank?"

"Are you kidding? But now Frank wants me to turn over all of my files to the goddamned idiot and brief him and all that crap. I can hardly badmouth him considering the situation I'm in because I'm afraid it'll just make me look worse. Frank acted like he was my big protector and emphasized that the files would come back to me as soon as I'm cleared. What a crock."

Pete thought about it for a while, then said, "Do you think it might be Cap who's setting you up?"

Tessler scoffed. "I thought about that, but he's not smart enough. He's nothing but a stinking leach and a liability to the department."

Pete studied him again for a while. "So what's next?"

"I'm meeting with Cap at ten tomorrow morning to turn over the files on my active cases and brief him on where we're at on each one. After that? I don't know. I just might to go a bar somewhere and get shitfaced."

"That won't solve anything."

"Yeah? I've seen you a few times when things haven't been going right in your life and it looked like you'd had a few."

Pete shook his head and looked at him. "We're going to knock this friggin' thing out of the ballpark, but to do that, we need a plan."

A hopeful look returned to Tessler's eyes and he stared at Pete. He said, "You know, after Frank dumped that ton of bricks on my head, I had to talk to somebody, and you were the first person who came to mind. Not because you're my lawyer or anything, mind you, but because I regard you as my friend. Probably the only *real* friend I have in this outpost of humanity." He chuckled before adding, "And to think, I'm saying that to the man my boss—if I can still call him that—regards as his number one enemy."

Tessler sat quietly, then laughed again, as though unable to get over the irony of it. Pete had to smile himself.

"Not to get ahead of you," Pete said, "but I think we need to do a couple of things right out of the box to get the ball rolling on your defense. First, we need to visit your old friend, Beryl, and see if we can get her to refresh her memory, as we lawyers like to say, on the marijuana thing. And—"

"I don't care if I ever *see* her again."

"I understand, but ignoring her won't solve your problem. We've got to start chipping away at Nichols' case, and she's a key piece."

"Do I have to go with you?" Tessler said.

"You definitely need to be there. It'll prevent her from waltzing around my questions. And the other thing we need to do is find some way to get those Venus security tapes. Do you know who owns the place?"

Tessler thought about it. "A guy named Frei I believe." He thought some more and said, "That's it. Simon Frei."

"You said that your department has been trying to shut the place down. You mentioned suspected drug activities as one reason. Are there other reasons?"

"A whole boatload. Suspected prostitution, suspected child prostitution, all kinds of nasty stuff."

"If you were going to pick one suspected activity where the owner might be sensitive to pressure, what would it be?"

Tessler thought for a while again. "Maybe the child prostitution thing. If we could develop evidence of that and word got out, the public outcry would be louder than the ice breaking up on a Michigan stream in March. Nothing gets the public stirred up these days like sexual exploitation of children."

"But I gather you haven't been able to come up with enough evidence yet."

"Not enough for Connie, anyway. Our undercover guy who's been hanging around the place says that it seems to him that some of the ladies who might be prostitutes look awfully young. I noticed the same thing. We raided the place maybe a year ago, and they must have had advance warning of it or something, because by the time our people went in, the only ladies in the place looked like they'd been drawing Social Security for ten years."

Pete chuckled at the characterization. "They cleaned things up, huh?"

"That's the way it looked."

"Do you know if Beryl works?"

"She said she does. I'm not sure where. Or what she does."

"Where does she live?"

"Manistee."

"Tell you what, I haven't been in Manistee for a while. After you've had a chance to unwind from your session with Cap, why don't you and I take a drive down that way. Maybe we'll get lucky and she'll give us some ammunition we can use to start punching holes in your friend Oilcan's case."

Tessler got up to leave. "I can't say I'm feeling good," he said, "but I'm feeling better than when I walked in. You're a good guy to have in your corner. You not only have ideas, but you act on them."

"Can I record what you just said and show a transcript to Harry?"

Tessler's eyebrows raised. "He doesn't agree?"

"You'll have a chance to judge for yourself at dinner tonight."

"Dinner?" Tessler said, looking confused.

"You're having dinner with Harry and me at Rona's Bay Grille."

"I am?"

"Unless you have plans you can't get out of. You didn't think we'd leave you alone at a time like this, do you?"

Tessler looked thoughtful. "Kelene wanted to do something and we were going to talk about it before I went to her house. I guess I could beg off saying something came up with my job. That would kinda be true."

Pete waited for his answer.

His face brightened. "What time?"

"Half-past six?"

"That'll work." He started toward the front door, and before he opened it, he said, "By the way, who belongs to that white Corolla parked next door?"

"A friend. She went for a walk along the beach. I'm surprised she's not back by now."

"I noticed the Wisconsin plates."

"That's where she's from."

"Did she add the brush? That can scratch the paint, you know."

Pete laughed and tried to sound casual. "She heard somewhere that we've had a lot of car theft up here. I think she wants to make her Corolla less conspicuous."

"Jesus, this is nothing like the chop-shop operations in Detroit or places like that. Is she joining us tonight?"

"I'll ask, but I doubt it. She's leaving at the crack of dawn tomorrow."

He nodded. "See you this evening."

Pete waited until he heard Tessler's Acura pull out of his driveway, then called upstairs to Angie who was already on her way down.

"That was very smooth."

He grinned. "Thank you."

"I heard most of your conversation. Another wrinkle in the investigation, huh?"

"A big one, unfortunately."

She eyed him for a moment. "Are you going to build a fire?" she asked. "It's cold in here."

He went to the fireplace, crumpled some newspaper and placed several pieces of kindling over it, then added a couple of birch logs. When the flames began to lick upwards, he replaced the screen and held his hands out to absorb the warmth. Angie came over and did the same.

"You saw and I'm sure heard Detective Tessler. Your Corolla caught his attention. Today Tessler, tomorrow someone else. You might take Harry up on his offer and store your car in his garage while you're here."

She didn't say anything.

"Should we do it before I join Harry and Joe for dinner?"

She stared at the fire. "Like I told you, I'm wondering whether I should just make a personal change of venue."

"Does that mean you've developed a plan?"

"Nothing specific."

"Where would you go then?"

"Out of the Midwest. Idaho or some place. Or maybe the east."

"And stay where?"

"A motel. Or maybe I could rent a house somewhere."

"Do you have money?"

"In my brokerage account."

Pete studied her. "Tell you what, let's move your car to Harry's garage until you come up with a more specific plan and decide definitely to leave."

TWENTY-FIVE

Lebo drove slowly through town, pretending to check out the buildings, although he was really trying to read Carmen DeMarco who'd been silent since they left Appleton. The manager of the car facility there had confirmed that Angie had rented a five-year-old white Toyota Corolla in August and prepaid for three months. He talked freely because both DeMarco and Lebo flashed credentials with false names showing that they were Chicago PD detectives who were tracking Angie because she was wanted for a variety of offenses in Illinois that included multiple felonies.

DeMarco stared straight ahead with tight lips as they cruised through Rhinelander. In an effort to loosen the atmosphere, Lebo pointed to the giant Hodag statue in front of the Chamber of Commerce building and said, "Jesus, look at that, will you?"

DeMarco's eyes flicked toward the statue, then resumed staring straight ahead.

"You'd never see something like that in Chicago."

Finally DeMarco said, "Stop the sightseeing tour babble and find the Oak Tree Boutique, alright?"

Lebo clammed up and continued down the main drag, passing shops with signs like Paws 'n' Clawz and Rollie & Helen's Musky Shop and Hunter's Haven. He spotted the store they were looking for and said, "It's coming up on the right."

He maneuvered the Escalade into a parking spot that had been vacated by a rusty pickup. DeMarco hopped out before the engine stopped turning over, and Lebo hustled to catch up. "I'll do the talking," DeMarco said.

When they stepped inside, they were greeted by an array of skirts and slacks and sweaters and outdoor clothing and assorted lingerie and sleepwear, all displayed on tables or piled neatly on shelves. Two saleswomen were on duty and they approached the closest one.

DeMarco flashed a smile and asked, "Are you the manager?"

The youngish woman grinned self-consciously. "No sir. See the lady back there?" She pointed toward an older woman with neatly coiffed gray hair and a Halloween-motif sweater who was rearranging seasonal apparel on a long display table. "That's the manager. She also owns the store."

They thanked her and headed the manager's way. "Expecting a big Halloween season?" DeMarco asked, showing his smile again and eyeing her sweater with appreciation.

"Hopefully there'll be witches flying everywhere and oodles of hobgoblins," she said, smiling back at him with small-town friendliness.

DeMarco nodded. "I'm Dick Viola and this is my partner, Hank Markov. We're with the Chicago PD." He pulled out his wallet and showed her his fake credentials.

The woman studied them and looked up at him, seemingly confused. "You're a long way from home, aren't you? Rhinelander isn't exactly a Chicago suburb."

DeMarco chuckled. "We go where the criminals go," he said. "And your name is?"

"Geneva Turner. Everyone calls me Gennie."

"Gennie — I hope it's okay if we use your first name — we're tracking a fugitive who we have reason to believe headed this way when she took off from Chicago. Is there someplace we can talk in private?"

Gennie Turner glanced around the store. There was only one customer and the saleswoman they'd just talked to hovered near her. "Of course," she said.

She led them to a small nook without a door at the back of the store. It was cluttered with files and stacks of papers and boxes. She cleared the side chairs and invited them to sit down. When she was seated behind her small metal desk, she said, "What's this fugitive charged with?"

"I'm not at liberty to go into details, Gennie," DeMarco said, leaning across the desk and trying to appear solemn, "but they're very serious offenses. Financial crimes, mostly, but she's also a suspect in someone's death."

"Oh, my. Maybe I should call our sheriff and have him join us. He usually stops for a snack at Jack's Diner about this time, but I'm sure he'd pull himself away from the pie for something like this."

DeMarco smiled again and said, "I don't think that'll be necessary. We just want to talk to you about some purchases we believe the perp, if you'll pardon my jargon, made at your fine establishment. Besides, we plan to talk to the sheriff separately."

"As you think best," she said. "What kind of purchases and when were they made?"

"I have a list here." He handed Gennie a copy of the credit card statement. "I also have a photograph of the woman." He slid a black-and-white photograph of Angie across the desk.

Gennie looked at the photograph and then at the credit card statement. "I remember this woman. Very nice lady. She bought a lot of clothes and other things from us."

"Did she give you a local address?"

Gennie looked at him sadly. "Even if she did, I couldn't give it to you. We don't release information about our customers without their consent."

DeMarco wasn't expecting that given his charm offensive. He lowered his voice and said, "This isn't an ordinary situation, Gennie. We're law enforcement and we're trying to catch up with a dangerous fugitive."

"I understand, but—"

"Look," DeMarco said, struggling to hold his temper in check, "either you check to see if the woman gave a local address or I'm going to have to make some telephone calls. Things start to get unpleasant if we do that. In an hour or two, I'll have a warrant signed by a judge that *compels* you to give us the information we're asking for now."

Color drained from Gennie's face. Finally she said, "I remember one pair of slacks the lady bought required alterations. She was staying somewhere around Eagle River, as I recall, and didn't want to drive back here to pick them up. We had them delivered."

DeMarco leaned forward again and said, "You must have her address then."

She appeared uncomfortable and scooted her chair back a bit to create more separation. "I'll have to check," she said. She went to a file cabinet and spent ten minutes searching through a drawer, her hands trembling visibly. DeMarco looked at Lebo and rolled his eyes.

"Here it is," Gennie said. She handed DeMarco some invoices with a handwritten slip stapled to them.

DeMarco studied the address for a moment, then flipped through the invoices. "Do you know where this place is?" he asked.

Gennie shook her head. "The county atlas might show it."

"You have one I assume."

She nodded and went to a bookcase that overflowed with an assortment of books and documents and files. She found a spiral bound volume and carried it back to her desk and glanced at them nervously. They waited as she checked the index and turned to a page in the atlas. Apparently striking out, she repeated the process. Lebo grabbed his throat with a mock choking grip. DeMarco looked away disgustedly.

"I think I found it," Gennie said, sounding relieved. She kept one finger on a page in the atlas and the other on the slip of paper with the address. DeMarco and Lebo moved behind her so they could see the map. The place they were looking for was on a short spur jutting off a county road that wound among several lakes. "It should be about here," she said.

"Mark it and copy that page," DeMarco said.

Gennie lugged the atlas to a machine that looked like the first-generation copier after the old mimeograph machines. She hit a button and the machine growled and squeaked until a sheet of paper crawled out. Gennie waved it in the air a couple of times to dry the ink and handed it to DeMarco before she stepped away from him again.

DeMarco checked the page and tucked it in a pocket. "You've been a great help, Gennie. We're going to get out of your hair so you can get back to business." He shook her hand and felt her clammy palm.

"Should I tell Sheriff Miller about this when I see him?"

"Like I said, we plan to stop and see the sheriff before we leave the area. It's best if he hears everything directly from us so he gets a complete picture."

After saying goodbye to the other saleswoman, they left and got into the Escalade and started down the street to find Sassi's Aesthetics.

"Do you think Gennie will hold off telling the sheriff?" Lebo asked.

"I don't care what she does. By the time old Sheriff Miller finishes his evening pie, we're going to be long gone."

Sassi's was at the beginning of the next block in a lavender-colored building with wide slabs of vertical siding. The sign in the front window said the place offered spa services that included manicures, pedicures, massages, waxes and sugaring, whatever the hell that was.

A bell tinkled when they walked into a waiting room with subdued lighting and the smell of incense. Music wafted softly from the sound system. Seeing no one, DeMarco clanged the bell on the stylish desk. A fortyish woman with long dark hair and eye lashes that probably caused a breeze when she blinked appeared from behind a velvet curtain.

DeMarco went into his charm routine again and introduced himself and Lebo. The woman batted her eyes a couple of times and sized them up. "How can I help you, gentlemen?"

"Do you own this establishment?"

"I'm the manager. The owner is in Arizona for the winter."

"Smart woman," DeMarco said, chuckling at his wisecrack and slapping Lebo's shoulder with the back of his hand. "What's your name Ms. Manager?"

"Irene." She batted her eyes some more.

"We're not here for a manicure or anything, although Lord knows we probably could use one. We're law enforcement officers from Chicago." He showed her his fake credentials.

She looked at them and handed them back.

"We have reason to believe," he said, "that a fugitive we're tracking might have patronized your spa in September and this month as well." He pulled out Angie's photograph and showed it to her.

Irene studied the photograph. "You said she's a fugitive?"

DeMarco nodded solemnly.

"She came in once a week for the past month or month-and-a-half," Irene said. "Each time a massage, a manipedi, the works. But nothing for the past ten days or two weeks."

"Where does she live, do you know?"

Irene shrugged and shook her head.

"So you wouldn't know if she left town?"

Irene shook her head again.

TWENTY-SIX

Pete took Angie back to his house after they dropped off her car at Harry's, then headed to town again to meet Harry and Joe Tessler. When he walked into Rona's Bay Grille, Harry was seated at their usual table sipping what was probably a single-malt scotch and water.

Pete sat down and said, "Thanks again for letting us borrow your garage."

"No problem, as the saying goes. Jesus, I'm not sure I would have recognized Angie if I hadn't known who she was. Even with that flannel shirt and floppy hat, she looked like a model."

Pete smiled. "She takes care of herself."

Harry peered at him over his half-glasses with a look that always telegraphed suspicion. "It's none of my business, of course, but do you two, ah, have something going?"

Pete smiled again and shook his head.

"Boy, that must be hard. A looker like that, all alone with you in a comfortable place on the lake, a fire going, maybe a glass or two of wine. You must take cold showers on the hour."

Pete shot him a look. "When Joe comes," he said, "be careful not to let anything slip about her. He knows none of this."

"I understand. But as I warned you, sooner or later a guy like that is going to pick up on something. That's the reason I suggested moving her car."

Pete saw Tessler walk in and waved to him and said in a low voice, "Remember what I said."

Tessler greeted them and sat down. He looked better than when Pete saw him that afternoon.

"I heard about what happened," Harry said. "I was really sorry to hear it."

"Yeah, embarrassing as hell." Tessler brushed a shock of black hair away from his forehead. "And a total crock, too."

"Look, the three of us are friends. Your suspension is news and my readers probably would be interested, but put your mind at ease. Pete threatened to burn down my building if a word about any of this makes its way into *The Sentinel*."

Tessler glanced at Pete appreciatively.

"I understand you think you're being set up," Harry said.

"What else can it be? That big oaf of an investigator Frank brought in must be getting tips from someone. It seems like he's hell-bent on screwing up my career, stringing together minor things and trying to make it look like I'm a serial murderer or something. I get the feeling all he wants is to hang the thing on me, collect his fee, and go on to his next sucker client."

Harry looked at him sympathetically. "Well, you have a lot of people in your corner. There aren't many sheriff's departments in rural areas like this that have the kind of big-city background and experience you bring to the job. You've been a real asset to this county."

"I appreciate that."

No one spoke for a while, then Harry said, "You know, I could talk to Cap off the record and see if he knows what's going on. We go way back and he's provided a lot of useful information over the years."

Tessler's face darkened. "I wish you wouldn't do that."

"Why?"

"I have a feeling sometimes that your friend Cap would just as soon see me gone."

"Oh, I doubt that," Harry said.

"This conversation is strictly off the record, right?" Tessler asked.

Harry nodded and continued to look at Tessler quizzically.

"I told Pete this before. Cap always seems to be an unhappy camper. You remember when Sheriff Haskins resigned to run for higher political office?"

"Sure."

"Cap was totally batshit when Frank was elevated to acting sheriff. He had seniority on Frank and thought *he* was the one who should have been tapped. Then the next election rolls around and Cap talked to everyone about how he was going to challenge Frank. It was all a bunch of hot air. His excuse for not running was that Frank had too much of an advantage because of his unfair elevation a couple of years earlier."

Harry thought back for a few moments. "I vaguely remember that."

"Why none of this got back to Frank I'll never know. The point I'm making is that whenever there's an opening and Cap doesn't get it, he's unhappy and bitching and holds it against the guy who got it instead of him."

"Umm."

"I told Pete about how he's been angling to get a detective position the past few months, trying to get me to support him by going to Frank and pitching an idea he has about expanding the department."

Harry frowned again. "I knew Cap grumbled now and then, but I thought it was just his personality. And as far as setting someone up . . . I never saw that in him."

Tessler stared around the room with a sour expression on his face.

Pete tried to steer the conversation away from departmental politics. "The special investigator Sheriff Richter brought in claims he has an affidavit from a woman Joe used to date—"

"I took her out exactly three times," Tessler interjected. "*Three* friggin' times!"

"Right," Pete said. "Anyway, the investigator claims he has an affidavit from her that portrays Joe in a bad light. We're planning to talk to her and find out where she's coming from."

"Where does she live?"

"Manistee."

Harry went into his thinking mode again. "I know a guy down there who runs a start-up newspaper—not the *News Advocate*—which is getting some traction because it digs up and prints dirt on people in the community. Drunk driving charges, citations for fishing or hunting without a license, that kind of thing. The paper contains a lot of other stuff, too, but people like it most because of the dirt it prints about their neighbors."

"Sort of a *National Enquirer* on the local level." Pete said.

"Yeah, kind of like that. What's the woman's name?"

Pete looked at Tessler, who muttered, "Beryl Wuyt."

Harry pulled out a pen and wrote the name on a napkin and tucked it in his shirt pocket. "I'll call in the morning and ask the guy I mentioned to check his morgue. That's newspaper-speak for archives."

Tessler nodded.

"Anything else you guys have in mind?"

"We're going to talk again tomorrow after Joe meets with Cap to turn over his files."

Harry's bushy eyebrows rose. "You didn't tell me about the files."

"Frank told me it's a *temporary* measure while I'm suspended," Tessler said, his face darkening again. "But it demonstrates what I was saying a minute ago. Cap sees an opportunity and he jumps on it, not worrying about who might get hurt."

Harry shook his head.

The conversation shifted to other things and Harry tried to convince Tessler to take up fly fishing, lecturing him on the equipment he should buy as a beginner. At one point, he hoisted himself from his chair and demonstrated proper casting technique to the considerable amusement of the other diners.

When their waiter came to ask about dessert, Tessler ordered peach cobbler with two scoops of vanilla ice cream. Even though Rona was at her book club meeting and not around to monitor his diet, Harry limited himself to a piece of key lime pie that he promised to share with Pete. When Tessler's cobbler came, Harry eyed it with obvious interest while picking at the key lime pie that he kept much closer to him than to Pete.

After Tessler left, Harry said, "Troubles all around, huh?"

"I guess."

"You're my best friend," Harry said, "and I hope I'm yours. You have a habit of getting yourself behind the eight-ball in these situations. I hope you'll be more careful this time."

TWENTY-SEVEN

Lebo leaned forward in his seat, as if being closer to the windshield would improve visibility, and alternately flashed his upper and lower beams as he navigated the narrow dark road. He kept an eye on the map as he drove, frequently glancing down at it.

"Crap," he muttered, "I think I missed a turn."

He jockeyed the Escalade around and retraced his route, relieved that DeMarco hadn't gone off on him again. DeMarco nervously played with his Glock 43 by ejecting its magazine and slamming it back in. Lebo's grip on the steering wheel tightened each time he heard the metallic click.

Lebo saw the fork he'd missed the first time and turned onto the single lane that was even narrower and less maintained than the road they'd been on. They bumped along and DeMarco sighted down the barrel of his Glock and moved it around like he was surveying a field of fire. Whenever the muzzle pointed too close to the driver's seat, Lebo was tempted to nudge it away, but he took a deep breath and kept driving.

They came to another fork with wooden signs that pointed both ways. Lebo braked to study the map and then veered left on Deerpath Lane. After he'd gone another hundred yards, he saw lights ahead through the trees.

"Cut your headlights and use the running lights," DeMarco said. Lebo followed instructions even though he was having enough difficulty seeing with his headlights on.

"If those lights are coming from where I think they are," DeMarco said, "I have a feeling that wifey and I are about to have a reunion." He played with his Glock some more and continued to snap the magazine out and jam it back in and sight along the barrel. Lebo's palms grew moist as he sensed what DeMarco had in mind and worried about how it would play with Vinnie. And whether he'd be blamed.

As they got closer, a cabin with light peeking from its windows took shape. It was a one-story structure with a rustic slab-shingle exterior and a front door flanked by a single window on the left and two others on the right, like at some point an addition had been tacked on. An older model Jeep Cherokee was parked to one side under a large tree. No white Corolla.

"Stop here," DeMarco commanded.

Lebo pulled over and looked at DeMarco. "Should I turn around? You know, in case we have to make a fast exit?"

"Forget it," DeMarco snapped in a snarly voice. "When we leave, we'll have plenty of time."

Lebo cut the engine and they started toward the cabin. "You take the left window and I'll take the ones on the right," DeMarco said in a low voice. "Make sure whoever's inside doesn't see you looking in. And watch for friggin' dogs."

DeMarco crouched down to stay below the window line with his Glock held against his leg. When he reached the cabin, he raised up to look in the lower corner of the first window. He saw an elderly man in a plaid shirt and suspenders sitting in a wooden rocker watching an old-fashioned television with rabbit ears on top. DeMarco shifted positions so he could observe the rest of the room, but didn't see anyone. He caught Lebo's eye and held up one finger and motioned for him to meet at the door.

"Did you see anyone other than the old man?" DeMarco whispered. Lebo shook his head.

"Maybe she's in one of the bedrooms. You take the old man and I'll check the back."

DeMarco knocked on the door with his free hand while continuing to conceal his Glock. He heard scuffling inside and clutched and re-clutched the grip.

The door opened and the man they'd seen watching television asked in a gruff voice, "Can I help you?"

DeMarco gave him a violent shove and sprinted toward the bedrooms with his Glock in the ready position. The first bedroom was empty and the second was as well. He returned to the living room where the old man was sprawled on the floor with a confused look on his face and Lebo standing over him. He clutched his hip.

"Where is she, asshole?" DeMarco leaned over and ground the muzzle of his Glock against his temple.

"I don't know what you're talking about," the man said in a whimpering voice.

"Angie DeMarco! Where is she?" He slammed his Glock against the side of his head.

The old man clasped his hands to his head and his eyes bulged and he rolled over and moaned. "I don't know what you're talking about," he said, sobbing.

DeMarco kicked his ribs and shouted, "I'm going to have another look around, asshole! You better regain your memory by the time I get back!"

He did a more thorough search this time and looked for signs that a woman had been there. In the first room, he ripped the comforter and top sheet from the bed and left them on the floor. Then he rifled through the drawers of the small chest and nightstand and checked the closet. He found nothing except a small duffel with the old man's spare clothes. He kicked at the bed on his way out and went on to the second bedroom and searched it as well. Nothing.

He stepped into the short hall and gazed at the old man who was still on the floor and alternately holding his head or rubbing his ribs and hip. He wondered what to do with the old fart. Then DeMarco stuck his head in the bathroom and looked around. A shaving kit, presumably the old man's, was on the vanity top and nothing else except a damp towel draped over the shower curtain rod. He used his Glock's barrel to move the curtain back, but the stall was empty.

DeMarco took a leak, and as he was staring down at the commode, he noticed refuse in the wastebasket. He zipped up and grabbed the wastebasket and dumped the contents in the sink. He sorted through it using the barrel of his Glock. His eyes fixed on a crumpled bag with the colorful logo. *Sonofabitch!* he screamed.

He bolted from the bathroom and pushed Lebo aside and stood over the old man and shoved the bag in his face. "See this, scumbag?" he shouted. "See the logo? This bag's from Sassi's Aesthetics! Now you've got five seconds to tell us where Angie DeMarco is!" He pointed the Glock at the old man's head.

The man raised his hands and said between whimpers, "I don't know what you're talking about."

"Sonofabitch!" DeMarco screamed. He moved the Glock closer to the old man's face and slammed the side of his head.

Lebo's alarm bells went off. "If you kill him, Carm," he said cautiously, "we'll never find out where she went."

"Shut your trap, Leebs!" He dropped to his knees and pressed the Glock's muzzle against the old man's temple and twisted it. "Tell me, goddamnit! Where is she?"

The old man tried to shove the gun away, and between more whimpers, said in a whiny voice, "I never heard of the woman you're looking for. Please."

DeMarco whacked him alongside the head again, screaming, "Tell me!" He slammed him a third time.

The man groaned and his eyes lost focus and his hands fell away from his head.

"Sonofabitch!" DeMarco beat on the man's head and face with the Glock, striking him repeatedly. Blood trickled from his nose and mouth and streaked his face. Then his body jerked violently and everything went limp.

DeMarco looked at him for a few moments before he rose to his feet again. His chest heaved and his eyes were unfocused.

Panicked, Lebo knelt and felt the old man's wrist. Then he slid his hand up and felt the side of his neck. "No pulse," he said.

DeMarco continued to look disoriented. He turned and went outside. Lebo stared at the dead man and tried to figure out what to do. After a few minutes, DeMarco came inside again and seemed calmer. "Let's get some rags and wipe this stinking place down and get to hell out of here," he said.

Lebo hurried to the kitchen and found a stack of dish towels. He soaked them in the sink, wrung them out and began to wipe everything they'd touched — countertops, wooden chair arms, door handles, light switches.

"Give me one of those rags, Leebs," DeMarco said. He took it to the bathroom and wiped everything including the toilet handle he'd touched when he flushed it. Then he wiped the light switches in the bathroom and bedrooms and used an elbow to turn off the lights.

"I think I got everything in here, Carm," Lebo said when DeMarco returned.

"Okay, let's get out of here before some idiot comes along and sees us. And take the rags. We'll toss them in the woods somewhere."

As Lebo was about to close the door and turn off the lights, he looked at the man on the floor and said, "I wonder who he was."

"What difference does it make? He's dead."

"I know, but —"

"We had to take care of him one way or the other when we left anyway. Did you think I was going to leave him alive when he knew we're looking for the bitch?"

TWENTY-EIGHT

On the way to Manistee, Pete said to Joe Tessler, "So Cap was humble as a Franciscan monk when you met him to turn over the files, huh?"

Tessler shook his head and muttered to himself. "Phony bastard. Every five minutes, he acted like he was going to start bawling because he felt so bad for me. Kept interrupting my presentation when I was trying to brief him on the cases, telling me how awful he felt about my situation and all that bull. I felt like puking."

"Completely overwhelmed, huh?"

"He couldn't even put on a good show. Third graders can act better than him."

"What do you think he'll do with the cases you turned over to him?"

"I'll tell you one thing," Tessler said, a bite to his words, "he better not screw anything up. Goddamn guy can't even fill out a speeding ticket without making about seven errors. The county attorney won't prosecute any of the tickets he writes because she knows they're so full of holes the driver's going to walk even if he doesn't have a lawyer."

"Are you going to keep an eye on the cases?"

"How can I? Officially, I'm not supposed to be in the building unless I come as a private citizen for personal business."

They passed the Little River Casino and Pete said, "Manistee is—"

"And here's something else. The guy is supposed to wear a uniform because he's only a deputy, right? So today at our meeting he shows up in civies like he's already been promoted to detective which I know he hasn't because the county board has to pass on his interim appointment and they won't meet again for another week."

"You're going to have to—"

"Then—we were meeting in my office because all the interview rooms were occupied—I swear the guy was casing it to see what changes he was going to make when he moves in. Disgusting."

Pete shook his head. "As I was saying, you have to guide me to Beryl's place."

"Go through town and take a left by the church."

Pete didn't say anything and continued on the winding road that passed over the river.

Tessler surfaced from his sulking and said, "How are we going to use the stuff about Beryl that Harry's newspaper pal dug up?"

"Try to put her on the defensive. See if we can get her to recant what she said in the affidavit."

Tessler was quiet for a while, then said, "Recant. That means take back, right?"

"Right."

"I kind of feel sorry for her in a way. She didn't strike me as a *bad* person."

"C'mon, Joe, don't go squishy on me. She lied and threw you to the wolves."

"Yeah, but Oilcan is *really* the bad guy here, isn't he? I bet he used her marijuana habit to pressure her into giving that affidavit."

"Look, if you're not up for this, just say so, and we'll turn around and find a place to get a bite to eat and I'll drop you at your place."

"I didn't say I'm not *up* for it," Tessler protested.

"Then get your game face on. Is this where I turn?" He jerked his head toward a white church with a spire just ahead.

"Yeah, that's it. Left there and go four or five blocks. I'll warn you when her place comes up."

Beryl Wuyt's house was an old white clapboard which like some others on the block, looked like it could use a coat of paint. Pete parked, and when they crossed the street, Tessler nudged him toward the side alley.

"Beryl has the second floor," he said. "Another woman with a couple of kids lives on the first. We need to take the outside stairs."

The rickety stairs struck Pete as a lawsuit in the making. Halfway up, Tessler whispered, "I see lights so she must be home. I'll take the lead. She knows me, obviously."

Tessler knocked on the door. They waited and heard noises inside. Finally the door opened slightly and a woman peered through the crack. Pete could smell the pungent aroma of marijuana.

"Joe," she said, sounding surprised. "What are you doing here?"

"We need to talk."

"You should have called first. I'm busy." She tried to close the door, but Tessler had his foot in the opening.

"Smoking your bong, Beryl?"

"What? You're crazy!" She leaned against the door, trying to close it, but Tessler pushed back and wedged it open wider.

"You can't just barge in! I'm going to call the police!"

"Call them," Tessler said. "I'll hang around, and when they get here, I'll be interested to hear how you explain this weed smoke. They'll probably tear this place apart and find your stash. They might not care a rat's ass about someone who smokes a bong once in a while, but the supply you keep will get their attention real fast. That's dealer quantity."

"I don't deal!" she screamed.

Tessler leaned against the door again and it snapped back against the wall. Pete saw Beryl Wuyt jump away. She had on a frayed terrycloth robe and her auburn hair adorned with a purple slash was damp.

Tessler grinned and said, "A little late to be getting up, isn't it Beryl?"

"Screw you. I just got out of the shower."

Tessler continued to grin. "This is my lawyer, Pete Thorsen. He's here to explain to you the consequences of giving false affidavits."

Her eyes widened. "What are you talking about?"

"I'm talking about the bullshit affidavit you gave Bernie Nichols saying I supplied you with weed."

Her eyes flicked between Pete and Tessler.

"Pete," Tessler said, "you want to explain the law to Beryl?"

"We're going to fight this in court, Ms. Wuyt. That means you'll be called to testify and you'll have a choice. Either recant what you said in your affidavit and admit it's a bunch of lies, or stick to your position and face perjury charges for lying under oath. Either way you're going to have a problem because I'm also going to advise Detective Tessler to bring a lawsuit against you for defamation. Your affidavit that Detective Tessler, a law enforcement officer, supplied you with marijuana not only is untrue, but since it's in writing and there's been publication, it's a clear case of libel. I don't know what the damages will be for maliciously defaming a law enforcement officer, but suspect they'll be substantial." Pete knew he might be laying it on a bit thick, but what the hell . . .

Beryl looked confused. Then she seemed to regroup and screamed, "Leave my house right now!"

Tessler looked at Pete and shook his head sorrowfully. "She was so much different the last time I was here, Pete, begging me to smoke weed with her before we went to her bedroom."

Pete feigned an aghast look. "She did that?"

Tessler nodded solemnly. "She got her supplies out and laid everything on the table. Three different jars of weed, a bong, rolling papers, the whole nine yards."

"I bet if we looked around, we'd find something."

Tessler grew thoughtful, then nodded and said, "Good idea." He walked over to a credenza and opened the doors and began looking through it.

"You can't come in my house and tear things apart!" Beryl screamed.

Tessler paid no attention to her.

"I warn you, I'm going to call the police!"

"Call them," he said. "We'll find your stash a lot faster with a little help."

"You slimy jerk!"

Tessler smiled. "Don't you just love a woman with spunk, Pete?" He walked to her bedroom and started looking around.

"Get out of my bedroom!"

"Oh, my, look what we have here, Pete," Tessler said when he opened a nightstand door. "It's the canisters I saw when Beryl invited me in before. And this lovely bong. The whole works, just the way I remember it." He used his cell phone camera to take photographs.

Beryl watched with slumped shoulders as he pulled item after item from the nightstand. She buried her head in her hands and began to cry.

Pete watched from the doorway and said, "Do you want to talk about that affidavit, Beryl, and see what we can do to set things straight?"

"It was that big guy, Bernie or whatever," she said between sobs. "He came to my house and must have smelled something. He claimed he was with the DEA and threatened to arrest me unless I cooperated, as he put it. He told me Joe is suspected of stealing drugs from the sheriff's department's evidence room and keeping some for his personal use and selling the rest. He knew I'd gone out with Joe a few times, and said if I'd give him an affidavit, he'd develop amnesia about the stuff in my apartment."

Pete looked Tessler's way and smiled.

"That night I was here," Tessler said, "I didn't bring any weed and suggest we smoke it, did I, Beryl? That was your idea and we smoked your stuff."

She sniffled and nodded.

"As I said a few minutes ago," Pete said, "falsely accusing another person is a serious matter. Would you like to recant what you said in the affidavit you gave Bernie? Recant means, basically, take back what you said."

"I'm afraid of that man."

"When all of this comes out, he won't be in a position to hurt you in any way. He's not with the DEA, he's a private investigator. He'll be lucky if he doesn't lose his license and go to jail over this."

She took her hands away from her face and looked at Pete with a pleading expression. "Are you sure?"

"Positive."

A flicker of hope showed in her eyes and she asked, "How do I recant, if that's the right word?"

"Do you have a computer and printer?"

She nodded. "In the other bedroom."

"Can I use it?"

She nodded again.

Pete disappeared into the adjoining bedroom, and when he reappeared with papers in hand, Tessler was sitting on the bed next to Beryl and her head rested on his shoulder.

"Beryl," he said, "would you read this and tell me if it's okay?"

She read through the statement a couple of times, then looked up and asked, "Does this part have to be in it?" She pointed to a paragraph that essentially described her supply of marijuana and the paraphernalia she possessed. Pete knew what her concern was and left the room again. Ten minutes later he returned with a revised version.

"This better?" he asked.

Beryl read it and nodded

"You're prepared to sign it then?"

She looked at Pete with concern in her eyes again. "What you said about Bernie what's-his-name, you're positive about that?"

"Yes. And we won't use your statement in court unless we need to."

Beryl pursed her lips and nodded and kissed Tessler on the cheek. "Sorry, Joe."

Tessler gave her a squeeze.

Pete looked at Tessler and said, "There's a notary seal in the glove compartment of my car. Would you mind running down and get it?"

When he was gone, Pete said to Beryl, "Look, this has been unpleasant for everyone concerned. But if you try to squirm out of this statement, I'm going to make damn sure you regret it."

She scowled at him. "Why are you threatening me? Joe understands what happened. He's forgiven me."

"I saw the way you were playing up to him. I'm not as easy to manipulate. The false affidavit you gave caused Joe a lot of trouble. I expect you to keep your word as we try to set the record straight."

"Jeez, you can really be unpleasant."

Pete just fixed her with a steady stare.

Tessler returned with the notary seal. He grinned and said, "What have you two been talking about while I've been gone?"

"Just where we go from here."

Tessler continued to grin and shook his head. "I'll tell you, doll, if you ever need a lawyer, this is the guy to hire."

They moved to the kitchen table and Beryl signed copies of the statement and Pete affixed his notary seal. On their way out, Tessler tried to kiss Beryl on the lips, but she apparently noticed Pete watching and quickly turned her head so he caught her cheek instead.

They got something to eat at a place in Manistee, and on the return drive to Frankfort, Tessler said, "I know I'm repeating myself, but in a way, I feel sorry for Beryl."

"Feel sorry for her, but don't fall for her crocodile tears."

"There's not a lot of give in you once you've made up your mind, is there?"

"Just being a realist. She was willing to do you in to save her own hide."

"I know, but . . ."

Pete shook his head again.

Tessler didn't say anything for a few moments, then, "At least you have to admit she's got style. Did you see that purple slash in her hair?"

"I saw it."

Tessler must have detected something in Pete's tone because he said, "What, you didn't like it?"

"Maybe it was the color. I might have liked it better if the slash had been green with silver glitter."

"Now you're kidding, right?"

"What I'm not kidding about is my advice that you stay away from her."

Tessler sighed. "I guess you're probably right. Besides, I'm seeing Kelene and I probably don't have enough free time for both of them. Or enough money."

Pete rolled his eyes and hoped Tessler didn't notice.

"Do you suppose Frank will drop me as a suspect and reinstate me after he sees Beryl's second statement?"

"I don't think we should show it to him yet."

His words seemed to jolt Tessler. "Why not? It'll show him that the affidavit Oilcan produced is false and what an ass the guy is. I'm anxious to get my badge and gun back."

"I know you are, but when we make our case, I'd like to have as much ammunition as possible."

Out of the corner of his eye, Pete saw Tessler slump in his seat. "Does that mean I have to continue to live with this friggin' suspension?"

Pete slapped him playfully on the shoulder with the back of his hand. "Hey, it's only been a day."

"Seems like a friggin' month," Tessler grumbled. "What's this *more* you think we need?"

"I have an idea."

TWENTY-NINE

Pete dropped Tessler at his house and headed for Venus. Tessler had suggested they stake out the club again that night, but he begged off, saying he had to get home. The truth was he wanted to size up the club by himself and see what kind of a plan he could come up with.

The lot was jammed just like the last time he was there, and he thought about the goons who'd taken down his license plate number that night and hoped it wouldn't be a problem. He drove up the center row so he could get a look at the doorman and make sure it wasn't one of them. The man didn't look familiar and Pete looped around and parked off to the side again.

He donned his "Save the Boat" cap and walked toward the door. No one was coming or going at the moment and he could tell he had the doorman's full attention.

"Members only" the doorman warned him when he got close.

Pete smiled and asked, "How do I become a member?"

"You local or just visiting the area?"

"Is Frankfort local?"

The doorman ignored his smart-alecky comment. "Membership for locals is one twenty-five."

Pete took out his wallet and forked over the money. The doorman examined the bills briefly, then dug around in his pocket and handed him a metal key. "Don't lose this," he said. "Otherwise, it'll be another buck twenty-five if you want to come back. Cash only inside." He opened the door for him.

He walked past the coat check area and pushed through the velvet curtain into the club. It was as Tessler had described. Cavernous with psychedelic lights flashing and a nude woman performing on an elevated stage. A staccato beat blared from the sound system.

He made his way to the bar and found an open stool. Before he could order a beer, he felt a warm body press against his back. He glanced around and saw a middle-aged woman trying to masquerade as someone half her age smiling at him seductively.

She slipped onto an adjacent stool and purred, "Buy me a drink, handsome?"

"Of course," Pete said, smiling back. "What would you like?"

"Champagne, honey. Don't *all* ladies drink champagne?"

"They certainly do."

When the bartender came, he ordered Coors Light and a glass of champagne. A minute later, he came back and plunked the drinks on the bar in front of them, not bothering to ask who was getting what. "Thirty bucks," he said.

Pete acted casual and handed him a pair of twenties. When the bartender waved one in the air, Pete shook his head and he walked away.

"Well," Ms. Snuggly said, linking an arm through his and raising her glass, "Cheers." Pete felt her leg against his.

"'Save the Boat,'" she said, taking his cap off and placing it on the bar and admiring it. "You must be a sailor."

"Of sorts."

"And look at that gorgeous hair." She ran her hand through it a couple of times. "A man with hair like yours shouldn't wear a cap."

He smiled and took another sip of his beer. "Come here often?" he asked. "That's the standard line for a place like this, right?"

"Once in a while. I have some psychic in me. I know when a *real* man is going to be here." Her leg pressed harder and she took another swallow of champagne.

Pete had been surveying the room as Ms. Snuggly went through her act. "Some of the ladies in here look kinda young," he said, trying to make his comment sound like a casual observation.

She seemed annoyed at having their conversation lurch in another direction. She leaned closer and said, "Too many little sluts if you ask me. I don't know why they let them in. Look at the way they dress."

Pete tried to keep a straight face and maintain eye contact and not glance at her cleavage. "Do a lot of them come in here?" he asked. As he posed the question, his eyes flicked toward a youngish girl with spikey pink hair and a mini skirt and stiletto heels.

Ms. Snuggly pushed away and looked at him and said, "You're not another of those pedophiles, are you?"

He chuckled and shook his head. "Gosh no. I like my women grown up."

She stared at him for a few moments. "I thought so. You look too normal. Not like some of the perverts in here." She snuggled closer again.

"I'm curious, though. Do a lot of young girls come in here?"

"Too many," she whispered as her lips brushed his ear.

"I'm surprised the place hasn't been raided."

"It has been. But you know how rats and mice disappear when the lights go on? That's the way the teenies are, too."

"Umm."

Ms. Snuggly whispered in his ear, "See that man over there? The one in the black suit who looks like an undertaker? That's Simon Frei. He owns this place. He likes them young. And I mean *young*. He's always parading around with some little tootsie, showing her off." The pink-haired girl he'd been watching had glommed onto Frei and firmly attached herself to his arm.

He watched them for a few moments, then asked, "Do you know Simon?"

"Sure," she said nonchalantly. "All the girls know him. You can't hang around here if you don't."

"Are you saying that the girls in here, ah, work for the house?"

Ms. Snuggly stiffened. "What kind of question is that?"

"Maybe that came out wrong. I didn't mean work *for* the house. I meant are *vetted* by the house so that the wrong people don't get in."

She pulled away again and her brows furled and she stared at him. "Are you a cop or something?"

"No," he said, chuckling.

"Why are you asking all of these questions, then?"

"This is my first time here. I'm a curious guy."

"Well, I thought we were having a nice conversation, but now I don't want to talk to you anymore. All you seem to be interested in is asking about other people." She took her last swallow of champagne and slammed her glass on the bar and walked away.

That was real smooth, Pete. Just when you were getting somewhere.

He slid off his stool and headed for the door. He didn't know whether Ms. Snuggly really knew the Venus owner, but he wasn't going to chance it. He'd seen before how things could unravel, and he didn't know how he'd explain if the owner confronted him with the two thugs who'd pounded on his window in the parking lot.

THIRTY

"Jesus Christ, Freddy," DeMarco said, "I ain't asking for the moon. I only want to get in contact with the guy we use at the Chicago PD when we need to track someone."

"To ask him to do your personal business, right? To track down that wife of yours now that you know she's still alive. That's the trouble with you, Carmen, you think too much about yourself and not enough about the organization and its business."

"That's bullshit. Who brought Frei around, huh? Me and Leebs, that's who."

"You think doing your job entitles you to special favors?"

"The way I see it, this ain't a special favor. It's using a resource to help someone who does a lot for the organization."

"Resources are unlimited, right? They just grow on trees like a bunch of friggin' olives."

"I didn't say that."

"Resources are *important*, and we conserve them for when we need them. It's hard to see how using them because a guy's in a pissing contest with his wife qualifies as need."

DeMarco was boiling inside and he was tempted to tell Pole to screw himself, but he maintained his composure. "Look," he said, "let me tell you how this benefits the organization. Suppose little wifey, who we now know is still out there someplace, puts two and two together and figures out, if she hasn't already, that I had something to do with the car bombing. She goes to the feds and tells them the story and about other things she might have picked up over the years. All of a sudden we got investigations coming out our rears, not just a couple of the local-yokels questioning *me*. They'll make the connection between me and Vinnie, so there's no way he won't be pulled in, too."

"I'm glad you've finally seen the light, genius. That's what Vinnie has been trying to get through to you. If you hadn't gone off on your own and played cowboy without taking into account the big picture, none of this would have happened. We got enough problems. Two nights ago, the FBI kicked down the door at our accountant's office and confiscated all the records and took his computers including a couple in back that were going to be sent out for repairs. They even took the friggin' wastepaper cans. They're looking for stuff to support tax charges."

"I appreciate that you've got problems. But my problem can't be ignored, either. I've been careful to keep business separate from personal, but who can tell what old wifey might know. She's a friggin' lawyer, remember. So it's not just me, it's the organization, too. Ending things the way they should be ended solves both problems."

Freddy Pole didn't say anything for a few moments, like he was thinking. Then he said, "I'll talk to Vinnie. No promises though."

"Could you do it quick? I'm sitting here on this friggin' park bench freezing my butt off."

"And I'm freezing mine on a goddamn patio with dead grape vines everywhere and nothing to break the wind. We have to communicate this way because *nothing* is secure these days. They've got something called a 'roving bug' now they can plant in your phone without ever having physical contact with it. Turns the friggin' thing into a microphone even if you don't have your cell turned on. That's how they got one of the New York families."

"Okay, okay, I understand."

DeMarco waited on the park bench for Pole to call back. He turned up his jacket collar to protect against the chilly wind and buried his hands in his pockets. His cell burred a half hour later.

"It's been arranged," Pole said. "Call this number at exactly 8:00 p.m. tonight and ask for Rudy." He gave him the telephone number. "Give him your wife's cell phone number. Our contact has access to a device called the StingRay. It pretends it's a cell tower or confuses the cell towers or whatever and can pinpoint the location of a phone. You get the location of the phone and you've got the location of the person."

"Thanks, Freddy, I really appreciate it."

"And Carm, this is the second special favor Vinnie's done for you. First the DNA guy and now the StingRay guy. I'd keep that in mind if I were you."

DeMarco sat in his den with Joey Lebo, his eyes glued to the time shown on his laptop's monitor. The slip of paper with Rudy's telephone number was on his desk, as was Angie's cell phone number. He drummed his fingers on the desktop as he waited for the appointed hour to show on his screen. Lebo, who'd been instructed not to turn on the television, sat on the couch flipping through *People* magazine and periodically glancing DeMarco's way.

When 8:00 p.m. showed, DeMarco immediately dialed the number Pole had given him.

"Yeah?" a gruff voice answered.

"This is—"

"Just give me the friggin' number."

DeMarco gave him Angie's cell phone number, reading the digits slowly to make sure he got it right. As soon as he finished, the connection went dead.

DeMarco stared at his cell phone. "What a prick!"

"What did he say, Carm?"

"He didn't say *anything*. He just cut me off when I tried to give him thirty seconds of background."

Lebo nodded and went back to his magazine.

DeMarco brooded for a few minutes, then pulled out his highway atlas and began to trace a route with his forefinger. "Come here, Leebs. I want to show you something."

Lebo did as requested and peered over DeMarco's shoulder at the map.

"Here's Eagle River," DeMarco said, "which is where we found that cabin we know she stayed at. From Eagle River, you can go one of three ways. You can go back south toward Chicago, which is where she came from. Two, you can go through this godforsaken part of Michigan," he said, pointing to the Upper Peninsula, "and then maybe south again unless she found another place to stay. Or three, she could go west," he said, dragging his finger in the direction of Minneapolis. "What would be your guess?"

Lebo studied the map some more, then leaned over and pointed to the Upper Peninsula.

DeMarco thought for a few moments. "I don't think so. She's too much of a princess to stay in a pissy wilderness area like that very long. Remember how she used to go to the spa in Rhinelander every week? I bet we find her in some more civilized area where she has the luxuries she's gotten used to."

"When is the StingRay guy supposed to get back to you?"

"Who knows? That's what ticked me off. All he wanted to hear was the ten-digit cell phone number. He cut me off as soon as I told him."

"Did you reach an understanding with Freddy about what comes next? After we catch her, that is?"

187

"We didn't talk about it."

"What's your plan, then?"

"It's evolving, as they say."

"What's that mean?"

DeMarco shot him a look. "A guy I know likes to say it's easier to apologize for something after the fact than it is to beg for permission beforehand."

THIRTY-ONE

When Tessler called back, Pete said, "I visited Venus after I dropped you off last night. I have an idea for getting our hands on those security camera tapes."

A pause, then, "You went to Venus? You said you needed to get home."

"I juggled things."

Tessler sighed. "Okay, so what's your plan?"

"I'd just got there when this working lady latched onto me and got me to spring for a glass of champagne. We—"

"How much did the champagne cost you?"

"Twenty bucks."

"Ain't that ridiculous? And it's nothing but colored water."

Pete chuckled. "Anyway, as I was saying, we talked for a while and I steered the conversation around to young ladies. She got snarly and told me they let too many of the young ones in. That was my observation, too. She—"

"Was the pink-haired girl there?"

"She was."

"Isn't she something? I wonder how long it takes her to get her hair to look like that? It can't look that bad when she gets up in the morning. How old do you think she is?"

"Don't know. She's probably younger than she looks if you strip off all that makeup. Anyway, she was hanging all over the owner of the place, who according to my more mature friend, likes them young."

"Simon Frei."

"Right, Simon Frei. Anyway, I asked some more questions and I guess I pushed too hard because she began to get suspicious. I didn't press my luck and just left when the opportunity presented itself."

"So, your idea is to work the young lady angle."

"Right. Do you think Kelene might be willing to help us?"

A pause, then, "Help us do what?"

"Pose as a working lady a few nights to see if she can come up with something we can use against Frei."

Another pause, longer this time. "I'm not sure I like what you're implying, Pete."

"I'm not implying anything. I'm just asking whether she might be willing to do an acting job to help us get information."

Tessler didn't say anything for a few moments. "If I asked her to do something like that, she'd probably think I viewed her as a lady of loose morals. That might not mean squat to you, but for me, it probably would be the end of our relationship."

"That's why we'd have to handle the thing delicately. Does she know that you've been suspended?"

"Well, yeah, I had to tell her. Whenever I go to her place to pick her up for a date or just hang out, she pats me down and likes to feel my piece, you know? A lot of women find that exciting. Gets their juices flowing. Then when I was there the other night, I didn't have my department-issue piece, obviously, and *also* didn't have my private sidearm. In other words, I was totally naked. She goes through her patting routine and didn't feel anything. I had no choice but to come clean."

"That makes it easier. She might be more willing to go along with my scheme if it gets your gun and badge back."

"Maybe. I'd have to ask her."

"Call me back. And Joe, put your salesman's hat on. This might be our best shot."

Pete was about to leave for Kelene Brill's house when Julie called. "Dad," she said in a voice that oozed excitement, "I only have like thirty seconds to talk, but I wanted to let you know that Effie and I are on our way to Leslie Lehr's apartment. Or I guess I should say Leslie Wallace's apartment because that's her last name these days."

"You found her."

"We *think* we found her. That mailroom guy I told you about? He came through after all. Leslie left a forwarding address with them when she left Harrison Stryker and he finally remembered and contacted Effie."

"That's great."

"Remember what I said about investigative technique? How asking questions and following up on every lead you develop can eventually pay off? I think that might be about to happen to us."

"You might try calling her first to make sure she's home. If she got another job, she might be working."

He heard her sigh, like his comment was so obvious she'd be embarrassed to even raise it. "We already called, Dad. Like *seven* times. We always get this recorded message that the number isn't in service. Going over there is our only choice."

"Sounds like it."

"Very quickly, when are you coming to Philadelphia like you promised so you can buy your daughter some nourishing dinners?"

"I'll have to get back to you in a couple of days. I'm juggling some things."

"I need you to bring a warmer coat for me, too. With colder weather coming on, I don't know how Rocky got by with just a crummy sweatshirt."

Julie was well beyond her thirty seconds, and when she finally signed off, Pete grabbed his keys and headed out, knowing he probably had a selling job ahead with Kelene. She'd apparently balked at the idea when Tessler raised it, fearing it might ruin her reputation if word got around that she frequented places like Venus. She agreed to talk about it, though. He rehearsed in his mind what he was going to say to persuade her to go along with his plan.

Tessler's car was there when he arrived, and when he walked in, he saw that Kelene had dressed for the occasion: a shocking pink sweater, form-fitting black slacks and multi-colored platform shoes. Stale tobacco odor lingered in the air even though neither Kelene nor Tessler was smoking.

"Pete," Kelene said, looping her arms around his neck and giving him a long squeeze. Tessler stood a few feet away, scowling, like he viewed the embrace as excessively friendly.

"Sorry I'm late."

Kelene disengaged from Pete and acted like she hadn't heard his apology. She continued to smile seductively and glanced between Pete and Tessler. "How about something to drink, boys?" she said.

Tessler's face morphed into a lopsided grin as he looked at Pete for guidance. Pete shook his head. "Thanks, just water for me."

"I'll have the same," Tessler said. He sounded disappointed.

Kelene disappeared into the kitchen and came back with two bottles of water and a mug of coffee for herself.

"So," she said, sitting down on the couch next to Tessler, "I understand you think I might make a good actress."

Pete smiled. "You know about Joe's situation, right?"

She patted the left side of Tessler's chest. "No gun."

"Somebody's setting him up. We believe you might be able to help us get his piece back. *And* his badge. *And* help serve justice as well."

"You want me to dress up as a hooker, right?" She screwed up her face to show her disgust at the thought.

"Think of it as a costume. It's just something so you'll blend into the scene at Venus."

She looked thoughtful for a few moments. "What if some big oaf comes on to me?"

Pete could tell she was more receptive to the idea than Tessler led him to believe. "That's good," he said encouragingly. "That means you've played your part well. But always keep in mind that your objective is to get close to the young girls working there. Cozy up to them, to use the vernacular, try to gain their trust. If we're right, some of them might be underage. We're looking for leverage to get the owner of the place to give us access to security camera tapes that we know exist."

"You say cozy up to them, like it'll be easy. I don't know much about the world's oldest profession, as they call it, but they'll likely view me as competition, won't they?"

"Maybe. But they're also more likely to talk to you than someone like Joe or me. Introduce yourself to them, show empathy for their situation, try to find out their ages. Always keep in mind that we're trying to establish that Simon Frei, who owns the place, permits underage girls to ply their trade there. And if possible, come up with evidence that he preys on them himself."

"Empathy. That's like sympathy, right?"

"Kind of."

Kelene reached for a silver case. She lit a cigarette with a flare and blew a stream of smoke over her shoulder. She took another drag and did the same. "If I agree to do this, what do I get out of it?"

Pete hadn't thought about it and asked, "What do you suggest?"

She turned thoughtful again. "I could use some new clothes."

"I'm sure we can work something out."

"I mean some *good* things. Not the kind of cheap stuff they sell locally."

"I understand."

She took another drag on her cigarette and blew the smoke away from them. "I wouldn't even know what to wear at this Venus place."

"When I was there last night," Pete said, "casing the joint, most of the working ladies wore clothes that were long on top and short on the bottom. Lots of glitz."

She blew another stream of smoke over her shoulder and said, "That sounds so sleazy."

"Remember, it's just to blend in."

She snuffed her cigarette in an ashtray and got up and walked toward her bedroom.

"I think she's going to do it," Pete said to Tessler in a quiet voice.

"I feel bad, taking advantage of her this way," Tessler said. "You don't think she'll be in any danger, do you?"

"If we had her wear a wire, I'd say maybe. But not the way we're planning to do it. The worst that's likely to happen is they'll toss her out of the place if they conclude she isn't really a working girl or isn't being friendly enough with customers."

"I don't *want* her being friendly with customers."

"Do you want your badge back or not?"

Kelene came back from the bedroom carrying a bundle of clothes. "Joe, if you'll move, I'll show you boys some things and you can tell me what you think."

When she finished arranging her display, Pete gazed at the array of miniskirts and glitzy tops, many with silver or gold threads running through them. "I didn't bring them out," she said, "but black or gray panty hose would probably work with most of these. Maybe red with one or two of the outfits."

"Perfect. And while you're at Venus, be sure to watch for a girl with pink hair who likes to hang around Simon Frei."

THIRTY-TWO

"Our man got in touch a couple of hours ago," Freddy Pole said. "He said the StingRay came up blank with the number you gave him."

"Came up blank," DeMarco repeated. "What does that mean?"

"Just what I said. Blank. Zilch. Nothing."

"How could that be?"

"I didn't ask him to write a fifty-page report, but he said either you gave him a bogus cell phone number or the owner of the phone has removed the batteries."

DeMarco thought about that. "I didn't give him a bogus number. Don't you think I know wifey's cell phone number?"

"She must have removed the batteries then."

"If she removed the batteries, nothing would work, right?"

"How would I know? I'm not a friggin' engineer."

DeMarco thought about it some more. "Okay, Freddy, let me think about it. If I need more help, I'll get in touch again."

"I remind you again, Vinnie called in favors from two people for you. Don't screw with this and cause him more problems. Oh, and we might need you and Leebs to visit Mr. Frei again. It seems you guys might not have gotten through to him the first time."

"Bull. When we left, the guy was licking the floor and begging to cooperate."

"I'm just telling you it might be necessary to refresh his memory."

When DeMarco walked back to his house, his mind was on locating little wifey rather than Simon Frei's balkiness. He walked in the door and heard the *Judge Judy* show blaring loud enough that if a window had been open, he could have heard it in the park a block away. He kicked the door and screamed, "Turn off that friggin' show!"

Startled, Lebo saw DeMarco's twisted expression and clicked off the television.

"That StingRay genius who's supposed to be able to do everything with his secret device? All we got from him is that I must have given him the wrong cell phone number or the batteries have been removed! Dumbass!"

DeMarco went to his desk and dug a cell phone from one of the drawers. He input a number and waited. Nothing. He tried the number again a few minutes later. Still nothing. Lebo watched and braced himself for another outburst. Instead, DeMarco calmly placed the cell phone on his desk and leaned back in his chair and appeared to think.

Lebo grew uncomfortable with the silence and wanted to say something, but knew better and let DeMarco stew. Finally he said, "She thinks she's outsmarted me. We'll see about that."

He got up and disappeared from the room. Ten minutes later, he returned and logged onto his computer, and after fiddling around for a while, jotted down the telephone number for Sears & Whitney.

DeMarco picked up the cell phone again and input the number. He waited until the operator answered and said, "Sears & Whitney, Marcia speaking."

"Angie DeMarco, please."

A long pause, then, "I'm afraid Ms. DeMarco is no longer with us, sir."

"Really. Since when?"

"Since August, sir. Ms. DeMarco was involved in a tragic accident."

"Accident?"

"Her car caught fire and . . ." The operator sounded choked up.

"That's terrible. I hoped to talk to her about a case she handled some years ago. Is there someone else I can talk to?"

"Maybe our docket manager?"

A pause, then, "I think I need someone more senior than that. Who's your managing partner?"

"That would be Mr. Johnson, sir."

"Could I speak to him please?"

"Your name, sir?"

"Ed Harrington. I'm a lawyer in Springfield."

After a pause, the operator returned to the line and said, "Mr. Johnson is on a conference call, sir. If you'll give me your telephone number, I'll have him return your call."

"On the phone, huh?" DeMarco said. "I'll tell you my problem. I represent a former client of Ms. DeMarco's who's presently in prison and we have an important court hearing in the morning. I'm going to argue that Ms. DeMarco screwed up at his trial and he's entitled to a new one. That's why I need to speak to Mr. Johnson."

"Oh my."

"I'll hold until Mr. Johnson is free."

She put him on hold, and a few minutes later, came back on the line and said, "I'm sorry, sir, Mr. Johnson is off the phone, but he has people waiting for him in the reception area. The best I can do is have him call you back."

DeMarco looked at the ceiling and tried to remain patient. "Look, Marcia, I need to speak to Mr. Johnson right now. Tell him that. It'll be very bad for your law firm if I'm not able to speak to him."

"I'll see what he says."

Five minutes later, a man came on the phone and said, "Steve Johnson, Mr. Harrington. How can I help you?"

DeMarco repeated his story about how Angie DeMarco had screwed up at his client's murder trial nine years ago, and said he was appearing in court in the morning on a petition for a new trial. He could sense Johnson's demeanor change as he laid out the story.

"Ms. DeMarco is dead, you know."

"That's what your receptionist said. But you and I both know her being dead doesn't get your firm off the hook if she messed up. Besides, I have it on good information that Ms. DeMarco *isn't* dead. I need to talk to her."

Johnson didn't say anything for a few moments. Then, "Who told you she's not dead? She died in a car fire in August. I was even at her funeral."

"I'm just telling you what people tell me."

"What people?"

"I'd prefer not to name names, but they're from Chicago and claim to know."

A pause, then, "What firm are you with, Mr. Harrington?"

DeMarco scrambled to come up with a name and flipped out, "Lane & Harrington."

"And what's the name of the defendant Ms. DeMarco supposedly represented?"

"His name is Manuel Jimenez. I don't know the original case number offhand."

"Doesn't ring a bell," Johnson said after a few moments. "Mr. Harrington, I've got people waiting for me. I'll check our files and call you back if I find anything. What's your telephone number?"

DeMarco gave him the number of his burner cell phone.

"Is that the number you're calling on? My receptionist said her screen showed unknown caller."

"It's my personal cell phone. I'm calling from my car."

"Got it."

"But Mr. Johnson, Angie DeMarco should call me. She's the one with knowledge of this case."

When he was off the call with Johnson, Lebo grinned and said, "That was damn slick, Carm, the way you handled the legal stuff. Where did you learn that shit?"

"You think I live under a rock or something? I'm trying to stir the pot and see if old wifey sticks her head out."

"Pete, Steve Johnson. A couple of hours ago, I got a call from a guy named Ed Harrington who said he's a lawyer with a Springfield firm named Lane & Harrington. He claims he's representing a client Angie once represented, Manuel Jimenez. I guess the guy's in prison and Harrington's trying to get a new trial for him. He asked to speak to Angie."

"Really," Pete said, jolted by Johnson's comments.

"I told him she died in a car fire, but he didn't seem to believe me. Then he said something that blew my mind. He claims that some people in Chicago told him that Angie is still alive."

Pete glanced at Angie who was sitting in a chair twenty feet away from him, reading. "That's ridiculous," he said, "we were both at her funeral. Who told him she's alive?"

Angie looked up as soon as the words came from his mouth.

"He wouldn't give me a specific name," Johnson said.

"Strange."

"And it gets stranger. After I finished a meeting with some clients, I went online and checked Martindale Hubbell and other lawyers' directories and didn't find any indication of a lawyer in Springfield named Ed Harrington or of a firm named Lane & Harrington."

"It could be a two-person firm," Pete offered. "Very small firms often don't want to spend the money to be listed."

"Possible, I suppose, but in my experience, most lawyers list individually in those cases because it's common for people looking for a lawyer in a particular city to check the major directories."

"True."

"I also checked our records and found no indication we ever represented a client named Manuel Jimenez."

"How did you leave it with him?"

"I promised to call him back if anything occurred to me."

"Did he give you a telephone number?"

"He did." Johnson gave it to him. "Our screen showed unknown caller so I wasn't able to establish that it was actually Ed Harrington calling. He said he was calling from his car on his private cell phone."

"What are you going to do?"

"What *can* I do? I'm just going to forget about it unless the guy calls back. But I thought I'd let you know because you and Angie were close. And you know what he said at the end of our call? He said, 'Have Angie DeMarco call me.'"

When Pete finished the call, he looked at Angie and said, "That was Steve Johnson in case you couldn't tell. A man named Ed Harrington called the firm and asked for you. He said he said he knew you were still alive because people in Chicago told him so." He summarized the rest of his conversation with Johnson.

When Angie stared at him blankly and didn't say anything, he asked, "Do you have any idea what that was all about?"

She shook her head.

"Someone obviously thinks you're still alive. Harrington claims he represents a man in prison you once represented. His name is Manuel Jimenez. Does that sound familiar?"

Angie shook her head again.

Pete thought about it for a few moments. "Maybe I should call this Ed Harrington back," he said. "Steve gave me his number."

Angie suddenly recovered her ability to speak. "Don't! It might be a trap!"

Her reaction fueled the suspicions churning inside him. He frowned and asked, "How would it be a trap?"

"I don't know. I just don't think you should call that man back."

"I don't understand."

"Don't do it, okay?"

THIRTY-THREE

"Kelene might have hit a home run for us," Tessler said. "Could you join us at her house?"

"How about a sneak preview?"

"It's best if you hear it from her in person. Besides, we have visual aids you'll want to see."

That got Pete's attention and he said he'd be right over. He left a note for Angie who'd gone for a walk along the beach attired in her floppy hat and a parka.

When he walked in, Tessler was sitting on the couch holding Kelene's hand. She was dolled up again and two fluted glasses containing what Pete assumed was champagne rested on the coffee table in front of them. It wasn't yet 11:00 a.m.

Kelene sprang from the couch and sashayed across the room toward Pete with a seductive look and purred, "Buy me a drink, handsome?"

Tessler grinned as he watched her. "Doesn't she have the routine nailed, Pete? We've been talking and I'm going to be her agent if she hits Broadway or heads west to Hollywood."

Pete nodded to show his appreciation of her acting skills. "I gather from the celebration that our ruse worked?"

"Yeah, but first you have to join us in a glass of champagne. You know, to recreate the atmosphere."

Having champagne or any other drink before noon was the last thing Pete wanted, but he agreed in order to get the show on the road. When he was seated across from them with a fluted glass in hand, he said, "Okay, darlin'," drawing out the word, "break a leg."

Kelene giggled.

"Start from the beginning, honey," Tessler counseled. "You know, when you walked up to the door of that place."

Kelene got to her feet, and after taking a sip of champagne, she put her glass down and went to the other side of the room, then turned and started back toward them. Tessler scrambled to his feet to play the part of an imaginary doorman. She said in a sultry voice that would make Mae West proud, "Hi, my name's Kelene. Do I need a ticket to get in?"

Tessler looked her over, patted her on the fanny a couple of times and said in a low voice that mimicked an agitated junk yard dog, "Check in with Simon when you get inside, doll. You need to understand the rules and get his okay to hang around."

"So I walk in this place," Kelene continued, "and the music is playing and all kinds of lights are flashing and this stripper is working the pole. I swear, guys are hitting on me before I'd gone ten feet. I gave them a wink and a little squeeze and said I'd be back as soon as I talked to the boss. I wandered around looking for Simon and all of a sudden this guy with undertaker clothes comes up behind me. He looked me over like he was judging a heifer at the county fair and ran his hand over me. I—"

"That's the part I don't like," Tessler said, scowling. "Goddamned pervert. He needs to keep his hands to himself."

"I was about to say that, darling. I almost kneed him in the jewels, but caught myself and remembered the reason I was there."

Tessler nodded solemnly and seemed mollified for the moment.

"Then Simon says to me in this creepy voice that sent shivers down my spine, 'There are three things you got to remember, doll. First, you're here only as long as I say you're here. Next, you better keep the champagne flowing, because if you don't, it's bye-bye. Last, if you hook up with a john, I get half.' Then he walked away."

"Now tell Pete about the driver's license."

"I cruised around the place, talking to this creep and that one, snuggling up them and getting them to buy me champagne, while—"

"That's the watered-down stuff they charge you twenty bucks a pop for," Tessler interjected, something Pete already knew.

"All the while I kept my eyes on the young girls in the place. It's hard to tell how old a person is these days with all the eye makeup and other gunk they wear, but some of the girls looked *awfully* young. Especially the pink-haired babe who kept attaching herself to Simon like a suction cup."

"Get to the makeup room, honey," Tessler urged.

Kelene continued with her story. "Just like you said, pink hair, do you believe it? That short spikey style that looks like it was combed with an eggbeater."

Tessler cranked his hands in a circle and urged her to get to the point even though his periodic interruptions delayed the production as much as anything.

"There's this room connected to the ladies' room where the women freshen their makeup and stuff. It has these small lockers along one wall where you can lock up your purse and other valuables if you want. I saw the pink-haired teenie go in there and followed her and pretended to work on my eyes just like she was doing, but I was really watching her. When she finished, she threw her purse into one of the lockers and walked out. Didn't take the key or anything, just threw it in there. I was going to take a quick look, but there were too many people coming in and out, you know?

"The next night, I was at Venus again. Ms. Pink Hair was there, too. I kept an eye on her again, and when she headed for the ladies' room,

I was right behind. She goes through the same routine as before, and when she throws her purse into a locker and didn't lock it, I waited until the room was empty and then grabbed that sucker and looked through it."

"Show Pete what you found, honey," Tessler said anxiously.

Kelene opened an envelope and handed Pete a Michigan driver's license with the girl's picture. The name on the license was Cindi Carr.

"You took this from her purse?" Pete asked, gazing at her with new admiration.

"Natch, honey," she said, slipping into her act again. "There weren't copy machines every ten feet for me to make a picture of it so I *confiscated* it as Detective Tessler would say."

"Look at the date of birth," Tessler urged.

Pete checked it and did the math in his head. He looked up at them and said, "Seventeen."

"Right," Tessler said, "and she won't turn eighteen for seven more months."

Pete smiled at Kelene who was refilling her champagne glass. She smiled back and did a little wiggle.

"Did she do good or what?" Tessler asked.

Pete nodded. "This is a damn good start."

That brought Tessler up short. "Damn good start? You aren't going to pull another one of those on me, are you?"

"I'm just saying we need to build on Kelene's great work."

Tessler stared at him blankly.

"Standing alone, all the license shows is that Venus permitted one underaged young lady in the place, which is probably a slap on the wrist at most. But if we can tie it to Simon like I think we might be able to . . ."

Now Kelene was suspicious. "You're not saying I have to go back to that place, are you?"

"No, you did a terrific job. Do you have any idea where Cindi Carr lives locally? The address on her license shows Detroit."

Kelene shook her head.

Tessler seemed to pick up on Pete's question. "Are you thinking about another, ah, visit?"

"It crossed my mind."

"There's a place near Thompsonville that caters to transients. We've made a couple of drug busts there. That could be where she lives."

The low-slung Sunrise Apartments building looked like it might have been a motel at one time. It was laid out in a horseshoe and a neon sign in front advertised daily, weekly and monthly rates. Pete and Joe Tessler parked in front and went into the postage-stamp office. A skinny young man with a pale complexion and shaggy hair sat on a swivel chair behind the counter perusing a magazine with great interest. He looked up and saw them.

"Hello, Elroy," Tessler said, "I thought when we talked last time you were planning to move on."

Elroy swallowed hard and his jaw muscle pulsed. "I want to call our lawyer."

"Go ahead," Tessler said, "but that'll just complicate your life. We're not here to bust this place again, but if you give us any guff, that's exactly what's going to happen. We only want some information about one of your guests."

"Who?"

"Cindi Carr."

Elroy swallowed again. "Our guest information is confidential."

Tessler gave him a baleful stare, then looked down at the old-fashioned guest book on the counter, spun it around and began paging through it.

Elroy grabbed for the book. "Our guest book is one of our business records. You can't look at it without a warrant!"

"Sue us," Tessler said, grinning as he flipped the book shut. "Unit 17," he said to Pete.

Elroy looked stunned and then said in a voice that sounded like he was just going through the motions, "I'll call and see if Ms. Carr is available."

Tessler shook his head. "Uh, uh, Elroy. We'll check ourselves."

Elroy fixed him with a petulant glare.

"I mean it, friend. If Ms. Carr gets any telephone calls before we get to Unit 17, the first thing I'm going to do is come back and stick your head in that commode and flush it for five minutes before I haul your ass off to jail to book you for obstruction of justice and a string of other charges long enough to make your nuts squeal."

Elroy stared toward the open toilet door.

On the way to Unit 17, Tessler looked at Pete and grinned. "I hope she lets us in. If we have to force things, it'll be the second time in days we strong-armed a female. We're going to start getting a reputation."

Tessler put on his game face and knocked on the door a couple of times and waited. When no one answered, he whispered, "You don't suppose she's already at the club, do you?"

Pete shrugged.

He knocked again, louder this time. Pete heard scuffling inside and then got the feeling someone was peering through the peephole. "Go away," a muffled female voice said, "I'm busy."

"Open up, Ms. Carr, sheriff's department," Tessler said.

"Go away!" she repeated.

"If you don't open up, I'm going to break your door down."

Silence, then rattling of the security chain. Tessler shoved when the door opened a crack and the pink-haired girl jumped out of the way. She looked pathetic in her ratty oversized tee-shirt and pale face streaked with eye makeup.

She stared at them with wide eyes and asked, "What do you want?"

"A seventeen-year-old girl shouldn't be working in a place like Venus," Tessler said, glancing around the pigsty of a room. "We need a statement from you and then you need to get away from here and get your tail back to Detroit."

"I don't have to talk to you."

Tessler ignored her and looked at the nightstand by the bed. He went over and picked up a couple of packs of condoms and examined them. After eyeing the girl again, he said, "Did one of your johns leave these here? Or is this your supply?"

"They were here when I checked in."

"Stop trying to horse us around, Cindi. We know everything about you. Your age, your address in Detroit, how much you have to give Simon Frei for tricks you land at Venus, the special favors you provide him, everything."

Her body slumped and she folded her arms petulantly. "I'm not talking."

"If you don't cooperate, Cindi, we're going to call the juvenile authorities."

She continued to glare at them defiantly.

"Is that your answer, you don't care?"

She didn't say anything.

"Okay," Tessler said, sighing exaggeratedly, "you're forcing our hand." He hauled out his cell phone and began to punch in a number.

"Wait."

Both of them stared at her.

"What kind of statement?"

"Do you have it, Pete?"

Pete handed her the one-page statement he'd prepared before they came.

Cindi Carr read it over. "What if I won't sign this?"

"Is there something in there that isn't accurate? Like maybe you're older than seventeen and you can prove it? Or you've never been to a place called Venus? Or you've never provided sexual favors for a man named Simon Frei? Or you've never sold yourself to other men? What part of it isn't accurate?"

She stared straight ahead expressionless.

"We're wasting our time," Tessler said to Pete, "I'm calling juvenile while someone's still around." He started to input a number again.

"Are you going to try to bring charges against me if I sign this?"

"Not if you sign it," Tessler said. "We just want you to get out of here and go back to Detroit like I said. Do you have relatives there?"

She didn't say anything.

"This is hopeless," Tessler said, raising his cell phone again.

"I can't get back to Detroit without money."

"How much?"

A pause, then, "A couple hundred?"

Pete left Tessler and headed for the office again. Elroy looked startled to see him, but Pete walked directly to the ATM in the corner and withdrew three hundred dollars and left again without speaking to him. Back in Unit 17, he held up the stack of bills so Cindi, who was now sitting on the rumpled bed, could see them.

"Ready to sign?" he asked.

Cindi stared at the floor and didn't say anything.

"Last chance, Cindi."

"I'll sign if I can get a hundred more."

"Done."

Tessler cleared off the nightstand and she signed several copies of the statement. Pete gave her the money.

"Get yourself cleaned up, Cindi, and pack and clear out of here. And don't go near Venus because we've got people watching the place and they'll pick you up if you do. Don't try to call Simon, either, because we have his phones tapped and you'll be interfering with a law enforcement operation. That's a separate offense in case you don't know."

On their way to their car, Tessler said, "It makes you wonder how a seventeen-year-old girl gets so far off the tracks that she winds up like Cindi."

Pete nodded. He was thinking about Julie and how lucky he was, at least so far.

"Scumbags like Simon Frei have a lot to do with it," Tessler said. "That's one of the reasons I need my badge back."

THIRTY-FOUR

T he satisfaction they'd felt after leaving Cindi Carr's room faded when they learned that Frei wouldn't be in until the next day. They'd been in battle mode and both were disappointed with the delay. Pete dropped Tessler at his house and took the road along the north side of the lake back home.

When he climbed the steps to his front door, he saw that the blinds were drawn again, something he'd grown accustomed to, and used his key to get in. Angie relaxed when she saw him, and after some perfunctory questions about their session with Carr, went back her book.

Pete went to the kitchen and made a sandwich and sat at the table and ate it. His eyes flicked Angie's way and he thought some more about the telephone call Steve Johnson had received and her reaction. She'd clearly been shaken, but hadn't been exactly forthcoming when he tried to discuss it. It made him wonder, though, whether there might be some justification for her jitteriness other than paranoia.

He finished his sandwich and went to the living room and sat down on the couch opposite Angie. "Any further thoughts about the call Steve received now that you've had time to think about it?"

She shrugged.

"It pretty clearly was a fishing expedition by someone who believes you might not be dead, don't you think?"

"Could be."

"If you had to guess, who would you say it was?"

She shrugged again. "One of the creep's enemies he's warring with, who else?"

"Which brings us full circle to the original question: how would someone know you didn't die in the car bombing?"

"Pete, for the tenth time, I don't know!"

He glanced at her, trying to read her thoughts. "It's interesting," he said, "that the caller seems to have focused on our law firm as the party in cahoots with you for faking your death."

"Yeah? So what's your point?"

"On reflection, that might be a good thing. No one associated with the firm except me knows the truth, so they won't have to lie if the caller contacts them again and presses his narrative that he knows you're still alive. You don't get caught in inconsistencies if you don't have to hide the truth in the first place."

"I wouldn't want something to happen to the firm because of me."

"Maybe you should confess the truth, then, and let the law find the bomber or bombers. I'm sure they're investigating as we speak."

Angie's eyes telegraphed her discomfort.

"As an intermediate measure, we could contact the Chicago PD and the FBI and tell them what happened so they can put taps on the firm's phones in case the caller calls back."

She seemed to think about it, then, "I don't want to do that."

"Why?"

"I agree with you that it was probably a fishing expedition. Talking to the Chicago PD might in effect be coming out of my foxhole. It might be exactly what they want."

"Okay, then—"

"Everyone knows there are a few dirty cops inside the Chicago PD, they just don't know who they are. If word gets back to the mob, I might be more vulnerable than I am now."

He breathed in deeply and then expelled the air. "Well at least the caller seemed focused on ferreting out *whether* you're in fact dead as opposed to where you *are*. Hopefully, we can keep it that way."

She frowned.

"The point I'm raising is my connection to the firm. I'm still listed on the firm's website—and, I assume, in the print materials—as Of Counsel. My address is probably there someplace, too. For people familiar with the firm, our association is hardly a secret."

"Maybe they already know about you."

"I don't think so," Pete said. "If the caller had put everything together, he would have called here instead of calling Steve. I believe there's still separation."

Angie's eyes gave away nothing.

"Which leads me to my final point. We talked in detail about what you did after you left Riverside. Can you think of anything else that might eventually point someone who's looking for you up here?"

"Such as?"

"The obvious thing is cell phone use. A couple of years ago when I was trying to help my old army buddy, I told everyone I was going to Chicago, but the sheriff who was after him found out I was really in North Carolina because of my cell phone usage."

"I haven't used my cell phone since I've been here."

"Here meaning the lake, I assume. How about after you left Riverside and went to northern Wisconsin?"

"I used it a couple of times. I had no choice."

"Did you ever check your Facebook page or surf the web?"

"A few times. Never here."

"Someone who knows what he's doing can pinpoint a person's location because of his cell. They trace it through the cell towers or something. But thankfully, that doesn't seem to have happened in your case or we would have had visitors."

"Lest you think I'm a complete idiot, I not only haven't used my phone up here, I've also removed the batteries. I know a little about cell phone tracing, too."

The asshole is hiding something, DeMarco thought, as he brooded over his telephone conversation with Steve Johnson. He went on the Internet and pulled up the Sears & Whitney website and scrolled through the list of partners until he came to Johnson's name. He read through his bio: graduated *cum laude* from Northwestern University, got his JD from the University of Michigan Law School, intellectual property practice specialty. Two terms as a trustee on the Wilmette Village Board.

He leaned back and thought for a few minutes. That's exactly the kind of guy dear little wifey would take up with. Snooty jerk who thought he was above other people, making a living by screwing others over and living high on the hog. Probably inherited his money from his old man.

DeMarco went down the hall and rummaged around her study looking for the pocket law firm directory he'd been unable to locate before. Still having no luck, he returned to his den and plugged into an online telephone directory and found Johnson's home telephone number and street address. He wrote them down and leaned back again and thought some more and drummed his pen on the desktop. Maybe he'd take a drive.

He used the toilet, set his house alarm, and walked to the detached garage and got into his rebuilt Dodge Dart. A tremor shot up his leg as the powerful engine sprang to life. He'd thought about taking Lebo along, but decided against it. The guy had been with him a long time, but recently he'd begun to question his loyalty. Too much sucking up to Vinnie. And to that jerk, Freddy Pole. Plus, some of their timid crap seemed to be rubbing off on him.

Weaving through traffic on the Tri-State, he thought about the way Leebs had worked over Frei and couldn't help but notice the gusto he brought to the job compared to the way he always preached caution when it came to his search for little wifey. He even had to take care of that old fart in the cabin himself even though it clearly was Leebs' job.

DeMarco cut over toward the lake, and when he entered the Village of Wilmette, he looked around at the houses as he watched for Lake Place. *North Shore*, he thought, feeling like puking. He didn't see anything so special about the houses or the neighborhood. Just a bunch of goddamn phonies.

Lake Place was a block-long cul-de-sac with Johnson's house at the end. He eyed the house, a brick colonial with white columns in front and a circle drive. A bicycle lay on its side next to the steps. People obviously were home because the place was lit up on both floors like a Christmas tree. *Just as I expected,* he thought.

He cruised past, looking in and watching for signs of movement. Someone passed in front of a window, but he couldn't tell whether it was a male or female. He continued around the circle and headed out of the cul-de-sac again and stopped a couple blocks away in front of two houses that were dark inside.

After ten minutes, he doubled back towards Johnson's house. As he was about to turn into the cul-de-sac again, he noticed a man in a trench coat and slouch hat trudging along with a briefcase clutched in his hand. DeMarco continued straight and watched in his rearview mirror as the man turned into the cul-de-sac. He pulled a U-turn and cruised past Lake Place in time to see Johnson upright the bicycle and go in his front door.

Well, well, DeMarco thought, *Mr. Johnson works late and takes the train home. Work,* crap. He probably was sucking up cocktails in some dark bar with his new lovely before he took the train home to play nice to Lucille and the brats.

He wasn't that familiar with the commuter trains, but he knew that trains serving the North Shore operated out of the Ogilvie Transportation Center. He'd have to keep that in mind if he decided he needed have a private conversation with Mr. Johnson.

THIRTY-FIVE

Venus opened at 1:00 p.m., so Pete and Joe Tessler timed their arrival for 2:30 p.m., thinking that Simon Frei would be in by that time to check up on things. They used their keys to gain entrance and went to the bar where each ordered a Coors Light. The pole dancer wasn't performing yet and the crowd was still thin. They'd been there a half-hour when they spotted Simon Frei across the room talking to one of the bartenders.

They waited for him to finish, and when he headed toward the back of the cavernous room, they slid off their stools and followed. Frei had vanished through the door by the time they got there. Tessler looked at Pete. Patting the left side of his jacket, he said, "No guts, no glory." He turned the knob and opened the door.

Pete followed him inside and closed the door. Frei apparently heard them and stuck his head out to see who it was. "If you're looking for the john," he said, "you've used the wrong door."

Now that they were closer, Pete noticed the Band-Aid on Frei's chin and the bruises on his face and red marks rimming his neck. Tessler obviously saw them as well.

"Gosh, Mr. Frei," he said, "you should be more careful. It looks like you lost a battle with a sausage grinder."

"This area is private."

"We want to talk to you, Simon. It won't take long."

Frei's eyes narrowed. "Are you more of Zahn's guys?"

Tessler shook his head. "You've lost me, Simon. We're here to talk about Cindi Carr."

He glared at them and after a pause said, "I don't know Cindi Carr."

"No? The seventeen-year-old with the pink hair? One of the girls you let peddle themselves in your establishment? And perform—how should I put it—*favors* for you here in your office?"

"That's bullshit."

"Really. You might want to read this." Tessler handed him a copy of Carr's statement.

Frei took the statement and glared at them again for a few moments. "If you're not Zahn's people, who are you?"

"We're just a couple of average citizens, Simon, trying to make it in this big world."

Frei's face darkened. "Cut the idiotic double talk. Tell me—"

"You have something we need, Simon, and you're in a pile of doo-doo. We're here to trade."

"I—"

"Read the paper, Simon."

He shot them another surly look before he scanned the statement. His face lost color and he ran his fingers over the Band-Aid. "This is all a bunch of bull," he said when he looked up again.

"I don't think so, Simon. Cindi's willing to confirm under oath everything she said in the statement, only in a lot more lurid detail."

Frei eyed them. "What do I supposedly have that you assholes want?"

"Security camera tapes from the past year. We'd like to borrow them."

A look of recognition crept over Frei's face. "You're the guy from the sheriff's office, aren't you? The one who's been suspended for stealing drugs. You don't have any more authority than a lousy street bum."

"Wanna bet?" Tessler had his cell phone in his hand.

Frei stared at him defiantly.

"I'm getting tired of waiting, Simon. You willing to trade or not?"

"No, I'm not willing to trade. Get out of my friggin' club!"

Tessler punched in a number and held the phone to his ear. "Sheriff Richter, please. Tell him Joe Tessler is calling."

Frei recoiled and said, "Okay, okay, let's talk. What's in it for me if I let you see the security tapes?"

Tessler lowered his phone. "The statement you're holding goes bye-bye and Cindi Carr vanishes."

"Where is she now?"

Tessler grinned at him and said, "Nice try, Simon. All I'll tell you is she's gone from the Sunrise Apartments, so don't bother looking for her there."

Frei stared at them some more. "I have investors, you know. They're not going to be happy when they hear about this."

Pete finally interjected himself into the conversation. "Then it's in your best interests not to let them know, right?"

"Oh," Frei said as he looked his way, "you *can* talk."

Pete didn't reply.

"Deal or no deal?" Tessler asked.

Frei seemed to consider it again. "What assurance do I have that you'll keep your side of the bargain?"

"My word."

"Which is worth exactly squat."

"What do you have now, Simon? You've got squat as it is. And if I make that call, we're going to really nail you this time. You'll be facing a string of charges from running a prostitution ring to teenage prostitution to pedophilia to contributing to the delinquency of a minor and a hell of a lot more. You'll be lucky if you see the light of day again."

"You talk big for a dickhead who's lost his badge."

Tessler stepped towards Frei and pushed him in the chest with his hands. "I'm getting tired of this, Simon."

Frei felt his chin again and said, "I don't even know how far back my security tapes go."

"We'll take our chances. Where are they?"

Frei led them to the adjoining room and opened a padlocked metal cabinet and stepped back.

Pete saw two shelves of tapes marked with dates. Tessler began stuffing them into canvas bags, and when he was done, Pete motioned with his head in the direction of Frei's office. Tessler said, "Oh yeah," and returned to Frei's office and climbed on a chair and began removing the tape from the overhead camera.

"What are you doing?" Frei demanded.

"Just making sure we have everything."

"I just changed that tape two days ago! Those tapes cost money!"

Tessler shrugged. "Bill me."

❖ ❖ ❖

Pete and Tessler left Venus with three canvas duffels stuffed with security camera tapes and a device that would let them play the tapes on a television screen. Tessler glanced Pete's way with a grin on his face and said, "That was easier than I thought it would be. But all the same, thanks for letting me do the heavy lifting."

"You're the pro. I just tried to stay out of the way and let the master operate."

Tessler's grin widened. "Hanging around with you, Thorsen, has improved my bullying skills a hundred percent. Wait until Kelene hears about this. She'll probably jump me before she has a chance to drink one of those Pink Silk Panties martinis."

"Before you let your imagination get out of control, we should check to make sure Cindi is gone."

"Good thinking."

When they got to Sunrise Apartments, they circled around the building to Unit 17 and knocked on the door a few times. When they got no response, they paid Elroy another visit. He apparently had had his fill of confrontation for the day and confirmed that Cindi Carr had checked out around noon.

On their way back to Frankfort, Pete said, "Did you pick up on it when Frei mentioned Vinnie Zahn's name? Twice as a matter of fact."

"Vaguely. I was busy trying to stay ahead of the guy and think of ways to pressure him. I might have missed a nuance or two."

"Zahn, as you might remember, is the mob guy who has the vineyard on the Leelanau Peninsula."

"Oh yeah. Paulie mentioned that when we talked about the car fire."

"Don't you find it interesting that Frei thought we might work for Zahn?"

Tessler appeared to think about it. "You know, Zahn could be one of the investors he mentioned. Sometimes the mob guys have legitimate businesses—and I don't mean to imply that Venus is a legitimate business, understand—they run dirty money through to launder it."

"Plus, they control most of the sex trade in the country."

"But even if there's a connection between Zahn and Venus," Tessler said, "that's a whole separate ball of twine, ain't it?"

Pete knew he couldn't get into Angie's situation so he just said, "I suppose."

When they got to Pete's office, they unloaded the tapes and set up their operation on his small conference table. He moved his flat-screen television over and together they managed to hook up the device they'd borrowed from Frei's office. Pete gave Tessler a spare office key so he could come and go as he wished.

Tessler admired their handiwork and looked at the three canvas bags. "Boy," he said, "this is going to keep me off the streets for a while. I'm going to rely on you to assure Kelene that I'm really working and not spending time admiring that pole dancer at Venus."

THIRTY-SIX

Julie was in the dumps when Pete called. The address for Leslie Lehr the former mailroom guy came up with turned out to be another blind alley. According to the building manager, Leslie moved out some time ago, and as far as he knew, hadn't left a forwarding address. She said they grilled him until his patience wore thin and it was clear he wasn't just being evasive.

They talked about what she could do next. He hadn't really thought about it and threw out a couple of things off the top of his head. From her reaction, he could tell that she didn't think any more of them than he did.

Toward the end of their conversation, she tried to pin him down again on when he was coming to Philadelphia. He had to hedge for the umpteenth time because of what he was involved in with Joe Tessler and Angie's situation. When he tried to interject a lighter note into their conversation by cracking jokes about the Rocky steps, her forced laugh made it all too obvious it wasn't going over well. He heard the baby start to cry in the background and she said she had to go.

Angie was in the kitchen rummaging around the refrigerator and Pete joined her. Her rollercoaster mood seemed to be in an "up" moment.

"For dinner," she said, "we have a choice between spinach pasta or—are you ready?—spinach pasta." She held up a bag of pre-made pasta she'd taken from the freezer.

A medium rare steak and a baked potato sounded better, but Pete waxed enthusiastically about the pasta. The plus side was it only took ten minutes to prepare. *And*, better yet, it involved minimal cleanup.

Pete built a fire and they camped out in front of the fireplace and nibbled on smoked salmon and crackers. He decided to take another run at the Vinnie Zahn issue.

"When we were strong-arming Simon Frei to get the tapes, he said something interesting. He asked whether we were Vinnie Zahn's men."

"Really."

"Since Zahn is a mob chieftain, I concluded from his question that Zahn might be trying to move in on him, possibly to use his club as a money laundering vehicle. The implication was that Frei and Zahn or Zahn's people had contact before."

Angie's expression was blank.

"When we talked about this earlier, you said you didn't know Zahn."

"I don't. But since then I've refreshed my recollection as we lawyers like to say because I knew it was only a matter of time before you cross-examined me again."

"And?"

"He's a mob guy like you said. I believe he operates out of Chicago's west side."

He decided to press a little harder. "According to one press account, he's also your husband's uncle."

She waved her hand dismissively.

"Are you telling me it's not true?"

"God, you're obsessed with this, aren't you?"

"I'm not obsessed, I'm just curious."

"Okay, here's the story as I remember it. The creep said he was adopted when he was two. His mother, if I can use that term, claimed some sort of relationship to Zahn. Maybe the creep put the uncle thing out there to make himself seem important. That would be typical. As I told you before, I tried to stay as far away from his sleazy life as possible."

Pete was considering what further probing he could do when the telephone rang. He answered and Joe Tessler said, "You won't believe what I'm sitting here looking at."

"Where are you?"

"In your office, of course."

Pete glanced at his watch; it was after 8:00 p.m. "So what are you looking at?"

"You should see for yourself. Do you have a half-hour?"

He rolled his eyes, and after apologizing to Angie for delaying dinner, headed for his office. The timing was unfortunate because he felt he finally was getting somewhere on the parts of Angie's story that bothered him. And it came as a relief that she didn't go off like a skyrocket when he probed about Zahn.

When he walked into his office, Tessler was hunched in front of the television watching grainy images play out on the monitor. Pete pulled up a chair and joined him.

"Remember those marks on Frei's face and neck?" Tessler asked. "I think I know how he got them. Watch." He began to replay the tape.

Frei and two men—one with a cone-shaped bald head and the other with stylish closely-cropped facial hair—appeared on the monitor. They were in Frei's office from what Pete could tell. The stylish one had commandeered Frei's desk chair and the other hovered over him like the grim reaper. They were talking, and while there was no audio, it was obvious the conversation wasn't exactly cordial. The bald man grabbed Frei with his enormous hands and began to work him over.

"Jesus," Pete said.

"Yeah, Jesus, indeed. Now watch this." Tessler changed tapes and it showed the same two men in Frei's office having another conversation.

The bald man stood close to Frei again, periodically jabbing him in the face with something. Frei raised his hands in self-defense, probably trying to protect his eyes, then fell backward when his chair tipped over. The bald man lunged at him and seized his neck with both hands.

Pete grimaced.

"It looks like Mr. Frei has some very nasty enemies," Tessler said

"Zahn's people."

Tessler nodded. "And our friend Simon doesn't seem to be seeing eye-to-eye with them."

Pete rolled his eyes. "That's an understatement."

"Do you think we ought to make copies of these tapes and turn them over to someone? The FBI, maybe?"

"Let's make copies, but sit on them for the time being. Like we talked about before, our primary mission is to get your badge and gun back, not try to take down the mob."

"I know," Tessler said, "but when you see something like that happening in our own backyard . . ."

When Carmen DeMarco called Steve Johnson again, he got no answer. *Must have taken the train home like a good little boy.* He wondered what Johnson's wife was like. Probably fooling around while hubby was at the office doing the same. With little wifey, maybe? His anger bubbled again and he punched in Johnson's number. Still no answer.

He flipped through the Sears & Whitney directory he'd finally found in wifey's study, looking for something that might prompt his thought processes. Partners, retired partners, of counsel, special counsel, associates, secretaries, librarians, legal assistants, administrative staff, tech people. What a friggin' bureaucracy!

Then his eyes fixed on a name he recognized. He stared at it for a moment before he opened his laptop and called up a list of area codes. *Sonofabitch!*

He circled the telephone number in the directory and dog-eared the page, then sorted through his cell phones until he found the burner he wanted. He breathing grew heavier as he entered the number.

"So what was the big emergency?"

"No emergency, but something interesting. Two of the security tapes show Frei being roughed up by a couple of goons."

"Running a sex joint is a rough business."

"I guess. But as Joe said, you don't expect that sort of thing in a community like this."

"Just because the water is pure and smog doesn't choke out the sun and the golf courses are pristine doesn't mean the male species stop scratching their itch."

Pete glanced at her. She had that needling half-grin on her face again.

"I'll get the pasta going."

Pete stretched and went to his music rack and considered the selections.

Angie called from the kitchen, "While you were out, you had a couple of phone calls. I didn't answer, obviously."

Pete checked the Caller ID. The two calls were approximately fifteen minutes apart, both from an unknown caller or callers. *Telemarketers again,* he thought.

Sam Cook began to wail and he wondered if he should try to steer the conversation back to Vinnie Zahn.

THIRTY-SEVEN

Pete went to his office the next morning and found Joe Tessler already there, reviewing tapes. Coffee percolated in the machine and Tessler had a steaming mug in front of him.

"Sleep well?" Tessler asked without taking his eyes off the television monitor.

"Not bad. How about you?"

"Okay, I guess. I kept waking up thinking I might be going blind from watching these friggin' tapes."

"Maybe you should take a day off."

"Bull, I don't have time. I need my badge back."

Pete began to sort through the mail that had accumulated over the past couple of days.

"If you're bored," Tessler called, "you can join me."

"Maybe later."

When Pete finished the mail, he said to Tessler, "I'm going to walk down the street to see our newspaperman friend for a few minutes."

Harry was huddled in the back of the office with his assistant when Pete walked in. He killed time until he was free by reading the latest issue of *The Northern Sentinel*. When Harry returned to his desk, he said in a voice so low Pete could barely hear it, "Anything new with our lady friend?"

Pete told him about the call Steve Johnson had received from a man who appeared to be posing as a lawyer and saying he heard that Angie DeMarco was still alive.

Harry's eyes widened over his half-glasses. "That's not good," he said.

"It certainly makes you wonder."

"I still think moving her might be the way to go. Get her out of the line of fire, so to speak, in case someone *is* hunting for her. Which there very well could be based on the call you described."

Pete shrugged. "I floated the idea. She seems to be keeping her own counsel and mulling over what to do."

"It's not just her I'm worried about, it's you, too. If someone is after her, you're smack dab in the middle of things if whoever it is finds out that she's staying at your house."

"Believe me, that's crossed my mind."

"Do something, then. You always pride yourself on being proactive. If there was ever a time, this is it."

Pete thought about it for a minute. "Let me raise it with her again and see what she says." Then he told Harry what he'd been doing to help Tessler.

Harry shook his head. "See, that proves my point. You stick your neck out for a friend and then don't do anything to protect yourself."

"That's an exaggeration."

"Is it? I don't have good feelings about all of this."

Pete didn't say anything.

"So what's your plan for Joe if you don't have one for yourself?"

Pete shrugged. "Depends what we find on the tapes. Our end goal is to meet with Sheriff Richter and persuade him to reinstate Joe. We already have a statement from Beryl Wuyt recanting what she told the internal investigator, Bernie Nichols. We hope to come up with more ammunition. Joe's chomping at the bit. If we have to, we'll go with the Beryl statement."

Harry nodded. "I hope it works out. If you can take out Venus in the process, that would be good. It's not healthy to have a cesspool like that in our community."

"Have you heard anything about the mob expanding into this area?"

"Nothing specific."

"A mob bigwig from Chicago named Vinnie Zahn bought a vineyard on the Leelanau Peninsula a year or two ago. His name came up when Joe and I had our session with Frei. It got me thinking."

"My uneducated eyes need tutoring," as an English friend of mine likes to say.

"I'm wondering what the connection is between Zahn and Frei. All I can think of is that Zahn might be looking for a money laundering vehicle and has moved in on Frei."

"That makes sense."

"There also may be a tie-in with everything else that's going on. I don't know if you read all of those news clippings you dug up for me, but a couple of them reported that Carmen DeMarco, Angie's husband, is Zahn's nephew."

Harry frowned. "I didn't notice that."

"I asked Angie about it again last night. She finally acknowledged there's some kind of relationship although she said Carmen might be puffing a bit to make himself look important."

Harry shook his head. "This thing is murkier than hell, isn't it?"

"I'm going back to my office to see how Joe is coming and then head home to check on my other charge."

"You ought to hang out your shingle as a caregiver."

Tessler had obviously been next door to pick up food, because when Pete walked in, a crumpled sandwich wrapper lay on the table in front of him and food odors hung in the air. He munched on chips while he gazed at the television monitor.

"See anything else interesting, Dick Tracy?" Pete asked.

Tessler finished chewing and took a swallow of water. "Let me show you something," he said. He changed tapes and then hit the play button and fast-forwarded a while. He stopped when a frame came up that showed a man in a bulky coat and a skull cap pulled low on his forehead talking to someone who appeared to be the doorman.

"This is the outside camera at Venus, obviously," he said. He pointed at the screen. "Who do you think that is? Not the doorman, the other guy."

Pete studied the grainy frame. "Beats me."

"Look closer."

Pete did, but still couldn't recognize the man.

Tessler said, "I'll back it up a bit so you can see the guy approaching the doorman."

He did and the camera picked up the man when he was twenty feet away walking toward the building. "Now do you recognize him?"

Pete studied the moving figure and shook his head again.

"Watch this." Tessler manipulated the tape until frames appeared that showed the man leaving the doorman and disappearing around the corner of the building. "Notice that the guy didn't go *into* Venus, at least not through the front door. He went around to the side, or maybe the back."

Pete stared at Tessler blankly.

"You know who I think that is? That asshole Cap, that's who."

Pete frowned. "All I see is a blob."

"How long have I been in the department, twelve years? Cap was there when I came. I've seen the fat jerk a thousand times, always shuffling along pigeon-toed like a goddamned gnome, talking with his hands. I tell you, Pete, that's him."

"You're not trying to talk yourself into something just because you have it in for the guy, are you?"

"I thought about that, but I don't think so. There's too much that's distinctive about the figure in these frames. Physical shape, mannerisms, everything. And I'll tell you something else, I happen to know that he has nothing to do with our undercover operation at the place. If he was there, it was for some other purpose, and the way he's sneaking around the back of the building, I don't think it was just to get a glimpse of a set of naked boobies."

Pete looked at him for a while, then asked, "How do you think we can use this?"

"I'm going to finish looking through these tapes and hopefully I'll find some other shots of him skulking around the same as in these frames. Then I think we take what we have from the security tapes and Beryl's statement and ask for a private meeting with Frank like you suggested earlier. Put it all out there and try to convince him that his special investigator pal is looking in the wrong direction."

Pete thought about that for a while. "Can you get some blow-ups of the figure you just showed me and any other frames you believe are him? Showing facial similarities would be important."

"I'd probably need some outside help," Tessler said. "There's this technical guy our department uses once in a while. He might be willing to do a little private work for me on the side."

Pete was tired when he pulled into his driveway. Cloud cover had moved in since the morning, and the lake was choppy and gray and uninviting. He didn't feel like doing anything except heating up a frozen dinner, building a fire and settling down with a good book and oldies playing in the background.

As usual, the drapes and blinds were closed, and everything was quiet on the surrounding lakefront. He climbed the stairs, and when he got to the top, he didn't bother testing the door, but fished in his pocket for his key ring. He inserted his house key in the lock and pushed the door open. Everything was dark inside, which seemed odd. Then he saw something move.

Instinctively, Pete pulled the door closed again and his heart beat faster and caution flags flapped in his mind. He fingered his cell phone and wondered if he should call Tessler. He jumped when the door opened and a familiar female voice said, "Sorry, Pete, I didn't mean to startle you."

He expelled air and stepped inside. He could barely see Angie after he closed the door. "Why no lights?" he asked.

"I was napping." She clicked on a lamp and the room brightened as the Energy Star bulb came to life.

Pete tossed his keys on the breakfast bar. His landline rang and he shook his head and reached for it in irritation, prepared to cut off the call at the first indication it was yet another solicitation.

"Don't answer that!" Angie called in a hoarse whisper.

He already had the receiver in his hand. Holding it against his chest, he said, "It's probably a telemarketer. I'll get rid of it."

He raised the phone to his ear just as Angie repeated, "Don't . . ."

"Good afternoon, Mr. Thorsen. Would you mind passing the phone to Mrs. DeMarco?"

Jolted, Pete's eyes fixed on Angie across the room. She stared at him and her arms were folded and she tugged anxiously at her sweater. "Who?" Pete asked.

"Angie DeMarco. Our mutual friend. I know she's there. I heard her voice in the background when you answered."

Pete's mind flashed back to his telephone conversation with Steve Johnson. "Who is this?" he asked, suspecting that it was the same caller.

"Angela Frances knows me."

"Listen, I don't know what your game is, but there's no one here named Angela Frances or Angie DeMarco. You must have the wrong number."

"I'm sure there is," the caller insisted.

"I'm not going to argue with you. If—"

"You don't want to get in the middle of this any more than you already are, Mr. Thorsen."

"If you make any more harassing calls, mister, I'm going to report it to the police. Goodbye." Pete hung up the phone.

He stared across the room at Angie again. "I'm sure you heard enough of that to get the drift. It was similar to the call Steve Johnson received only this time the caller didn't say he *heard* you were alive, he acted like he *knew* you were. He even said he heard your voice in the background."

Angie avoided his eyes.

The telephone rang again. Pete stared at it for a moment, then ripped the connection cord from the wall. His upstairs phone continued to ring.

"What the hell's going on, Angie? And don't give me more bullshit about warfare within the mob."

THIRTY-EIGHT

Tears began rolling down Angie's cheeks and she wrapped her arms around her upper body again as though seeking warmth.

"My husband wants to kill me," she said.

Her words didn't even come as a shock to him. They were more of a clarification because he'd suspected all along that there was something not quite right with her story.

"The car bomb was intended for you, not your husband, wasn't it?" he said.

She nodded.

"And your husband was behind the bombing."

She nodded again.

He stared at her for a minute before a wave of anger swept over him. "Jesus Christ, Angie, why did you lie?"

She sniffled and wiped her eyes. "I was scared. And embarrassed."

"Scared and embarrassed?"

"I thought things would work out when I came here. I didn't think there was any way the creep could track me from the cabin. Like I said,

I didn't use my cell and even took the batteries out. I never used a credit card."

He looked at her disgustedly. "They worked out alright! Now your psychotic husband is after *both* of us!"

She avoided his eyes again.

Pete collected himself and asked, "Why is he trying to kill you?"

Angie's eyes darted around and she mumbled, "He's crazy."

"*He's crazy.* That tells me a lot." His eyes burned holes in her.

More tears, then, "He's been accusing me of things. Having affairs, concealing money from him."

He breathed in deeply and expelled the air. "And?"

She didn't say anything.

"Is he right, Angie?"

"Yes." She dabbed at her eyes.

"I suppose I shouldn't ask, but I will anyway. Who have you been involved with? Someone from Sears & Whitney?"

She shook her head.

"Who then?"

"It's personal."

"Bullshit, it's personal! Things stopped being personal when you lied to me and involved me in your stinking mess!"

"It's a judge, okay? I'm not going to tell you his name."

Pete rolled his eyes and shook his head. "I gather Carmen doesn't know specifics, just suspects something."

"He'd go after him if he knew who it was."

"How long has this been going on?"

"The affair?"

"The affair. The accusations. This whole mess."

She laughed bitterly. "When has it *not* been going on? The creep has been accusing me of things since the day we were married, most with no connection to reality. He started on me about the affair a couple of years ago, calling me all kinds of lovely names and threatening me. He was smart enough not to hit me because he knew I was wired at the state's attorney's office and would have had him locked up before he could blink."

"Have you been in contact with the judge since the bombing?"

She shook her head and bit her lip. "I didn't dare. Things were cooling anyway. He was probably happy I was gone so he wouldn't have to try to explain to his wife."

Pete stared at her some more. "Angie, you're a lawyer and a smart woman. Why didn't you divorce Carmen and get your life on an even keel again?"

"You don't understand. The creep isn't a normal human being. If you do something to him he doesn't like, or if he even *thinks* you've done something, it's a blood feud for life. He never forgets or forgives, and he's going to get even no matter what. If I'd divorced him, maybe everything would have been fine for a year or two. Then one day I'd have a mysterious accident."

"So it was Carmen against you and not you getting caught up in warfare between two mob factions."

She nodded.

Pete glanced at his watch. He didn't know where DeMarco had called from, but assumed it wasn't Frankfort, because if it was, he would have been at his house already. He knew he had to move things along and make some decisions, but felt a need to have a complete picture.

"How do you think Carmen discovered you're still alive?"

She shrugged and wrapped her arms around her upper body again.

"You must have *some* idea. You've had plenty of time to think about it."

"I had to use my cell phone a couple of times like I told you. I don't know why he would have picked up on that, though. More likely he discovered I was using my credit cards. A couple of weeks ago, the bank called me on my cell and said someone with my last name had been asking for information about charges on my statement. They wouldn't give him any information because he isn't on the account, but that must be how he discovered I was in Wisconsin. I'd instructed the bank to switch me over to electronic billing, but maybe a paper bill come through before the change and the creep saw it."

"And that's the real reason you became spooked and left Wisconsin."

She nodded again.

"And you're sure you didn't leave a trail when you came here?"

"I was careful."

He thought about the call a few minutes ago. "Before the call I just took, have other calls come in while I've been out?"

"The two I mentioned last night. Then today the landline has been ringing nonstop, which never happened before. I checked Caller ID after each call and saw they were all from an unknown caller. I didn't have to be a genius to figure out who it was."

"And Vinnie Zahn is Carmen's uncle just like we talked about, right?"

She nodded again. "He was at my wedding. And, I suppose, my funeral."

Pete's lips tightened and he said, "Final question. That day on our bike ride, was your concern real or fake?"

"Real. I thought the guy might have been the scumbag I saw around our house once in a while. But as time passed and nothing happened, I concluded it probably wasn't. If the creep thought he had me, he'd be there personally."

Pete breathed in deeply. "Well, it's clear we have to get out of here and figure out a plan."

"I have a plan."

"Fine, you can tell me about it at Harry's if the call I'm about to make goes the way I think it will."

She looked at him with a frightened expression and seemed immobilized.

"Pack up and let's get the hell out of here. And be sure to take all your stuff. If someone breaks in, I don't want him to find any evidence that you've been here although I don't know why I'm worried about that after what your husband just said on the telephone."

❖ ❖ ❖

Pete pulled into Harry's driveway off the alley behind his house and parked in back of his Explorer. Harry must have been watching for them because he bolted out his back door before the engine stopped and wrenched open the passenger-side door and hustled Angie into his house. He came back outside.

"Should I call Millie and reserve a cabin?" he asked Pete in a low voice.

"Before we get into that, I need to fill you in on the details." He told him the whole story, and when he finished, Harry seemed more troubled than ever.

"You must have been as disappointed as hell the way she lied to you," he said.

Pete looked away disgustedly. "I'm beyond disappointed. It's not just her that has a problem. Now it's me as well. If Carmen's the madman Angie claims he is, there's no way I'm not on his radar screen. That was the message I got from him on the telephone, too."

"So what do you think?"

"Angie says she has a plan. I'd like to talk to her about it but I need time to assess things. Can we stay here tonight?"

"Sure."

"In case you're worried, I don't see any way Carmen could figure out we're here. You have no connection with Sears & Whitney, which is the way I suspect he zeroed in on me. It also seems to fit with his earlier call to Steve Johnson."

Harry nodded and turned thoughtful. "You know what I'm thinking?" he said. "Maybe it's time to bring Joe Tessler into this thing."

"He has enough problems of his own right now. Besides, Angie might be skittish about widening the circle of people who know what's going on."

"The cat's out of the bag on that one. The guy she's got to worry about already *knows* she's alive and is after her. And don't forget, Joe *owes* you for what you're doing for him."

THIRTY-NINE

Joey Lebo walked into DeMarco's den and said, "What's up?"

"I figured out where she is."

Lebo looked at the open road atlas in front of him. He hadn't heard anything about Carm's obsession for a full day and had hoped his boss's anger had dissipated.

"Right here," DeMarco said, jabbing the atlas with his forefinger. "A place called Frankfort, Michigan. You know how I know?"

Lebo stared at him blankly.

"That's where an asshole named Pete Thorsen lives. He was with little wifey's law firm until he bailed a few years ago. Him and her were thick as friggin' thieves, always going to places like Gibsons Steakhouse, supposedly to talk about firm business. Business, what a goddamn joke."

Lebo nodded.

"I've been calling the asshole all day. Finally he answers, and I asked for Angela Frances. He played dumb, like he'd never even heard her name before. Wasn't even smart enough to go into an act and say she was dead. Then he hung up on me when he couldn't think of anything to say."

"Mmm."

"We need to take another road trip, Leebs. I smell this thing coming to a head real soon."

Lebo nodded again.

"Let's hit the road first thing in the morning. If someone finds out we're in northern Michigan, we just say we're checking up on Venus to make sure our boy Frei is continuing to play ball."

"Are we having problems?"

DeMarco grinned. "Maybe yes, maybe no. You got to see your business partner up close eyeball to eyeball to know for sure."

After Lebo left DeMarco's house and drove a few blocks, he took out one of his burner phones and punched in a number.

Pete walked into his office and saw that Tessler had brought in more food to fuel his tape-viewing marathon. Tessler seemed surprised to see Pete since he'd left only a few hours earlier.

"I called the techie," Tessler said. "He's coming first thing in the morning to show me how to create stills and do the enlarging. I hoped he'd comp me because of all the business the sheriff's office sends his way, but the bastard is charging me a hundred bucks."

"Look at it this way. It could turn out to be the best hundred you've ever spent."

"Yeah," Tessler said, still not looking happy, "I suppose. What brings you back at this hour?"

"If you can break for a few minutes, I have something else I'd like to talk to you about."

"Thank God," Tessler said, expelling air and stretching. "It'll give me a chance to rest my eyes. You don't mind if I close them while you talk do you?"

"Not as long as you listen." Pete laid out Angie's predicament and went into considerable detail to make sure the nuances came through.

Tessler frowned. "When did you say she showed up at your house?"

"About ten days ago."

"And that day I stopped at your house to tell you I'd been suspended? I had absolutely no idea she was there."

"Things have gotten uglier since then. The calls I mentioned leave little doubt her husband knows Angie's at my house."

"And her husband's a 'made guy,' huh?"

"That's what I understand. And if I didn't mention it, he's also Vinnie Zahn's nephew."

"The mob boss."

Pete nodded.

Tessler shook his head several times. "So what do you want from me?"

"I know you're up to your eyeballs with your own problems, but I need help. Carmen DeMarco sounds like a homicidal madman. Reading the tea leaves, I probably rank right there with Angie as a target because I assume he believes I'm the one she's been carrying on with."

"Are you?"

"No," he said, skipping over the tryst that night. "Apparently it's some judge in Chicago."

"A judge. She's not a bottom-feeder, is she?"

Pete shook his head.

Tessler appeared to think. "Do you still have that piece I gave you when you thought someone might be after you a few years ago?"

As soon as the words were out of Tessler's mouth, Pete realized he'd neglected to take the Ruger when he vacated the house with Angie. "It's on my closet shelf," he said sheepishly.

"You need to dust that baby off and keep it handy."

"Good point."

"I also seem to remember you have an alarm system at your house," Tessler said. "Do you arm it regularly?"

"I let the service lapse."

Tessler nodded. "Well, those systems aren't foolproof, anyway. If somebody who knows what he's doing wants to get in, he's going to get in. And you have to assume this DeMarco guy and whoever he has with him know what they're doing."

"Your observations are making me feel a lot better," Pete said dryly. "But what I was leading up to is, do you think I'd have any luck getting a deputy to watch my house?"

Tessler turned thoughtful again. "I doubt it," he said. "The most you could hope for would be for someone to drive past once in a while. The department is short-handed as it is, and your relations with Frank wouldn't exactly help."

"That's kind of what I thought."

"Are you staying there tonight?"

Pete shook his head. "Harry's."

"You ought to consider booking a room there until things sort themselves out."

Tessler seemed to pick up on Pete's disappointment and added, "Don't get me wrong, I'll help you on the side."

"Any ideas?"

Tessler went into his thoughtful mode again. "I think the first thing we should do is find out if anyone's snooping around your house. When I was with the Chicago PD, we set a trap for a guy we suspected might try to break into a house. We moved the people who lived there to another location and left everything else the way it normally would be. Cars in the garage or outside, lights on timers so they'd go on and off at different times just like if people were home. Then we rigged the doors so we could tell the next morning if someone had been in the house."

"Did it work?"

"It's a sample of one, but it worked like a friggin' charm in that case."

Pete thought about it. "Would I have to leave my car?" he asked. "If I do, how can I be certain I won't be blown to smithereens when I finally start it? That's how DeMarco tried to get Angie."

Tessler frowned. "That's a problem, I agree."

Pete thought about it some more, and decided to give Tessler's idea a try. A car bomb was a risk whether he stayed in the house at night or not. At least Joe's idea might show break-in attempts. He walked down the street to the hardware store to buy some additional timers and just made it before closing time. Tessler followed him home and helped him set up his house for the night.

FORTY

Joe Tessler was watching tapes again when Pete got to his office the next morning. He was disheveled, his eyes looked bloodshot, and everything about him screamed fatigue. A raft of dirty coffee mugs sat on the table along with a stack of glossy nine-by-twelve photographs.

"You just missed Ian," Tessler said, tapping the photographs. "He came early because someone else called and insisted on a 9:00 a.m. appointment." He shook his head. "Those technical guys must make a bundle with all the demand and the prices they charge."

"Anything interesting in that pile?"

Tessler almost dripped saliva. "Oh, one or two things. Let me show you."

He spread a dozen glossies on the table and arranged them with care. Then he stood back and eyed Pete with a satisfied expression. Pete studied the glossies. To him, the blobs looked like enlarged blobs.

Seeing Pete's reaction, Tessler said, "Let me lead you through them." He pointed to one enlargement. "See that little hook nose? See those flabby jowls and elephant ears? See the girth? That's him! No friggin' doubt about it!"

Pete nodded.

"And that's just one. See the others? The same damn thing."

"And I assume the other stills are of Frei in his office."

Tessler grinned. "Frei getting the crap beaten out of him, Frei engaging in all sorts of things with a minor girl, the works."

Tessler plunked down in a chair with a smug look. "Should I call Frank and tell him we want to see him?" he asked.

"I've been thinking about that. I think Connie Chapman should be there, too. And you probably shouldn't be."

Tessler looked surprised. "Why?"

"You'll have to work with Frank in the future if everything turns out the way it should. If Frank balks initially, I don't want you to trade words with him that might taint your relationship going forward."

Tessler's eyes narrowed and he searched Pete's face for signs he might have missed a spot when shaving that morning. "You don't have any doubt this is going to work, do you?"

"I think we've got a good case."

Tessler stared at him some more and a scowl settled over his face. "Boy, you sure know how to dump ice water on a guy's morale."

"I don't mean to. And don't misunderstand, I have positive feelings."

Tessler sulked a while and then said, "Okay, are you going to call Frank?"

"I think going through Connie might be better. My relationship with her is good and she seems to be able to control your boss."

Tessler sighed. "Okay, you're the legal-eagle."

Pete moved to his desk and dialed Chapman's number. A paralegal or someone answered, and after putting him on hold a couple of minutes, the county attorney came on the line.

"Mr. Thorsen, it's been ages."

Pete laughed. "You know what they say about idle hands and the devil's workshop."

"Which workshop are you in this time?"

Pete chuckled again. "I need to meet with you and Sheriff Richter as soon as you're available."

"About what may I ask?"

"I'm Joe Tessler's lawyer. He hired me right after he was suspended."

"The sheriff is Detective Tessler's boss. Why don't you just meet with him?"

"Because some of what I'm going to say goes beyond Mr. Tessler's suspension and I think you ought to be there."

A pause, then a sigh, then, "I could meet later this afternoon, say 4:00 p.m. I don't know if Sheriff Richter is available."

"Hopefully he can *make* himself available. If I can't meet with you today, my law partner is pressuring me to call a press conference for tomorrow morning to lay out Detective Tessler's position. He thinks we've got a damn good case. I've been holding him off, but . . ."

Pete heard another sigh. "You have such a delicate touch, Mr. Thorsen. I'll call Frank and get back to you."

When Pete hung up, Tessler was grinning again. "I couldn't hear the other end of that conversation, but I really liked the part I *could* hear. And you'll have to introduce me to that law partner of yours."

"Connie said I have a 'delicate touch.'"

Tessler's grin threatened to split the flesh of his haggard face.

Pete puttered around his office until Connie Chapman called him back and confirmed the meeting for 4:00 p.m. in her office. He looked at Tessler and said, "Now you've got a choice. You can go home and sack out for a couple of hours or you can go with me to see if I had visitors last night."

"Let's go to your place. I owe you. Sleep is just a luxury."

When they got to Pete's driveway, Tessler pulled to the side of the highway and parked. "Let's walk in," he said. "I want to see if there's evidence that another vehicle has been in your driveway."

They walked on the brown grass along the side of the driveway and watched for tire tracks in the patches of loose dirt. None were visible.

"Just an idea," Tessler said, "but we might consider smoothing the dirt when we leave so we have a better chance of identifying new tracks."

Pete nodded.

Everything was quiet around the house. The lights were off, which meant the timers worked, and there were no signs of breaking-and-entering. Tessler checked his shoulder holster and walked around the house with Pete. Nothing seemed out of order.

"Let's take a look inside," Tessler said. "See if our little trick worked."

After Pete unlocked the door, Tessler patted his sidearm again and eased the door open a crack. The tennis ball was still on the floor behind the door where he'd positioned it and the bag with a racket on top, part of the ruse to explain the ball, rested on the sofa back. He opened the door wider so they could get in and the door bumped the tennis ball and it rolled away. Tessler moved quickly to the back door and saw that the ball they'd left there was still in place as well. A quick search of the house revealed nothing.

"What do you think?" Tessler asked.

"Standing in this room, all I hear is the voice of that guy who called ringing in my ears."

"Spooky, huh?"

Pete didn't say anything.

"Want to get the Ruger?"

Pete looked at him. "Maybe it's not a good idea. I'd probably just shoot myself in the foot."

"From what I saw on the range that day, I'd say you're competent enough that's not likely to happen. I think you ought to get it."

Pete went upstairs and found the shoebox in his bedroom closet and came back down. Tessler saw the box and nodded.

"You go out first," Tessler said, "and I'll position the ball and then slip out." He grinned. "Not implying I'm thinner than you or anything."

Pete found an old broom in his shed and smoothed the parts of the driveway with loose dirt, then stood back and assessed his handiwork. Tessler pointed out the broom marks that might be a red flag. Pete got his blower, and after a dozen bursts, they let the dust settle and agreed it looked better.

Pete looked at his Range Rover. "It's probably a poor time to think about it, but I wonder if I should take my car and then redo the driveway."

"Remember, the reason we left it last night was to make it look like you were home. I think we should do the same thing tonight."

"I feel lost without my wheels."

"And I feel lost without my badge. You said I had to let things play out and the same goes for you."

Pete knew Tessler was right and followed him out to the highway where his Acura was parked. He glanced back at his Range Rover and wondered how comfortable he'd be getting into a vehicle that had been left unattended in a part of the lakefront that was mostly void of people. It was hard to shake the image of the bomb that had been intended for Angie.

Tessler dropped him off at Harry's house, and before he got out, they talked some more about his meeting with Connie Chapman and the sheriff. Tessler emphasized again that he was more interested in getting his badge back than in punishing someone else, although he allowed that it was a close question when it came to Cap.

Pete had a couple of hours to kill before he had to leave for Connie's office and he spent it chatting with Angie after he'd stowed the handgun in his duffel.

"So what's your plan?"

She shrugged. "Go east somewhere, or west. Change my appearance and my identity and go from there."

He nodded. "Do you have money?"

"In my Schwab account. And yes, it's secure. It's all electronic and I'm the only one with the password."

Pete nodded again. "I told Joe Tessler about your situation."

"What a surprise."

"If things go south all of a sudden, we're going to need all the help we can get. He's law enforcement, remember."

"He's a dirty cop."

"He's wrongfully *accused* of being dirty."

She didn't say anything.

Pete went to the kitchen and got a bottle of water and came back.

"I told you my plan," she said. "What's yours?"

"I'm staying. My roots are here."

"I'm not sure you know what you're up against."

He didn't say anything.

"I'm sorry I dragged you into this mess, Pete. If I hadn't come here, none of this would have happened."

He didn't say anything.

"Just staying isn't a plan."

"I have a meeting this afternoon to see if I can get Tessler's suspension lifted. Then I'm going to turn to my situation. Or *our* situation if you're still here."

FORTY-ONE

ete's mind was still on his conversation with Angie and on her psychotic husband when he pulled up in front of Connie Chapman's building. A cruiser he assumed belonged to Sheriff Richter was in the side lot. He went inside and found them in a conference room next to Connie's office. Richter scowled when he walked in. Connie smiled and offered him coffee or water.

Pete hadn't seen Richter for a while, but it didn't take long for his memory to be refreshed. The sheriff was a workout freak, and with his massive upper body, he resembled an inverted triangle. His biceps strained against the fabric of his tailored uniform which was short-sleeved despite the chilly autumn weather. His cherubic face made him look younger than he actually was, and as always, his dirty-blond hair was carefully trimmed and moussed.

"Where's Joe?" he asked.

"He's not coming. He authorized me to speak for him."

The sheriff's face darkened a shade and his lips tightened. "Not coming? I put off plans because I thought Detective Tessler might have something to say that I should hear and now I find he doesn't care enough to be here."

The plans Richter was referring to, Pete thought, probably involved his daily workout at the local health club. He avoided making a snide comment and said, "I'm the one who suggested he not come so blame me if you want. I thought we'd be able to talk more candidly without him here."

"We've got this—"

Connie Chapman's plain, makeup-free face had been an inscrutable mask during the exchange between Pete and the sheriff, but now she said, "Why don't we hear what Pete has to say, Frank." She motioned for him to proceed and reminded him that she still had work to do that evening.

"I've got two main points," Pete said. "First, there's the conduct of the man the sheriff hired to investigate the evidence room matter. Then—"

"Conduct?" Richter said, straightening like he was about to spring from his chair. "If you came to bad-mouth Bernard Nichols, you can forget it. The man has sterling credentials. A long career with the FBI, in private practice in Detroit since then where he's been involved in some very big cases, solid references. I checked him out myself."

"I checked him out, too, Sheriff. The feedback I got is that he's a shoot-from-the-hip artist who cuts corners and manufactures evidence when it serves his purpose."

Richter looked ready to explode. "That's a crock!" he said.

"Is it?" Pete asked. "Here's the statement from one of the so-called witnesses Nichols came up with in this matter." He gave the sheriff and Connie Chapman photocopies of Beryl Wuyt's first statement.

After they'd had a moment to scan it, Pete said, "I went to see Ms. Wuyt and asked her about the statement. She said Nichols threatened her and bullied her into giving the statement, which she now admits contains numerous falsehoods. Here's what she gave me recanting virtually everything she said originally." He handed them copies of her second statement and gave them time to read it.

"The most important thing," Pete said, "is that Ms. Wuyt now states unequivocally that Detective Tessler never at any time provided her with drugs. On the contrary, she admits the drugs were hers and that she was the one who needled Detective Tessler until he tried a joint."

Richter's head was down as he poured over Wuyt's second statement. Finally he looked up at Pete. "And what kind of threats did *you* make to get her to sign this?"

"None. All I did was explain the consequences of making a false statement about another person, particularly where the statement libels a law enforcement officer."

Richter seemed at a loss for words.

"As I understand it, Sheriff," Pete said, "the false statement by Ms. Wuyt is one of the primary things relied on to suspend Detective Tessler pending completion of Nichols' investigation. It was offered to show that Mr. Tessler not only is a drug user, but also that he was in possession of a supply of drugs that Nichols claimed came from the evidence room. Both things are untrue."

When Richter didn't say anything, Connie Chapman said, "What's your second point, Pete?"

"Nichols has also been trying to paint Detective Tessler as a bad guy. He produced stills from security camera tapes that allegedly show the detective in Venus, the sex joint near Thompsonville, which I understand is notorious for drug activities. Nichols claims he's identified Detective Tessler being there at on at least twenty separate occasions. I questioned Mr. Tessler about this—he's embarrassed, by the way—and he admits he's gone there occasionally over the years, as have a lot of other upstanding citizens of this community from what I understand. He's single, as you know, and the way he put it to me was he might go there when it was a choice between that or going home to an empty house.

"His visits took place over a five-year period, too. Using Nichols' number, that comes out to four times a year. Less, actually, because a couple of times Detective Tessler was there standing in for the department's undercover guy."

"You can't deny that the place is a drug hothouse," Richter said suddenly.

"I believe I just said it was. My point, though, is that Detective Tessler had nothing to do with it. All of the stills that allegedly show him at the club show him drinking beer or wandering around with a bottle in his hand."

Richter didn't say anything.

"On the other hand, you might want to look into another member of your department." Pete slid the glossies he had with him across the table to the sheriff. Chapman leaned over to get a better look.

"In case you haven't guessed," he said, "those stills also came from the Venus security camera tapes. They show the front door of the club and the adjacent outside wall and corner. See anyone you recognize, Sheriff?"

Richter shuffled through the stills. "These photographs are so blurry and grainy they're practically worthless," he muttered.

"Exactly like the stills Nichols produced that allegedly show Detective Tessler inside Venus. But if you look closely, I think you'll see someone you know. And unlike Detective Tessler, he's doing suspicious things, talking to the doorman and then sneaking around the corner of the building. Like he's going to another door or meeting someone. He doesn't appear to be there just for a good time."

"Who's the figure, Frank?"

"Let's talk about it later," Richter muttered.

"It sure looks to me as if someone is trying to set up Detective Tessler, lady and gentleman. And Bernard Nichols, who's more interested in another scalp on his belt and his fee than ferreting out the truth, is his accomplice, wittingly or unwittingly."

No one spoke until Connie Chapman said, "Anything else, Pete?"

"Two things. I'd like to emphasize that Detective Tessler loves his job and enjoys the people he works with. His name has been dragged through the mud enough. He just wants to get back to work.

"The other doesn't relate directly to Detective Tessler, but I came across it while looking into his situation. I believe someone is trying to move in on Venus and take over. The mob controls most of the sex trade. Maybe it's them."

FORTY-TWO

When Pete got back to Harry's house, he called Joe Tessler to give him a report on his meeting with Sheriff Richter and Connie Chapman before he went inside. Tessler peppered him with questions and pushed for his best guesstimate of whether he thought the outcome would be favorable. Pete declined to speculate, saying only that he was pretty sure he'd gotten their attention.

He used the key Harry had given him to open the door, and when he walked in, he saw Angie on one of the couches reading a book. Like his house, the drapes had been closed and the only light came from a lamp on an end table next to her. She closed the flap on her purse, something he'd gotten used to.

"How did it go?" she asked.

"Okay, I think. I'd say it's fifty-fifty," he said, repeating the assessment he'd just given Tessler.

She nodded and went back to her book. He went to the kitchen for a bottle of spring water, and when he returned, said, "It's smart to keep a gun handy."

Angie looked up and frowned.

"The gun in your purse," he said.

She looked at him balefully and didn't say anything.

"Are you still considering leaving in the morning?"

"Yes."

"You might want to put it off for a day or two. Now that I've done what I can for Tessler, I'm working on some things and need a little time to see if they come together."

"What things?"

"Some ideas to get us out of this mess."

She stared at him some more. "The creep probably called from Chicago and he'll be here soon if he's not already. His number one mission is to get me. I told you my plan for 'getting out of this mess,' as you say. If you have a better one, you'd better share it with a little more specificity than saying you're working on some things."

"You shouldn't be in any danger as long as you stay here."

"That's what I thought when I left for northern Wisconsin, too. And when I came to your house. There's nowhere to hide from those people."

"If you leave and go somewhere else, there's no guarantee he won't find you there, too. Plus, you'd be giving up everything and your whole life will be down the drain."

"It's down the drain now."

Harry walked in and said, "Rona will be home in a few minutes." He looked at Angie and said, "We have to be careful, so I've arranged to have dinner brought in for the four of us rather than going out somewhere. If you guys will make your choices from this menu, I'll call the orders in and have the food delivered."

When they'd made their dinner selections, Pete guided Harry into another room and said in a low voice, "Angie's still stuck on leaving in the morning. I tried to talk her into delaying for a couple of days while I see if I can work something out, but I don't think she's buying it."

"What are you working on?"

"I don't want to talk about it here. I'll fill you in later."

Rona arrived, and after some small talk, Harry uncorked a bottle of Pinot Noir and started pouring. Both Pete and Angie declined. The atmosphere was awkward as they made small talk and tried to keep things upbeat. Pete mostly listened. His mind was on the call to Adam Rose.

Their food came and they moved to the dinner table and ate mostly in silence. Harry glanced Pete's way occasionally and Pete could tell he was itching for a private conversation.

The after-dinner conversation revolved around Chicago and the experiences they shared. Finally, it became clear that everyone was wearing down and they decided to call it a night.

When Angie and Rona went upstairs, Pete said to Harry in a low voice, "Is the alarm system you installed a couple of years ago still active?"

"I pay the bills every month. I rarely arm it, though."

"Arming it tonight might not be a bad idea."

"Does that mean you're worried?"

"I want everyone to feel we're taking every precaution we can."

"What's this plan you're working on?"

"It involves Vinnie Zahn. I'm trying to work out the details."

Harry grew pensive. "Something like you did a few years ago?"

"But more complicated."

DeMarco and Joey Lebo crept up the driveway and watched for signs of movement inside the house where several rooms were lit up. There weren't any. When they came to the Range Rover, DeMarco touched the hood in a couple of places. "Cold," he whispered. "It hasn't moved in a while."

They staked out trees twenty-five feet apart and stood in the shadows and continued to watch the house. Lebo put his oversized hands in his fleece pockets and his thoughts drifted back to their visit to Venus that afternoon. *Where was the pink-haired babe?* he wondered. *And the lady who seemed stuck on him during their first visit?* Jeez, he really could use some recreation.

DeMarco came over and said in a low voice, "More of Thorsen's games. Leaving his vehicle here and everything so we'd think he and little wifey were around. I bet if we went inside, the place would be empty."

"You think?"

"We're going to outfox old lover boy. Do you have those sensors with you?"

"In the vehicle."

"Get one."

Lebo disappeared out the driveway and returned five minutes later.

"Put it under there someplace where he's not likely to look if he should do some inspection work," DeMarco directed.

Lebo inched his way under the Range Rover and affixed the sensor, then wormed his way out again. He dusted off his clothes and said, "He'll never find it there."

"I can just see her face when lover boy shows up and we're right behind him."

FORTY-THREE

"Someone's been here," Tessler said as he examined the tracks in the dirt.

"How many?"

"Two I'd guess. If I was used to tracking friggin' animals through the forest, I could probably tell you for sure." He walked a little farther, staring at the patches of exposed dirt in the driveway as he went. He stopped when he came to a large bare spot and stared at it. "Yeah," he said, "two it looks like. See those tracks? One set looks bigger than the other, doesn't it?"

Pete studied the tracks. They did appear to have been made by different men. The tracks also seemed headed toward his Range Rover, a fact that unnerved him.

Tessler seemed to read his mind and dropped down and rolled over on his back and worked his way under the vehicle. He spent five minutes examining the undercarriage and squirmed out again.

"Don't see anything," he said as he dusted himself off. "But that's only using the eyeball test. If I were reinstated, I'd have access to the department's under-vehicle inspection device and could tell you better."

"They plant bombs under hoods, too, don't they?"

"They plant them everywhere these days. The friggin' terrorists have websites that provide roadmaps for every crazy in the world. They're how-to-do-it courses in violence."

Pete thought about it for a few moments. "Should we check?"

"Do you plan to take the vehicle with you?"

"I haven't decided."

"I think you should leave it as part of the bait. See what we catch."

Pete glanced at his house. "How about inside?"

"We can take a peek."

Pete unlocked the door and let Tessler go through the same gymnastics he had the previous day. Everything was the same as they'd left it, including the balls by both doors. Nothing was out of order upstairs, either. Tessler repositioned the ball by the front door.

They raked the dirt in the driveway and used the blower like they had the day before, then walked out to the highway where Tessler's car was parked and headed back to Frankfort. "Are you up for a quick early lunch?" Pete asked.

Tessler grinned. "At our favorite spot?"

"Of course."

"You know, I saw Kelene last night after about a gazillion years, and when we finished fooling around, she counted my ribs and swore I'd lost weight. Maybe we can pick up a couple of doughnuts besides our usual sandwiches and chips so I can start packing on pounds again."

Pete got the food, and on the way to the Elberta overlook, Tessler held a doughnut in one hand while controlling the steering wheel with the other. No interlopers were in the lot so Tessler parked directly in the middle. He looked at peace with the world as he gazed out at Lake Michigan and worked on the rest of his lunch.

He crumpled his sandwich wrapper and asked, "Do I seem more relaxed than I did yesterday?"

"Yeah, you do," Pete said.

"It's the Far Eastern spiritual stuff Kelene is teaching me. Helps me control my anxiety and appreciate the beauty of the universe a lot more."

Pete nodded. "Does that mean you've decided to let the chips fall where they may as far as your suspension is concerned?"

Tessler reached for the last frosted doughnut. "Oh hell no. I want my job back."

When Pete didn't say anything, Tessler added, "I can't help wondering what's taking Frank and Connie so long, though. I thought I'd hear something by now."

"It won't be twenty-four hours until later today."

"I know, but it's so friggin' clear. They relied on a horsecrap statement everyone now knows is false, plus they've got pictures of another member of our department skulking around Venus acting like a drug dealer on a corner in the hood."

"I'll check with Connie if we don't hear by the morning."

Tessler nodded.

"On another subject, did I mention that Vinnie Zahn, the mob chief, is Angie's husband's uncle?"

"I heard that somewhere. From you, from Paulie, someone."

"Remember the Les Brimley murder?"

"How could I forget? Poor bastard was staked to the ground on his own golf course and bludgeoned to death."

"Brimley's widow hired me to advise her on financial matters relating to his estate, and during the process of getting up to speed, I discovered that the mob had been financing Brimley's project. I gave his widow some advice the bad guys apparently didn't like, and next thing I knew, my stepdaughter was being harassed at her boarding school. I was forced to meet with Zahn and broker a truce."

Tessler looked at him and shook his head. "That I *didn't* know."

"I'm thinking of trying to meet with him again and see if I can get him to lean on his nephew to back off his vendetta against Angie and me. He lives on a vineyard on the Leelanau Peninsula these days if my information is right."

Tessler appeared to think about it. "That's risky, isn't it? Those guys are all psychopaths and the dude at the top is the biggest one of all. You might wind up buried in an Indiana cornfield."

"But what if—"

"Plus you don't know the extent to which Zahn can actually *control* his nephew. It's not like the old days when godfathers ruled their fiefdoms with an iron hand."

"It worked last time because I had leverage. I'm thinking of trying the same thing this time."

"I know, but still . . ."

"What the hell choice do I have, Joe? The psycho is probably right here in our town, or will be shortly. I'm scared shitless to go in my house without an armed escort and I'm not able to drive my own car. I'm even nervous when I walk down the street."

"I realize it's not a good situation."

"Here's my idea of leverage. Zahn seems to be under siege right now, particularly by the feds who are trying to pin income tax evasion charges on him. The last thing he probably wants is to have a murder investigation to deal with. Or to have light shined on Venus and what he's trying do there and the club's sleazy activities. Drugs, prostitution, child prostitution . . ."

"Assuming he *is* trying to muscle in on Venus."

"Right, but it sure looks that way."

"So what's your plan?"

"The first part is easy. I'd appreciate it if you'd call your pal Rozinski again and find out if Zahn still controls mob operations on the west side of Chicago and in this area. If he doesn't have a strong grip anymore, it probably makes no sense to try to persuade him to put the clamps on his nephew. If he does, I'm going to try to set up a meeting with him. I suspect he'll remember me. Before that, you and I need to visit Simon Frei again. Are you finished with the tapes?"

"Almost."

"Finish up and call your tech guy and get him to come out again and reproduce any additional frames you think we might need."

FORTY-FOUR

DeMarco gazed around his room at the Longfellow Motel on the outskirts of Manistee. *Cheap friggin' place,* he thought. He kicked at the coffee table and heard it crack when it jumped six inches. He stalked around the room and nervously ejected the Glock's magazine and jammed it back in and sighted down the barrel.

They'd just spent three hours in that hick town Frankfort, visiting Thorsen's place again with the same results as the night before. His vehicle was still in front of his house, stone cold again, and the place was lit up, but as far as they could tell, no one was inside. They'd driven around the lake, too, and scrutinized every vehicle in sight. Nothing. No sign of little wifey, no sign of her white Corolla, no sign of Thorsen.

To top it off, Lebo had tried to get him to stop at Venus again. For a "little recreation" as he said. He'd put the kibosh on that goddamn fast. Friggin' idiot, can't keep his mind on business for more than ten seconds.

DeMarco took the burner phone from his jeans pocket and tried Thorsen's number again. The usual voicemail garbage came on and he found the sound of lover boy's voice annoying. He muttered to himself and checked the time. Freddy had instructed him to call at 10:00 p.m., and as usual, had treated him like a worthless lackey. It was always go here, be there, call at such-and-such a time. What a jerk!

He kicked the table again and dialed Lebo's room on the house phone. "Come down here, Leebs. We need to talk about some things before I have to call my master, Freddy the Clown."

A few minutes later, there was a knock on his door, and after checking the peephole, DeMarco let Lebo in. He'd changed into a collarless ribbed gray shirt that looked like it was the top part of a pajama set plucked right out of a dirty clothes hamper. DeMarco looked away disgustedly.

"We need to figure out a way to make Thorsen move," he said. "Any ideas?"

Lebo shrugged.

Demarco glared at him. "Why is it that every time I ask for ideas you just shrug your shoulders? Are you telling me you don't give a crap?"

"I'm not saying that, Carm, I just haven't focused on it."

"Well *focus*, okay? Should we torch his house? That would probably bring him back, wouldn't it?"

Lebo appeared to consider that. "That might draw a lot of attention, though."

"More attention than a car bomb? That sure as hell got a lot of people's attention and everything worked out, didn't it?"

"Yeah, but Vinnie and Freddy Pole think—"

DeMarco had been fiddling with his Glock again and interrupted Lebo. "Vinnie and Freddy, Vinnie and Freddy," he said mockingly. "Sounds like a friggin' vaudeville team. You seem more interested in keeping those jokers happy than in completing our mission."

"It's not that, but sometimes they have a point."

"*Screw* their point!"

Lebo was sitting on the edge of the bed and recoiled a bit at DeMarco's latest onslaught. He collected his thoughts and said, "I was reading this *Field & Stream* magazine when you called. There was this article about guys who hunt deer and the way they build blinds to hang in until a deer comes by and then, *bam!* Maybe we could do something like that. There are woods across the road from Thorsen's house."

"Yeah and freeze our butts off while we're waiting."

Neither spoke for a while until DeMarco said, "Maybe we could take over one of the houses next to Thorsen's place and watch from there. That would be like a hunting blind, but you know, a lot more civilized. Sooner or later, Thorsen's going to show at his house."

Lebo nodded eagerly. "I bet that would work. We'd have to find a place to hide our vehicle of course. But we wouldn't have to have it like instantly in case Thorsen leaves because of the sensor." He didn't say anything, but hoped the house they took over had a working television set.

DeMarco checked his watch again and saw that it was time to call Pole. "I'm going to report in with Freddy the Clown so keep your trap shut while I'm talking."

"I thought you were supposed to call from outside for security reasons."

"Do you really think someone is going to bug a cheap motel room in the middle of nowhere?" He punched in the number and got Pole on the line.

"How did it go with Frei?" Pole asked.

"He's with the program a hundred percent. No rough stuff necessary, only some reinforcing of his knowledge of procedure. How to handle deposits, stuff like that."

"So you think we can rely on him?"

"An insurance policy I can't give you. But if you want my opinion, the guy finally seems to have his head straight."

"Are you guys back in Chicago?"

"We're still up north. Leebs' Caddy picked up a nail and it took us half a day to find a yokel up here who could fix it. We're probably going back tomorrow."

A pause, then, "Your delay doesn't have anything to do with that other stuff, does it?"

"Personal stuff you mean?"

"Well?"

"We'll check in with you when we're back in town, Freddy." DeMarco ended the call and looked at Lebo. "Do you believe that guy? Just can't get off the personal business even with everything else that's going on."

Lebo shook his head.

"I can't wait," DeMarco muttered. He picked up his Glock and examined it and sighted down the barrel again.

FORTY-FIVE

"I'm going to my office to meet with Tessler," Pete said to Angie, not saying anything about the fact she was still there after their conversation the previous day. "Call me on my cell if you think there's a problem."

She nodded.

He was about to leave when he thought about the Ruger, and went upstairs and retrieved it from his duffel. He examined the gun and loaded it and slipped it into his jacket pocket. He wondered if Angie would notice after his comment about the gun in her purse.

His cell phone burred when he was halfway to his office.

"Pete," Tessler said in an excited voice, "Frank just called. He wants me to come in and meet with him at 11:00 a.m."

"Great, are you in my office?"

"Yeah, I just finished the tapes."

"I'm three minutes away. Don't leave."

When he walked in, Tessler looked more ebullient than he had in days. "I got this positive feeling," he said.

Pete shook his head a couple of times. "God, that would be a payoff for all our work, huh?"

"You must have made a helluva presentation."

"Hopefully our arguments resonated. Did you reach Rozinski yet?"

"I did. He swore me to secrecy about the locals partnering with the FBI in their war against the mob—something I and half the rest of the world already knew—and that they monitor all kinds of communications that take place within the organization. The mob guys try to conceal things, but the task force still picks up bits and snatches that they put together to try to create the big picture. According to Paulie, there's no doubt that Zahn is still the main guy and is able to keep his troops toeing the line."

Pete nodded. One down.

"I've been giving some more thought to it, Pete, and I don't want to give the impression I'm a nervous Nellie or anything, but I've still got reservations about what you're proposing to do."

"Let's see what we get from Frei and then decide."

He pressed the point. "I know what you told me about the other time you cut a deal with Zahn. But that didn't involve a blood relative. Rozinski tells me Zahn's old man came from Sicily and blood runs real thick over there. This isn't like him losing a few bucks on a juice loan. Here you'd be trying to get him to put the screws to one of his kin so he'll call off his vendetta against a cheating wife. That's a whole different animal."

"I agree. It's a longshot."

Tessler checked the time again and said, "I better get going. I don't want to be late for my meeting with Frank. Wish me luck."

Pete nodded. "If I decide to take a run at Frei, are you willing to go with me?"

Tessler looked like he'd been put on the spot and wasn't sure how to respond. "I'll call you after I meet with Frank," he said.

When he was gone, Pete began to sort through the file he'd accumulated. Frei already knew about Cindi Carr's statement because they'd used it to pressure him into letting them review the security tapes. That was still the most damning piece of evidence against him. He didn't have evidence of the other things like run-of-the-mill prostitution or drug deals. Or of his suspicion that the mob intended to use the club to launder money from other sources.

Pete sorted through the stack of glossies and separated out the ones of Cindi in Frei's office and those showing the goons roughing him up. The photographs of Cindi stoked his anger again. He got two large manila envelopes and inserted the glossies of Cindi Carr in one and everything else in the other.

For the first time he could remember, he watched every car that passed with a wary eye and scrutinized every pedestrian he encountered on the two-block walk to Harry's office. When he walked in, Harry said, "How's Angie doing? I left the house before she came downstairs. I guess she decided not to leave."

"She's still there but not what you'd call real communicative."

Harry tightened his lips and shook his head in a sympathetic gesture.

"Joe's meeting with Sheriff Richter as we speak. Hopefully that'll work out the way it should. I need to get back to the office because we'd talked about doing something this afternoon, but I have a question for you as a journalist. If I came to you with a story about so-and-so running an establishment where a lot of bad things went on, what kind of corroboration would you require before you went with the story?"

"You're talking about Venus, aren't you?"

Pete nodded.

"Depends."

"Assume I had photographic evidence and statements from a relevant party to back up my story. Would you require a second source in those circumstances?"

"Every situation stands on its own. If the photos and statements were persuasive enough, I might not feel I needed a second source. It's awfully hard to answer in the abstract."

"You sound like a lawyer hedging his bets."

Harry shrugged. "Sorry."

Pete rolled his eyes. "Well, I have to get back to my office."

"You going to be around for dinner tonight?"

"As far as I know."

"Let's do a repeat of last night and have food brought in."

Pete picked up a sandwich on the way back to his office and ate it with his cell phone on his desk and his landline within reach. Tessler called shortly before 1:00 p.m. "I'm in my car because I didn't want anyone to overhear this conversation. Frank lifted my suspension and I have my badge and gun back."

Pete tucked the phone between his shoulder and chin and clapped. Pete couldn't see his grin, but heard it in his voice when he said, "Thanks."

"I'm twenty minutes away from you," Tessler said, "and I thought I'd stop by. Have you eaten yet?"

"Just finished."

"If I can impose, would you mind picking up the usual for me?"

Ebba was surprised to see Pete walk into her establishment for the second time in an hour and chided him for doubling up on lunch. He disengaged from her verbal assault just as he saw Tessler's car go past.

In his office, Tessler unwrapped his sandwich and began chomping away.

"When Kelene feels your ribs tonight, she's going to feel something else."

Tessler grinned and slapped his upper left side. "Yeah, I'm fully dressed again."

"You've had your private piece," Pete reminded him.

"I know, but different pieces have different feels, you know? It wasn't the same."

Pete nodded as if he understood.

"In your meeting," he said, "did Frank say anything about Nichols?"

"No, and that bothered me. I know the internal investigation is continuing because Frank said so, but he didn't say a word about Oilcan. I didn't want to raise it, either, because I didn't want to do anything that might upset the apple cart so to speak. Asking a lot of questions might sound like I was worried."

They talked about his reinstatement a little longer. Then Pete said, "Not to change the subject, and I don't want to rush you, but did you find anything else on the tapes you'd like to reproduce?"

"A couple of things."

"Let's get Ian over here ASAP, then."

"What's the rush?" Tessler asked as he popped more chips into his mouth. "I'll make sure he does it before I take the tapes back."

"I'm planning to visit Mr. Frei this afternoon and the excuse I'd like to use is that I'm returning his tapes."

"Oh, okay," Tessler said after he'd swallowed. "I'll call him."

"Tell him it's a bit of an emergency. Make something up."

Tessler called, and when he'd finished talking and put his cell phone down, he said, "We're lucky and caught him when he has a hole in his schedule. He's coming right over."

Pete nodded. His mind was already on how he was going to play it when he met Frei.

Tessler finished off his chips and tossed the empty bag into a nearby wastepaper can. He wiped his mouth with a napkin and said, "I'll go with you if you want."

Pete looked at him and nodded.

"I feel like I owe you for getting my job back."

"You don't owe me anything. You already paid my fee, remember?"

"Oh, yeah, I keep forgetting that," Tessler said, grinning. "That dollar bill I borrowed and then gave back really blew a hole in my finances."

Ian arrived while Pete and Tessler were discussing strategy for dealing with Frei. Tessler showed him what he wanted, and a half-hour later, the techie plopped another stack of glossies on the table and left with a second check in hand.

"As I understand it," Tessler said, "what you're after is Frei's admission that the mob led by your friend, Mr. Zahn, has muscled in on Venus, right?"

"That and any other nasty stuff we can wring out of him."

When Tessler called, Frei balked at seeing them again and said to just leave the tapes with the doorman. Tessler said that wouldn't work because they had something else they needed to talk to him about. After a lot of questions and some toing and froing, Frei finally caved.

Pete and Joe Tessler pulled into the Venus parking lot shortly before 4:00 p.m. The doorman must have been told to watch for them, because when he saw them coming, he called someone on his cell phone and opened the door to let them in. The familiar music and psychedelic lights greeted them. The pole dancer was already performing, too, which seemed to elevate Tessler's spirits even more. Frei was standing at the bar talking to a man, and when he saw them, he motioned for them to follow him.

They set the canvas bags on an empty desk in the outer suite and went into Frei's office. He sat down in his desk chair and said, "Okay, out with it. I have someone coming in fifteen minutes." He steepled his hands and waited. The marks on his face and neck had healed a bit.

Tessler took the lead again and said, "Your face and neck look better." He tried to hold his grin to a smirk.

Frei scowled. "You're wasting my time and yours."

"It wasn't what we were looking for, Simon, but we couldn't help notice some interesting things when we reviewed the tapes." He slid the thicker envelope across to him.

Frei didn't move. "What's this?" he asked.

"Have a look."

Frei removed the glossy stills from the envelope and shuffled through them. He tried to remain stoic, but appeared shaken by the photographs.

Tessler leaned forward and pointed to one of the glossies. "Do you believe the hands on that dude? I'd sure hate to have them around *my* neck."

Frei recovered from his initial surprise. "What are you showing me these for?"

"That's you on the floor with those giant hands wrapped around your neck, isn't it Simon?"

He scoffed. "That's not me."

Tessler glanced at Pete with a sly grin. "The hands must have affected something in his psyche, Pete. He doesn't recognize himself anymore. His clothes, his hair."

Pete shook his head sadly.

When Frei didn't say anything, Tessler said, "The mob is trying to muscle in on your club, aren't they?"

"I really don't know what you're talking about."

"Touchy, isn't he?" Tessler said, glancing Pete's way again.

Frei glared at them. "This is the second time you guys came in here and made a bunch of nutty statements. I let you look at my security tapes when I didn't have to. This time you've worn out your welcome."

Someone knocked on Frei's door and a man stuck his head in. "Sorry to interrupt, Simon, but the decorators are here."

"Hear that?" Frei said to Pete and Tessler. "I've got to go."

Pete spoke for the first time. "We know the Chicago mob has moved in on your operation, Simon. Those were Zahn's people working you over. It must be a very rocky relationship."

Frei licked his lips and glared at them.

"Don't worry," Pete said, "all we want is to hear directly from you what we already know."

"You guys are wired, aren't you?" Frei finally asked.

Both Pete and Tessler shook their heads.

"Prove it."

"We're not going to take our clothes off if that's what you're asking. You'll have to trust us."

"Bullshit I'm going to trust you."

"Zahn has taken over your operation, hasn't he?"

"Leave or I'm going to call security."

"We're not leaving until you answer our question."

"You've got no authority to ask me anything. A suspended cop and some friggin' civilian."

"I'm not suspended anymore, Simon." Tessler flashed his badge.

Frei glanced at it and his jaw muscle worked.

"Okay," Tessler said, "if you don't want to talk to us, fine. Maybe you'll change your mind when we come back with a warrant for your arrest. The press is going to have a field day, too, when these photographs mysteriously show up in their mailboxes. And these as well." Tessler slid the second envelope with the stills of Cindi Carr across the desk.

Frei continued to glare at them and didn't touch the second envelope.

"You're going to have a ton of visitors," Tessler said. "Our department, the state guys, the FBI, the DEA. You're going to be the most popular person in the county. There won't be enough lawyers in the state of Michigan to defend you."

Frei still didn't say anything.

"Oh, and your problems will be compounded because Vinnie Zahn is going to really be unhappy, too. I'm sure the newspaper stories will include a lot of stuff about him and how the mob is involved with your place and uses it to launder money. You'll have to go to Zanzibar to get away from all the people who want to tack your nuts to the wall."

Frei's jaw muscle twitched some more and he didn't seem to know what to do with his hands.

"Once again," Pete said, "has Zahn moved in on your club?"

"All I'm going to say is that I have one or more business partners."

Pete and Tessler looked at each other and grinned. "I think he means yes," Pete said.

On their way out, Tessler said in a low voice, "Satisfied?"

"Let's talk about it outside, but that's probably the most we're going to get."

FORTY-SIX

On the way back to Frankfort, Joe Tessler chortled about the way they'd tag-teamed Simon Frei. "Jesus, that was like Muhammad Ali in the ring with that lightweight, Ron Lyle. I'd pop him with a jab and you'd step in with a left hook, then I'd jab him again."

Pete chuckled. "While he didn't actually *say* that Zahn is his new business partner, it was stamped all over his face. He's just more afraid of him than he is of the law."

"So what's the next step?"

"Try to get in touch with my old pal, Vinnie. Oh, and show the photographs to Angie. When we were in Frei's office, I kicked myself for not thinking of it sooner. It might have saved us a trip to Thompsonville."

Tessler shook his head. "I hope you know what you're doing," he said again. "With Zahn I mean."

"That makes two of us. But at least I've got some history dealing with him."

Tessler dropped Pete off at his office and said, "Tomorrow is my first day back on the job, and I'm going to be busy as hell getting up to speed

273

again. I hope that idiot Cap hasn't screwed anything up since he's had his paws on my files."

"He hasn't had time, has he?"

"With him anything is possible. We need to stay in close contact until this thing is done on your end, though. Call my burner number if you need anything. And I'll check in with you periodically."

Pete went into his office and put his feet up and thought about Zahn. It was 6:00 p.m. Too late to start making calls today, he convinced himself. First thing in the morning, though.

Before he locked up, he made copies of the glossies that showed the hoodlums working over Simon Frei and stuffed them in a manila envelope. Then he called Adam Rose.

"How's the Big Easy?" he asked.

"Cooling down a bit."

"Is the black bunting from Fats' funeral celebration down yet?"

"You should have seen this place. It was Mardi Gras times ten."

They caught up a while longer and then Pete asked, "Are your lines secure?"

"As secure as you're going to get in this cyber world where not even your bathroom habits are private. We have everything swept once a day."

Pete told him about the bind he was in without mentioning names on either side. "I've got something in the mill," he said, "but it probably has a ten percent chance of working out. Two of us are up against it if it doesn't. I might need the services of a freelancer."

They continued to talk in obscure language.

"It would have to look like an accident," Pete said, "because I don't know how the chief would react if it looked like his nephew had been hit and I don't want to substitute a new problem for an existing one."

"I understand."

"What's the consideration likely to be?"

"Low six figures."

Pete promised to stay in touch.

❖ ❖ ❖

Rona and Angie were talking when he got to the house. The conversation seemed forced like it had the previous night.

He tossed the envelope on an end table and went to the refrigerator and came back with a bottle of spring water. He dropped into a wing chair and leaned back and let the tension drain from his body.

"Rough day?" Rona asked.

"Joe Tessler got reinstated."

"Wonderful!"

"He's not out of the woods because the investigation is ongoing, but it's a giant step in the right direction."

"I'll bet he's ecstatic."

Pete nodded.

Harry came home, and while he was chatting with Rona in the kitchen and calling in dinner orders, Pete retrieved the manila envelope from the table and sat down next to Angie. "I'd like to show you something," he said.

He removed the glossies from the envelope and handed them to her. "Look through these and tell me if you recognize anyone."

Her eyes fixed on the top photograph and she breathed in like someone had jabbed her ribs with a sharp object. She clutched the glossies and examined the next one and the one after that. She looked up at him with wide eyes. "Where did you get these?"

"They're stills from security camera tapes at Venus."

She shuffled through the glossies again. "That's the creep," she said in a voice that sounded far away.

"The guy in the chair."

She nodded.

"How about the second guy, the one working over the man on the floor?"

Angie glanced at the glossies a second time. "That's one of the goons who works for the creep. I don't know his name. He's the one I thought might have been behind us on the bike trail."

Harry and Rona had come out of the kitchen and were watching them. Harry sensed something and came around to the back of the couch where he could see the photographs. He tapped Pete on the shoulder and said, "That's what you were talking about this morning, isn't it?"

"It's related."

"Are the dates on the bottom of these photographs the dates they were taken?" Angie asked.

Pete nodded.

"My God, he's been operating right in our backyard while I've been here!"

No one said anything.

Angie stared at the glossies some more. "Look at him," she said. "He's enjoying it while his goon pal tortures that man. The creep *likes* hurting people."

The room was quiet.

"I need to get out of here," Angie said. "I should have left this morning. Or two days ago."

"If you want to go, Angie, go. We'll help you carry your stuff to your car. But I'm staying. I have a plan and I intend to see if it'll work."

"What plan? The only plan I've seen is what you've been doing to help your detective buddy."

Pete's fuse was burning. "Your husband works for Vinnie Zahn, Angie, something you know better than the rest of us. I believe I have some leverage and plan to get on the telephone tomorrow morning and try to set up a meeting with Zahn and see if I can get him to call off his dogs. I need a little time to see if I'm successful."

"You expect to deal with Zahn? You're out of your mind. He's the biggest murderer of all." She shook her head.

"I dealt with him once before."

Angie continued to look at him as though he'd lost it.

Harry jumped in. "Five years ago, Pete met with Zahn on his yacht. He brokered a deal to get Zahn's people off the backs of him and his daughter. He took all kinds of precautions ahead of time."

Angie just stared at them.

"If Pete feels he needs a few days to try to work things out," Harry continued, "I think you owe it to him. He's not the one who created this mess."

Angie's disdainful look was now directed at him.

"Let her make her own decision, Harry," Pete said. "I don't have time to fight with her anymore." He left the room.

Harry followed him and tugged at his sleeve and said, "Don't be too hard on her, Pete. She's under a lot of stress."

"Stress? You and Rona are under stress, too, for sticking your necks out and letting us stay here. I'm under stress because she lied to me and got me mixed up in the mess she's made of her life and now her psycho husband is after me in addition to her."

"I know but . . ."

"This whole affair has given me new insights into the woman."

Harry looked at him for a while. "As if this mess couldn't get any worse, I checked Angie's Corolla yesterday and it's almost out of gas. We have to assume her husband knows the kind of car she's driving and might be looking for it. We also have to assume he's here now based on what you guys said. I don't think it would be real smart for her to drive around town or wait at a station to gas up. He might spot her. That would be a total disaster."

"Maybe you should point that out to her."

"You think?"

"I've had enough of her for the time being."

FORTY-SEVEN

"Alison," Pete said, "this is Pete Thorsen. I talked to you about Conti Vineyards a few years back."

A pause, then, "Yes, of course."

"I know that vineyard has changed hands since we talked. Who owns it now?"

"Actually, it's changed hands *twice*. The man who bought it at the time you were interested went bankrupt and then some other outfit bought it in a court-supervised sale."

"That's Vinnie Zahn, right?"

Another pause. "That doesn't sound right," she said. "Just a minute." Pete could hear her talking to someone.

She came back on the line and said, "Old Country LLC owns it now. It's been renamed Isabella Vineyards."

"You don't have their telephone number, do you?"

She looked up the number and gave it to him.

"Thanks, you've been a big help."

"I don't know if Isabella Vineyards is for sale again, but I can check if you want. I *do* know that another prime property on the peninsula will be coming on the market in two weeks. Coldwell Banker Schmidt Realtors has the listing as a matter of fact."

"Hold off contacting Isabella. I might be interested in looking at the other one, though. I'll get back to you."

Pete gazed out at the bay a few minutes and then took a deep breath and dialed the Isabella Vineyards number. He got a recorded greeting that gave the days and hours the vineyard was open, and left a message asking that Vinnie Zahn call him. He left his office number and his cell phone number and added a reminder that he and Mr. Zahn had met a few years ago aboard his yacht, *Isabella II.*

He stared out the window some more and the doubts that had kept him awake most of the previous night crept back. Angie was still in her bedroom when he left for the office and he wondered if she'd be there when he returned. She was badly rattled by the situation and obviously not able to consider options in a rational manner. Instead, she lashed out, usually at him. He fumed over her self-centered attitude and lack of gratitude.

Restless, he began editing his draft manuscript for *The Fjord Herald* even though his heart wasn't in it and the words on the screen were a blur. He kept plugging along, wondering if his telephone was going to ring. Finally it did and his heart jumped until he saw from the Caller ID that it was Julie.

"Dad," she said without preliminaries, "I just received the strangest call. A female voice said, 'Leave me alone. I'm not going to warn you again.' Then she was gone. That was it."

It took a few seconds for Pete's mind to focus on what she was talking about. "Who was it?" he finally asked.

"That's what made it so weird. She didn't identify herself. She just said the words and then hung up."

"Do you think it was Leslie?"

"That's what Effie and I think. If Effie had heard the voice, she would have known right away, but I've never met Leslie and the call lasted like five seconds."

"What's your plan now?"

She sighed. "Continue doing what we've been doing, I guess. Follow up on every lead we get, go back and talk to people we've talked to before and find out if they've had any contact with Leslie or know of anyone who has. That sort of thing."

"If it was Leslie who called, why do you think she said what she said? It almost sounds like a threat."

"Effie and I talked about it. There's this story about a newspaper heiress who was kidnapped by a cult fifty or sixty years ago. They brainwashed her into embracing their beliefs and turning against her family and friends. Maybe something like that's going on here."

More than anything, Pete wanted to persuade his stepdaughter to come home, but he knew that was the last thing she should do in view of the mess he was in.

"Dad, I keep asking and asking. When are you coming to Philadelphia?"

"Sorry, Sweetie. I've been helping Detective Tessler with a job problem he has, but as soon as that's resolved, I'm on the plane."

When he was off the phone with Julie, he glanced at the wall clock and saw that it had been two hours since his call to Isabella Vineyards. Like five years ago, he was determined to make a pest of himself until he got through to Zahn. He steeled himself and tried the number again. He left the same message when he got the voicemail greeting.

Joey Lebo zipped his parka tighter around his neck, adjusted his stocking cap and stared out the window at Thorsen's house. They'd been watching since the previous day and hadn't seen any sign of movement. No one had come for the dark blue Range Rover, either.

He glanced back at DeMarco who was stretched out on the couch under a pile of blankets, napping. *When he wakes up*, he thought, *maybe I'll ask him how much longer we're going to watch Thorsen's house.* Lebo was relatively healthy, at least as far as he knew, but the way the chill penetrated his body conjured up visions of pneumonia. He also had to find a time to make a call. Maybe when DeMarco took over the surveillance duties, he'd take a walk along the beach to stretch his legs.

Pete had just placed his fourth call to Isabella Vineyards and left the same message as the other times. He drummed his pen on his desktop and wondered whether he'd eventually get a call back. When he didn't, it was almost a relief because it meant the time of reckoning had been put off for a while longer.

He wondered where Carmen DeMarco was. And his henchman with the enormous hands. He shuddered and thought about the Ruger in his jacket pocket and wondered if he'd have the guts to pull the trigger if it came to that.

Pete thought about Adam Rose some more. Rose was a former Navy SEAL, and he knew that if he were in his position, DeMarco would become the hunted instead of the hunter. But he also knew that wasn't him. One way or the other, though, he intended to get through this.

He glanced at his wall clock and saw that it was nearly 5:00 p.m. He thought about calling it a day and walking over to Harry's house, but at the same time, he didn't know whether Harry or Rona would be there yet and wasn't thrilled with the idea of being alone with Angie given the tension between them the last few days. He also hadn't been out to his house in a while and wondered about things.

He called *The Northern Sentinel,* and when Harry answered, asked, "Do you mind if I borrow your car for an hour? I'd like to drive past my house."

"Do you suspect a problem?"

"Not necessarily. I just feel more comfortable checking once in a while."

After telling Harry what he wanted for dinner, Pete walked the few blocks to Harry's house and cut through the side yard to the garage in back, noting the closed drapes and blinds again, like the house had been winterized. He used his spare key to fire up the Explorer and backed out to the alley. He wondered if Angie was able to hear the engine from inside.

Pete took the scenic route home along the water as he frequently did. Most of the leaves were off the trees, and across the end of the lake, he could see his house and the neighboring houses. All were dark except for two windows at his house, one on the first floor and another on the second, where lamps turned on by the timers peeked through along the edges of the drapes. The timers were a good investment he noted with satisfaction. The north shore was brighter where a sprinkling of lights winked at him in the gathering dusk.

He turned right when he reached the highway and pulled up next to his driveway. He walked in as he and Tessler had done while being careful to stay on the grass. He scanned the dirt, but saw no tire tracks or footprints.

The Range Rover appeared undisturbed, too. He went up the front steps of his house and checked the door. It was locked and he saw no evidence that someone had tried to get in. He went around the house, and when he got to the back door, checked it as well.

Pete walked back to the highway and got in the Explorer and started the engine. He decided to drive around the lake to give himself time to think before he faced Harry and the others.

FORTY-EIGHT

"Where the hell have you been?" DeMarco screamed.

Lebo was jolted by the ugly tone. "I told you I was going for a walk to stretch my legs, Carm," he said defensively. "I've only been gone a half-hour."

"I've only been gone a half-hour," DeMarco snarled mockingly. "The most important half-hour of our friggin' lives and you're not here! Get the Escalade, we've got to move!"

"What—"

"Get the friggin' Escalade! I'll meet you on the road."

Lebo saw the crazed expression on DeMarco's face, and decided not to ask any more questions. He patted his pocket to make sure he had the keys and dashed outside and ran two houses away to where his Escalade was parked under a rickety carport. He jumped in and backed toward the highway. He cranked the steering wheel, intending to swing past Thorsen's driveway to pick up DeMarco, but saw him running down the highway toward him and waving his arms. Seconds later, DeMarco wrenched the passenger-side door open, jumped in, and screamed, "Go! Go!" He pointed north.

Still confused, Lebo stomped on the gas pedal and increased his speed to ten miles an hour over the posted limit.

"Faster, goddamnit!"

Lebo gave the Escalade more foot and they careened around bends in the winding highway and then accelerated on the straightaways. DeMarco leaned forward and scanned the road ahead of them.

"Did Thorsen show up?" Lebo screwed up the courage to ask.

"Yeah, genius, he showed up! He was walking around his house, admiring it, looking at his vehicle. Then he left again, but I couldn't follow him because you had the friggin' car keys and were walking along the lake like some goddamn tourist."

Lebo had taken DeMarco's abuse since they were kids, but he still chafed at his words. "Did you see what he was driving?" he asked.

"A piece of shit gray SUV of some kind. A Ford I think."

"An Explorer?"

"I think so."

A deer crossed the highway in front of them and Lebo jammed on his brakes and swerved sharply left to avoid it. The sudden change in direction sent DeMarco slamming against the door. Lebo glanced his way nervously and muttered, "Sorry."

They sailed past the sign for Crystal Drive that ran along the lake on the north side. "Turn, for crissakes, turn!" DeMarco screamed.

Lebo braked and backed up and got on the drive. They'd gone a mile when tail lights appeared in the distance. Lebo accelerated to catch up, but when they got close, he saw it was an Infinity sedan and swerved around it. DeMarco leaned forward in his seat again, watching for more tail lights and checking out every vehicle that was parked on the road or next to a house. They caught up to two more vehicles by time they reached the small town of Beulah, but neither was what they were looking for.

The business district was largely deserted except for clusters of vehicles around a couple of the restaurants, so they drove through the back streets and kept their eyes peeled for a gray Ford Explorer. They saw several gray vehicles, but all were different makes or were sedans or pickups. They took the highway to Frankfort and then cruised down the main drag and around the backstreets of the town like they had the first time they were there, again without success. Finally, they gave up and got a pizza for dinner and headed for the west end of the lake again.

After dropping DeMarco off at the mouth of the driveway that led to their commandeered house, Lebo continued on to the rickety carport and then walked back. He worried about DeMarco's mood. He'd been subdued on their way back from town, and Lebo had learned from experience that was usually the lull before the cyclone. *It wasn't his fault, goddamnit!* He was going to push back if DeMarco gave him any more crap about it.

DeMarco had not only closed the venetian blinds on all of the windows, but also had hung a blanket over the one that faced Thorsen's house. Checkers from the game-board table were scattered around the floor and had been replaced by the open pizza box and a flickering fat candle. DeMarco had on his gloves and sawed at a slice of pizza with a knife and fork and popped it into his mouth. His Glock rested on the corner of the table close to him.

Lebo took in the scene, then got utensils of his own and sat down across from DeMarco. He donned his gloves and helped himself to a slab of pizza.

They ate in silence. After five minutes, DeMarco said without looking up, "You know, you screwed up our best chance to get that asshole Thorsen to lead us to where wifey is hiding."

Lebo resisted rolling his eyes. There it was again. Classic DeMarco, blaming someone else when things didn't go exactly the way he thought they should.

"We went through this, Carm," he said, trying to sound confident. "You knew where I was going."

DeMarco finally looked up with vacant eyes. "You didn't say you were going to be gone when Thorsen showed up."

"C'mon, man, you know it wasn't my fault."

"It's almost like you were trying to sabotage me, Leebs. If you'd been here, we could have tailed Thorsen and finished the job and been on our way back to Chicago."

Lebo just stared at his pizza.

"You better eat while the food's still warm, Leebs," DeMarco said after a while in the same icy tone.

Pete drove down the alley and parked the Explorer in front of Harry's closed garage door. Before he went inside, he called Tessler on his cell phone. Tessler sounded more upbeat than he had in days and told Pete about his day, including about how Ernie Capwell had left the files on his desk with a note saying he'd be happy to answer any questions Joe might have. Then Tessler described in detail his plans for a celebratory night with Kelene Brill.

Tessler finally got around to asking Pete about whether he'd been able to contact Vinnie Zahn.

"I called four times and left messages, but no luck so far. I'm going to start calling again in the morning. That's what worked the last time I dealt with him—make a pest of myself until he caved and agreed to see me." He didn't say anything about his call to Adam Rose or his backup plan if his calls to Zahn didn't bear fruit.

"If you *do* get through to him and set something up, do you think you should have backup?"

"I'd love to have backup, but I don't know how I'd pull it off." He told Tessler about the letters he'd left with Harry when he met with Zahn on his yacht and said he planned to do something similar this time.

"That makes me feel better," Tessler said. "Not good, but better."

"On another subject, do you remember our conversation about the portable under-vehicle bomb detection device your department has?"

"Of course."

"Could you sign it out so you'll have it handy? I'd like to start using my own vehicle again, but not without precautions."

"Do you want to set a time now?"

"Let's wait until tomorrow. But if Zahn gets back to me, there may be a short window and I don't want to miss it."

Pete signed off with Tessler and let himself in the back door. Harry was in the living room having cocktails with Rona and Angie. Pete got a glass of Pinot Noir and joined them.

"Everything okay?" Harry asked.

"I think so."

"What's your plan for tomorrow?"

"Continue to call and see if Zahn will get back to me." He didn't say anything about his plan to up the ante.

Angie sat on the couch with one leg tucked under her and her wine glass in hand. She didn't say anything, but he suspected she was sitting there thinking she knew his plan wouldn't work.

After checking with Harry, Pete went to his study and plugged in his laptop and began preparing instructions for him just in case. He also drafted a detailed letter to the U.S. Attorney for the Western District of Michigan and the head of the FBI's Detroit Regional Field Office.

In the middle of his work, he sensed someone standing in the doorway. He glanced up and saw Angie. "Sorry to disturb you," she said, "but I wanted to tell you how much I appreciate everything you've done for me. I know I haven't always sounded grateful."

"Let's see if it works."

"Anyway, thanks."

He nodded.

"If you don't have something set up by the end of the day tomorrow, I'm probably going to take a chance and leave."

He nodded again.

FORTY-NINE

When Pete got to his office the next morning, he fussed around for a few minutes, then screwed up his courage and called the vineyard again and left another message for Vinnie Zahn. This time he included a cryptic reference to Venus that he hoped Zahn or one of his henchmen would pick up on. He planned to call again at 11:00 a.m. if he didn't receive a call back.

To kill time, he reviewed the letters and related instructions for Harry he'd drafted the previous night and made some changes. He proofed them again and addressed envelopes and assembled everything together with sets of the glossies.

He propped his feet up on his desk and eyed the material and wondered if it would come together. His landline rang and he anxiously checked the Caller ID. It was Julie again.

"Hi, Dad, long time no talk."

He chuckled. "It's never too soon for you to call, Sweetie."

"I was thinking, since you've got things going on for the next couple of days, maybe I'll take a flight to Traverse City tomorrow afternoon and hang out at the lake until you're free. Assuming you're willing to spring for a ticket, that is. I need to get away from here for a while and think."

A chill washed over him. "Could you delay your trip for a few days?" he asked.

Silence, then, "Is something I don't know about going on, Dad?"

"Like what?"

"Like do you have someone there you don't want me to meet or something? First you put off coming to Philly and now you put me off again when I want to come home. Maybe I should call Wayne and see if *he's* available."

"I'm not putting you off, Sweetie, it's just that things are complicated right now."

"Oh, that explains a *lot*."

"Tell you what, I'll call in a day or two and we'll arrange something. Either I'll come out there or you can come home."

"Alright, Dad, I'll have my phone on." The connection went silent.

Pete's lips tightened and his jaw muscle pulsed. It was 11:00 a.m. He breathed in and dialed the vineyard's number again. He got the recorded greeting and left the same message he'd left earlier that morning.

He got a bottle of spring water from his refrigerator and propped his feet up again and stared at the bay some more. *Angie,* he thought bitterly. If she were here, he'd throttle her and leave her in the goddamn street. She could apologize twenty-four hours straight and it wouldn't be enough.

He took deep breaths to calm himself. His landline rang again. His head jerked around to see the Caller ID. An unknown caller.

He took another deep breath and answered.

"If you want to talk to Mr. Zahn," a raspy voice said without an introduction of any kind, "come to his vineyard at 4:00 p.m. this afternoon. You know where it is?"

"Yes."

The call ended without further conversation.

Pete was stunned. *It worked!* Then reality began to set in and the same icy feeling he'd had when he walked aboard Zahn's yacht years earlier returned. Second thoughts ricocheted around in his head.

Enough of this crap, he thought as he collected himself. He grabbed the phone and called Joe Tessler to ask him to pick him up at his office at 1:00 p.m. Then he took the envelopes on his desk and headed down the street to Harry's office.

Harry eyed him when he walked in and frowned. "You feeling okay?"

"Yeah, fine."

"You look a little peaked."

"I'm meeting Zahn at 4:00 p.m."

Harry's eyes bulged. "I'll be damned."

"Remember the drill we went through last time? I'm taking out the same kind of insurance policy this time." He handed him the plain envelope. "Glance at this to see if everything is clear."

Harry studied the instructions and the letters to the U.S. Attorney and the FBI and looked up. "Are you planning to show all of this to Zahn?"

"I'm going to play it by ear."

"It's almost a declaration of war, you know."

Pete shrugged. "That isn't my intention. I just want Zahn to put the clamps on his crazy nephew."

"I know, but . . ."

"I've got to get going, Harry. Joe is picking me up in a few minutes. I'm going to start driving my Range Rover again."

"You know what I'd do?" Harry said. "I'd keep the letter in reserve in case I couldn't persuade Zahn without it. Maybe you can hint at some of the things in the letter. That might be enough."

"I'll think about it."

Tessler was already there when he got back to his office and waited in the car while Pete packed his briefcase. Pete inserted a copy of his letter to the government officials and a set of the glossies in a plain manila envelope and tucked it in the briefcase. He fingered the Ruger in his jacket pocket a moment. He was certain he'd never get in to see Zahn with a gun on him, but at the same time, he knew he had to take it. He stowed it in his briefcase along with the extra magazine and spare ammunition.

On the way to Pete's house, Tessler kept up a steady stream of banter about his first day back on the job. Pete tried to listen politely even though his mind was on his 4:00 p.m. appointment.

Tessler parked along the road, snapped the trunk lock, and pulled out the device.

"It looks like a minesweeper," Pete said.

"That's kind of what it is."

"Do you know how to work it?"

Tessler shrugged. "I had twenty hours of training just like everybody else in the department."

"That's not what I asked."

Tessler grinned at him. "The thing is supposed to be able to sniff out explosives. I'm counting on it having a better nose than I do."

As they walked up the driveway, Tessler periodically pointed to indentations he thought might be a man's tracks. "The problem," he said, "is that this dirt's so fine that a little wind can blur things."

When they got to Pete's Range Rover, Tessler walked around the perimeter with his bomb detection device. Getting no reading, he dropped to his knees and rolled over on his back and visually inspected the undercarriage. "I'm going to charge you for my dry-cleaning bill," he called to Pete. "Rolling around in this dirt is ruining my wardrobe."

Tessler pulled the bomb detection device under the vehicle with him and ran it around the undercarriage. Five minutes later, he slid out from under the vehicle again and passed the device over the hood area. "Seems to me it's clear, but why don't you pop the hood so I can inspect the engine area."

Pete stepped back and hit the "unlock" button on his key, then opened the door gingerly and pushed the hood button. The hood snapped open a couple of inches. Tessler opened it all the way and visually inspected the engine and then let his device hover over everything for a couple of minutes. He shook his head. "I'd say it's clean. Want to try it?"

Pete would have preferred not to be the guinea pig, but he slipped into the driver's seat and inserted the key and turned it. The engine came to life. Pete got out of the vehicle again, but let the engine run.

"So far, so good," he said. "Should we check the house?"

"Might as well."

Pete turned his key in the lock and opened the door a crack. Tessler opened it a bit wider and stuck his head in and said over his shoulder, "Doesn't look like you've had any visitors." Pete followed Tessler inside and they checked all of the rooms. Pete went upstairs and checked there, too. Then they left the house and Tessler replaced the ball.

Pete thanked him and checked the time. It was after 2:00 p.m. He didn't want to keep Public Enemy Number One waiting.

FIFTY

Neither DeMarco nor Lebo spoke as they motored east and kept an eye on the moving dot on the screen. They deliberately stayed a mile back so there was no risk that Thorsen would spot them.

Occasionally Lebo glanced DeMarco's way, casually, as though he were interested in something along the right side of the highway. DeMarco's jaw worked and his mouth was tightly clamped and he stared straight ahead except when he checked the monitor. When DeMarco got pissed at him in the past, he'd usually be over it in a couple of hours and would slap him on the shoulder and remind him of their school days together and tell some story or other and they'd laugh. But not this time. Lebo felt a need to vindicate himself by saying he *knew* Thorsen would come back to his house, but kept his mouth shut.

After another five miles, DeMarco muttered, "I wonder where the asshole's going? We're headed towards Traverse City."

Lebo remained quiet and drove.

They came to an intersection and followed the moving dot north. At the bottom of Grand Traverse Bay, the dot zig-zagged around and continued along the west side of the water. They continued to follow.

DeMarco fished a map from the glove compartment and studied it. "That vineyard where me and Vinnie had our sit-down isn't far from here."

Lebo nodded.

The moving dot passed the small town of Suttons Bay and continued north for ten miles before turning west. DeMarco looked around as they followed. The countryside began to look increasingly familiar.

"He can't be headed for the grape farm," DeMarco muttered.

Lebo, still wary of igniting another cyclone, remained quiet.

"You think that's where he's going, Leebs?"

Lebo breathed in and hoped his voice sounded natural. "I don't know what else is out this way," he said.

"*Nothing* else is out this way!"

The moving dot turned north again, and after a short distance, stopped. Lebo caught up and when they got to the entrance to Isabella Vineyards, he pulled to the side of the road. They saw the Range Rover at the top of the hill near the fountain.

"See, he's at the goddamned vineyard!" DeMarco said. He banged his fist on the dashboard. "What the hell's going on?"

Pete used the gargoyle door knocker to announce his arrival. The door opened almost immediately and a squarish man with bristly hair who was dressed in a black turtleneck and black slacks said in a raspy voice, "Mr. Thorsen?"

Pete nodded and the man let him in. He stared at the envelope in Pete's hand. "What's that?" he asked.

"Something for my meeting with Mr. Zahn."

The man took the envelope and peered inside and shook it and felt both sides. He tossed the envelope on a nearby table and said, "Leave your keys and any other metal stuff on the table and pass through the arch."

He complied, and after not setting off alarms, one of the two men standing by the wall patted him down and had him unbutton his shirt so he could check under it and examined his belt. Apparently satisfied, he nodded to the man in charge who disappeared down a hallway.

Pete got dressed again and gathered his possessions and waited. After a few minutes, the man came back and motioned for Pete to follow him. When they rounded a corner in the hallway, Pete saw a silver-haired man in a wheelchair waiting for them. A blanket was folded neatly over his legs and upper torso. Pete was surprised by how much Vinnie Zahn had aged in five years.

"Pete," he said, rolling forward a few feet, "it's been a long time. You're looking good."

"You too, Vinnie. Thanks for making time for me."

Zahn nodded graciously. "If it's okay with you, we'll sit outside on my patio. It's a little chilly these days, but the sun is shining and the heating coils are on."

He maneuvered his wheelchair toward a handicap-accessible door and rolled down the ramp to a small cobblestone patio that was surrounded by immaculately maintained flower boxes. Except for the fountain, it mirrored the piazza at the front of the house. Zahn stopped his wheelchair next to a rectangular wrought iron umbrella table and motioned for Pete to sit across from him. Opera music began drifting from the outdoor sound system.

Zahn worked his remote to increase the volume, and said, "Franco Corelli, one of my favorites. Are you an opera aficionado, Pete?"

"I enjoy it, but I wouldn't say I'm an aficionado. I prefer the symphony."

"Ah, yes, we both come from Chicago, home to one of the world's finest orchestras. The present music director, Riccardo Muti, is from Napoli you know. Beautiful city. Have you been there?"

"I have." Pete knew from his first meeting with Zahn that his style was to engage in small talk before getting to the subject.

"How's that daughter of yours? She must be what, eighteen years old now?"

Pete felt another chill when he mentioned Julie. Zahn always seemed to know everything about him, like he'd researched all aspects of his life before their meeting.

"Eighteen," Pete said, confirming his recollection.

"I'm sure she's a very lovely young lady. Pete, do you mind if I turn up the sound a bit more? Some people find music distracting when they're talking, but you strike me as a healthy man who still has good hearing and can handle both."

Pete motioned for him to go ahead, and a second later, the voice of the great Italian tenor filled the air like they were in an opera house. Pete suppressed a smile. He suspected that Zahn was as interested in interfering with listening devices that might be surreptitiously eavesdropping on their conversation as he was with the music.

Zahn closed his eyes for a few moments, then opened them and gazed around at the rows of dormant grape vines that covered the gentle hills. "My grandfather had a vineyard in Sicily, you know. Whenever I sit out here, I think about him and how much he'd enjoy me following in his footsteps. You'll have to come back during the growing season and I'll arrange a special tour and a private tasting."

"That would be nice," Pete said.

"Well," Zahn said, "I'm sure you have other things to do today so maybe we should get to the purpose of your visit."

"You have a nephew named Carmen, I believe. He was married to a former law partner of mine, Angie DeMarco, who died in a car fire in August. If I'm not mistaken, you were at her funeral sitting in the front row with the rest of the family."

Zahn shook his head sorrowfully. "A tragic situation," he said. "Lovely woman in the prime of her life. Thank God they didn't have children." He crossed himself.

"Carmen seems to believe Angie isn't dead."

Zahn frowned. "Really."

Pete nodded. "He called my old law firm a week ago and asked for her. As I understand it, the managing partner told him she'd died in an accident, but he said a couple of people told him she was still alive. A few days later, he called my house and asked to speak to her. I tried to explain, but he said he *knew* she was there."

Zahn studied him. "Are you sure it was Carmen that called?"

"I'm sure."

More frowning. "If it *was* Carmen, why would he call you?"

"Let me back up a moment and say that he didn't just call once, he called nine times according to my Caller ID. As for why he called me, I really have no idea. All I can think of is that he remembered my name because Angie and I practiced law together for years."

"So how did you leave it with him?"

"He argued with me and kept insisting that he knew Angie was at my house. Finally I hung up on him."

"Since you're here, I assume you're going to tell me that didn't end it."

"It hasn't. He sounded threatening when I talked to him on the phone that day, and since then, my phone has rung constantly. I haven't answered unless I knew for sure who it was, but I'm certain the person doing all the calling was your nephew. Then I discovered that someone has been prowling around my property. Putting two and two together, I don't have to be a genius to figure out who it might be."

Zahn shook his head several times. "I know that death of a beloved spouse can do strange things to a person's mind. Looking at the positive side, though, those things usually are temporary. Symptoms of grieving I think they call it. Angela just died, what, two months ago? If Carmen had something to do with the things you described, I'm sure it'll pass."

"Maybe, but I'm not so sure. He sounded threatening when I spoke to him on the telephone. I want it stopped, Vinnie, and I thought you were the one who could do it."

Zahn scoffed and waved his hand. "Why me, Pete? Carmen is a grown man with his own life and business. I haven't even seen him since the funeral. I'm here on this lovely vineyard, confined to a wheelchair, doing my best to make wine that lives up to my grandfather's high standards."

"Let's stop playing games with each other. We're alike in some ways, and one is that we both do our homework. I know about Carmen's dry-cleaning business, but I also happen to know he spends most of his time working for you, helping you negotiate business deals with Venus and other places. And enforcing things afterward."

Zahn shook his head. "You've lost me, Pete."

"Really? Take a look at this." He slid the envelope across the table. Zahn's eyes flicked down at it.

"Go ahead," Pete said, "take a look. I think you'll see someone you know. Several people in fact."

Zahn pulled the glossies from the envelope and flipped through them, then frowned again. "These are so bad you can't even tell who the people are or what they're doing."

"I'll help interpret, then. The man on the floor getting pounded is Simon Frei, who owns Venus, the sex club near Thompsonville. The one doing the pounding works for you, but I don't know his name, at least not yet. The one in the chair is Carmen DeMarco, your nephew."

"What's your purpose in showing me these, Pete?"

"To show that I know a lot about you. And about Carmen. Maybe you've moved up here, but I know that you've got the same choke-hold on your organization as ever. I know that the feds are trying to pin tax evasion charges on you. I also know why you moved in on Venus. As I said, I know that Carmen is one of your key men and does a lot of—how shall I put it?—your less delicate work. Should I go on?"

Zahn's face was impassive, but his eyes were lumps of ice. "This is like a rerun of our *Isabella II* visit. I extend hospitality and you make threats."

"I'm sorry if you regard them as threats. All I said on the *Isabella II* that if A or B happened, then X and Y were going to happen, too, and it wouldn't be good for you or your business. I'm saying the same thing now. And I'm asking you to control your nephew and keep him away from me. If you don't, I intend to fight back and I don't think you'll like the result."

"The sun's going down and I'm getting chilly. Maybe we should end this conversation, Pete."

Pete got up from his chair and stared down at Zahn and said, "I'm not a crusader, Vinnie, but I've got everything set up so that if anything happens to me, or anyone close to me, the U.S. Attorney and the FBI will be all over you within hours. I don't think you want to compound your problems because of your nephew's twisted delusions."

The man in black had come outside and was standing next to him. "I'll show you out, Mr. Thorsen," he said.

FIFTY-ONE

Pete turned out of the vineyard and headed back to M-22 feeling he'd played his hand as well as he could have. And relieved that it was over. He called Harry and told him he was on his way back. Harry pumped him for details about his meeting, but Pete put him off until he got to his house. Then he placed a call to Joe Tessler and left a message that said essentially the same thing.

Driving home, Pete replayed the meeting with Zahn minute-by-minute, trying to remember his verbal and nonverbal reactions to each of the cards he'd played. His only conclusion was that he had absolutely no idea what Zahn would do, if anything, or when he might do it. He reflected on Tessler's comment about Sicilian blood being thick and the thought depressed him.

He thought about his backup plan, too, and whether he should cut to the chase and call Adam Rose now. If he made the call, it had to be one-hundred-percent untraceable and he couldn't tell anyone. Not Harry, not Angie, not Joe Tessler, not anyone. Adam no doubt had the drill down to a science, including communications with the freelancer and the flow of money. He knew he'd probably never be the same if he went forward with it, but at least he'd be alive. And Angie would be alive, and the risk to Julie would be gone. Or would it? He thought about the Sicilian blood thing again.

As Pete mulled it over, he wondered how he'd know if Zahn bought his not-so-veiled threats. He wasn't so naïve as to think he'd receive a telephone call from him. Pete also wondered where DeMarco was and what he was doing. And whether anyone, including his mob chieftain uncle, could control him. He thought of measures he could take to hedge his bets until things shook out and became more clear.

Dusk was settling over the area as Pete waited for the stoplight at the Interlochen intersection to turn. Just after it flashed green, his cell phone burred. He pulled into the parking lot of one of the business establishments on the righthand side, thinking it might be Tessler calling him back on one of his burner phones.

Before he could say anything, the voice that was permanently etched in his memory said, "Good evening, Pete, out for an afternoon drive in the wine country?"

The words jolted him. How the hell did DeMarco get his cell phone number? His landline and office numbers were listed in the local telephone directory, but not his cell phone number. And how did he know he'd been at Isabella Vineyards? Unless Zahn had called him as soon as he left and told him.

"Goddamnit!" he thought. He ended the call without saying anything and pulled out of the parking lot onto the highway and headed west again. His speed had climbed to seventy miles an hour when he punched in Harry's number on speed-dial.

Harry started to say something when Pete interrupted him and said, "Someone I'm practically certain was Carmen DeMarco just called me on my cell and it's clear he knows all of my movements this afternoon, including my visit with Vinnie Zahn. Maybe he's been tailing me, I don't know. If Angie's still there, you've got to get her out right now. Have her pack her stuff and then head for Millie's place. I'll join you as soon as I can."

"But—"

"Just *do* it, Harry! I can't talk anymore!"

"What I wanted to say," Harry said, "is that Rona's on her way home. She stopped at a store to pick up some things."

"Take her with you!"

Pete gripped the steering wheel with both hands and swerved around one car after another, hoping there weren't any cops working that stretch of the highway. Five miles later, his cell phone burred again and Pete glanced down and saw that it was Harry. He was forced to reduce his speed to answer.

"I can't reach Rona, Pete! Her cell must be off!"

"You need to leave right now! I don't know where DeMarco is, but I don't want him to walk into your house and find Angie there. I'll be there in a half-hour and I'll take Rona to the restaurant or someplace."

"They're closing early tonight."

Pete's thoughts were muddled and he was finding it difficult to concentrate. Then he said, "Doesn't she have a sister?"

"Yeah, near Arcadia."

"I'll take her there, then. I need to take a roundabout route to throw DeMarco off anyway."

"You'll get her, then?"

"Yes, I'll *get* her! Now let me get off the friggin' phone so I can drive!"

Honor was just ahead and the truck in front of him had reduced his speed. Pete cut into the opposite lane and went around it and slowed as he passed through the small town. Then his cell phone burred again as he was increasing his speed. He glanced down and saw that it was an unknown caller. It might be Tessler, but he wasn't about to slow down to answer.

Platte Road, which he often took going home, was coming up. He thought about what to do and continued on toward Beulah, concluding he'd be better off on a highway with more traffic. His cell phone burred again a couple of miles farther on. Another unknown caller. When he slowed for Beulah, he picked up his phone, and called up his voicemail. The same voice said, "Smart move going through Honor, Pete. We wouldn't want you to get a speeding ticket."

Pete slammed his cell phone down on the seat. *The sonofabitch must be right behind me.* He hit Tessler's speed-dial number, but got his voicemail yet again. He considered calling the general telephone number for the sheriff's office, but decided that would be futile. He knew from experience that by the time he answered a barrage of questions from the dispatcher, he'd just lose valuable time with no guarantee of success.

He turned right on the highway to Frankfort and gave the Range Rover more foot. He regularly checked his rearview mirror. There were several vehicles behind him, all with their lights on, but he didn't know if one of them was DeMarco. He came to the hill that coasted into town and turned right at the blinking light. He'd planned to go up the alley behind Harry's house, but at the last second changed his mind and took Forest Street. He needed to create some diversion and maybe Rona could help.

Pete parked in front of Harry's house and got out and glanced at the street behind him. He didn't see any vehicles other than those parked on the side of the street when he drove past. He slipped the Ruger into his jacket pocket and ran to the door on the side of the house and tried it. Locked. He banged on the door while periodically checking the street. Getting no response, he used his key to gain entry and stepped inside. Everything was quiet.

"Rona," he called, "it's Pete." He walked down the hall off the living room and called again. No response. *Shit*, he muttered.

Her cell phone number was on his speed-dial and tried it. No answer. He left a message saying he was at her house and asked her to hurry home because something had happened. Then he tried Tessler's phone again, but still got no response. He shook his head and walked back to the living room. Staying out of the line of sight from the street, Pete pulled the cord to close the bay window drapes. Then he peered out the side and scanned the street, but saw nothing unusual. He checked the time; he'd been in the house ten minutes.

Pete continued to wait and periodically checked the street. Then he heard the overhead garage door rumble. He stepped into the kitchen and took his Ruger out and held it close to his thigh and stood in a darker area where he could see the back hall. The overhead door rumbled again and then Rona stepped in and closed the door behind her. Apparently sensing something, she called, "Harry?"

Pete stepped out where he was fully visible and said, "It's me, Rona. We've got to leave right away. I'll explain in the car."

Rona stared at him and didn't move. "What's wrong?"

"There's no time, Rona. I'm taking you to your sister's."

"Tell me what's happening!"

"Someone has been following me. Harry has taken Angie to Millie's Fishing Camp on the Au Sable River."

Rona had her hands to her face and still hadn't moved. "I knew something like this would happen!"

"Rona, please. We have to go."

She stared at him blankly. "What should I take?"

"There's no time to pack."

She exhaled in exasperation. "How about my coat? Is that okay?" Her words had bite to them.

"Yes," he said softly, guiding her toward the door. "We're going out the front because I'm parked on the street. Take my arm when we go down the steps and walk to the car. Try to look natural in case someone's watching."

"Oh my God!"

"Ready?" Pete asked, his hand on the door handle.

She took a deep breath as Pete opened the door and they stepped into the chilly October night.

Pete had his hand in his jacket pocket as they walked toward his Range Rover.

❖ ❖ ❖

"There they are," DeMarco hissed.

They watched the couple come down the front steps and head for the Range Rover parked at the curb.

"Wait a minute," DeMarco whispered in an agitated voice as the woman slid into the passenger seat and closed the door, "that's not her."

"That's definitely Thorsen, though. I recognize him from when him and that other guy checked out his car."

"That's Thorsen," DeMarco said, "but not wifey dear. She's shorter than that broad and that ain't her hair unless she's wearing a friggin' wig."

Lebo frowned at him.

When the Range Rover was gone, DeMarco said, "I'm going to have a look inside that house." He left the shadow of the large tree, and after surveying the area, crossed the street and went to the side door of the house. He held his Glock close to his leg and knocked on the door with his free hand. No answer. He knocked again. Still no answer. He tried the door, but it was locked.

DeMarco said to Lebo in a low voice, "Get your tools."

Lebo slipped across the street again and went to the alley behind the two dark houses where his Escalade was parked next to a dumpster. He found his small case and closed the hatchback as quietly as he could. As he headed back, he became nervous again as he wondered about DeMarco's intentions.

It took him five minutes to get the door open. They went inside and DeMarco instructed him to stand watch while he looked around. He came back and said, "Just as I suspected! Her crappy rental car is in the garage, but everyone's gone!"

"Maybe—"

"I should torch this friggin' place!" DeMarco said, not bothering to whisper anymore. "Show them who they're screwing around with." He kicked a chair and sent it skidding across the room.

"Jesus, Carm, if we torch the house we might burn down half the town."

DeMarco whirled and stepped toward him and shoved the Glock in his face. "There you go with that timid horseshit again! We've known each other for a long time, Leebs, but maybe I need to get a consigliere who's not afraid of everything that moves!"

Lebo shrugged awkwardly. "Just raising considerations."

"Screw your considerations!" DeMarco said. "The only consideration I have is making sure she gets what's coming to her!"

Lebo didn't respond.

"Let's get going," DeMarco said. "Thorsen probably thinks he's lost us because we didn't follow right on his ass when he left this house. Boy, is he in for a friggin' surprise."

FIFTY-TWO

P ete arrived at Millie's Fishing Camp almost four hours after he left Harry's house. He'd dropped Rona off at her sister's place, then started east on an array of two-lane roads and zigzagged across northern Michigan. Every so often, he'd double back and find an old farmstead or dirt road to park in with his lights off and watch for signs of a vehicle following him. There weren't any and he also didn't receive any calls on his cell.

He knew the layout of the camp well as a result of having stayed there many times over the years. Instead of checking in at the log cabin that doubled as Millie's office and living quarters, he drove around until he spotted Harry's gray Ford Explorer parked at the far end of the camp. The camp was dark except for one cabin near the entrance.

He pulled in next to the Explorer and walked to the cabin and rapped on the door. A muffled voice that sounded like Harry's said, "Who is it?"

Pete identified himself and Harry opened the door. He walked in just in time to see Angie put her Beretta back in her purse. He plunked down in a worn fake-leather chair and looked at them.

307

"Thanks for getting Rona to her sister's place."

"You talked to her?"

"An hour, hour-and-half ago. She's scared senseless to go back to our house in view of what happened."

Pete didn't say anything, but gazed at Angie and asked, "How are you doing?"

"Okay."

"Have you had anything to eat?" Pete asked Harry.

"Millie made us sandwiches when we checked in and threw in two blueberry muffins. I'm afraid everything's gone, though. I have some trail mix in my SUV if you're hungry."

"In a while maybe. We need to figure out our next step." He summarized his meeting with Vinnie Zahn.

"Do you think your plan will work?"

He shrugged. "I got his attention. He didn't look too happy with me when I left."

"Do you think he'll try to control Carmen?"

Pete shrugged again. "Maybe the calls I kept getting on the way back to Harry's house were because Carmen had been following me since I picked up my Range Rover, or maybe they were because Zahn got in touch and alerted him to what I was up to. If it's the latter, we're back to square one."

"If you had to guess, which would you say it was?"

"I'm out of the guessing business."

"I know you," Harry said, "you've got a backup plan."

Pete's eyes flicked around the rustic cabin before settling on Angie. "Maybe Angie should leave like she was thinking about doing. Get out of the area, but stay in touch. We can get her a burner phone. Then wait until we see how things shake out."

"That might solve *one* of our problems. But how about you? And how about Rona and me? That madman probably knows about our part in this thing, too. That scares the crap out of me."

Pete didn't look at him.

"Do you think we're safe in this cabin?"

"I thought we would be, but now I'm not sure. I'm not sure what's going on."

After a moment of silence, Angie said, "What Pete's admitting, Harry, is that he knows he screwed up. His plan to meet with Zahn never had a chance of working in the first place. Zahn's a bigger scumbag than his nephew, if that's possible, and relying on his word is like relying on the weather forecast a year from now."

Harry stared at her over his half-glasses.

Pete steeled himself and was tempted to unload on her. He had to decide whether to make a second call to Adam Rose, though. And figure out what to do until the backup plan was executed.

Harry looked at each of them for a while, then said, "I'll get the trail mix."

Pete went to the bathroom and stood with his hands on the vanity and stared at his haggard face in the mirror and struggled to get his emotions under control. He splashed water on his face and toweled himself off. When this was over, he'd already decided he didn't care if he ever saw Angie DeMarco again. Her latest attack had reinforced his resolve.

The sound of the cabin door slamming open jolted him and he heard a rush of footsteps and then angry shouts. Angie screamed, then screamed again, and something crashed against a wall. A thump echoed through the cabin, like a sack of grain hitting the floor, and then more angry shouts. Pete's heart thumped and he thought about the Ruger in the pocket of his jacket that was draped over a chair in the living room. He stood there, frozen, and finally turned the bathroom door handle, hands shaking, and peered out.

A man he assumed was Carmen DeMarco hovered over Angie who'd fallen backward in her chair and was holding the side of her head. A second man with a nylon stocking over his face yelled and DeMarco jerked his head around and spotted Pete. His eyes were crazed and his face was contorted with rage. He swung his Glock around to point it at Pete's midsection.

"Looky here," he said in a mocking tone. "Mr. Thorsen himself. We finally get to meet after all our chats on the telephone. Get out here, lover boy, and hands behind your head!"

Pete complied. Then DeMarco stepped closer to him, and after glancing Angie's way, slammed his Glock against the side of his head. Pete saw the blow coming and dropped a hand to protect himself, but was too late. The blow sent him reeling. His vision blurred and nausea swept over him and he fell against the table in the dining nook. He grabbed it to steady himself and could barely remain upright.

"You stinking animal!" Angie screamed. DeMarco smirked and walked over to her. She cowered against the wall and raised her hands to protect herself, but DeMarco's boot caught her shoulder and then grazed the side of her head. She screamed in pain.

DeMarco stood over her, leering, and said, "What's the matter, honey, you afraid of what I'm going to do to lover boy?"

Angie looked up at him defiantly. Blood trickled from her mouth.

He kicked at her again.

Pete's vision cleared a bit, and in a burst of rage, he lunged at DeMarco.

DeMarco stepped back and swung his Glock again and this time caught Pete squarely on the temple. The room went black and a new wave of nausea flooded over him. He staggered around for a few moments, trying to stay on his feet, then crumbled to the cabin floor. He laid there, head throbbing, unable to focus his eyes, vaguely aware of voices around him, but too dazed to make out what they were saying. Then he felt his arms being wrenched behind him and his wrists being bound. He pulled at the restraints, trying to loosen them, but the will to fight drained from him. He fell back and closed his eyes.

When his vision had cleared a bit, he looked around the room and saw Harry lying on the floor ten feet away with his hands trussed behind him. His glasses were missing. Across the room, Angie had been tied up as well and cowered against the wall.

DeMarco sat in a wooden chair, Glock in hand, staring at her with a twisted smile. The man with the nylon stocking over his face stood next to the door with his pistol drawn.

DeMarco must have noticed Pete stir because he glanced his way. "You awake, lover boy? I've been waiting because I didn't want you to miss the big show. You able to concentrate on things now?"

Pete didn't say anything.

DeMarco leaped to his feet and kicked at Pete. His boot caught him in the ribs and Pete writhed in pain.

"I asked you a question, asshole!"

Pete still didn't say anything.

DeMarco kicked him again. "Answer, goddamnit!"

Pain seared Pete's side and rippled through his body. He had enough control of his senses to know it might be best not to say anything again, but he blurted out, "You're going to get what's coming to you, DeMarco!"

"Ha!" DeMarco said gleefully to the nylon stocking man, "Lover boy *can* talk. That must mean he can see and hear, too."

DeMarco walked over to Angie again and gazed down on her, leering. "Okay, wifey dear, now that everyone's awake and alert, want to hear what the rest of the night has in store? I know how you like to go to the theater and pretend you're some hoity-toity bigshot, so I apologize that I didn't have a chance to prepare a fancy program for this production. You're just going to have to settle for my oral presentation.

"For openers — I think you call it act one — I'm going to sample that little treasure of yours while lover boy here watches and dreams about what he's missing." He leered at her again.

Angie spit at him.

"Oh, fiery!" DeMarco said, obviously enjoying himself. "Do you think she's learned that from spreading for every asshole in the county, lover boy?" He leered some more and his hand snaked out and grabbed her thigh.

She kicked at him, screaming, "Leave me alone, you lunatic!"

DeMarco laughed and grabbed at her again, then backed off. "And after wifey and I have had our fun, we're going to go into act two, as they say." He picked up his Glock from the table and walked over and pointed it at Harry. "I'll probably start with the fat man first." He pointed the gun at Harry's head and said, "Pop!"

He turned to Pete and kicked him in the ribs again. He glanced Angie's way and said, "Now I'm really getting charged up. I think that just plugging lover boy between the eyes would be too simple, don't you? Maybe taking a shot or two at his nuts might be the way to go." He aimed the Glock at Pete's crotch and said, "Pop! Pop!" Then he leaned over and ground the muzzle against Pete's head.

He glanced at Angie again. "Think you'll enjoy act two, honey? I sure hope so because I've devoted a lot of thought to it. But act three is what's going to make this production special. This is your turn to take the stage, and at first, I thought maybe I'd just end things with a bang. You know," he said, aiming the Glock at her head, "Pop! Pop! Pop!"

DeMarco lowered the gun and feigned a thoughtful look. "But then I thought, that really isn't very dramatic, you know? Finally it came to me. What if a fire started in this quaint little cabin and everything in it went up in flames? The fat man and lover boy here and my beloved wife, all together. You missed that the first time. This would kind of be a do-over, you know? But back to act one."

After leering at Angie some more, DeMarco placed his Glock on the table again, then turned and lunged at her and pinned her legs under one of his arms while wrenching off her shoes with his free hand. She kicked and swore at him and tried to roll away, but he held firm. He smiled cruelly as he reached up and grabbed the waistband of her slacks and yanked. The button popped loose and the zipper split and he began ripping off her slacks. He tossed them to the side and stared at her and said with faux disappointment, "I was hoping to see something from Victoria's Secret, wifey dear. That's where whores get their undies, isn't it?"

"You lousy slimeball!" Angie screamed.

DeMarco slowly unbuckled his belt and continued to leer. "That isn't a very respectful name for your husband, is it?"

When his trousers were around his knees, he sprang at her and began to force himself on her.

"Pete! Help me!" She screamed and kicked and tried to fight him off.

Pete had been struggling with the restraints that bound his wrists. There was no give. The man in the nylon stocking seemed fixated on DeMarco and Angie and wasn't watching him. He worked himself around so his head faced DeMarco and rocked back to stand up. He rushed at DeMarco, screaming as he went. Demarco saw him coming and put out a hand and gave him a violent shove. Pete sprawled backwards on the floor again. DeMarco jumped up and kicked at Pete, rage showing on his face. Each blow sent excruciating pain tearing through his body.

DeMarco stood back, panting, then grabbed his Glock and pointed it at Pete's head. "I should finish you off right now, sunshine, but that would be too easy. I want you to see what I'm going to do to your whore."

Pete tried to draw in air, but with each breath, another burst of pain shot through his body again. *Some ribs must be broken,* he thought. His head throbbed mercilessly, and he wanted to raise his hands and hold it, but was unable to move.

DeMarco turned back to Angie. He tossed his Glock on the table with a clatter and lunged at her and pinned her to the floor. She started screaming and kicking again and rolled over on her side to protect herself. DeMarco wrenched her back flat.

Pete struggled to free himself. Across the room, he saw the nylon stocking man, his face just a blob, staring at DeMarco who was on top of Angie. He seemed tentative, like he didn't know what to do. For a while he didn't move, then slowly stripped off his gloves and slipped them in his jacket pocket and began creeping toward DeMarco. Those enormous hands, the ones Pete had seen in the security camera frames, flexed. When he got close, he lunged forward and grabbed DeMarco's neck and squeezed.

DeMarco released Angie and tried to pry the nylon stocking man's hands loose. In the hush that settled over the cabin, all Pete heard was gasping and wheezing and attempts to suck in air as DeMarco struggled to break his grip and tried to get at his Glock. Pete lay there, not daring to move, mesmerized by what was playing out fifteen feet away.

After a couple of minutes, DeMarco's hands fell away and he stopped kicking and his body relaxed. The nylon stocking man loosened his grip and DeMarco slumped to the side before he toppled over.

The nylon stocking man rose to his feet and stepped back and stared at DeMarco's body for a long time as if it had just dawned on him what he'd done. Then he seemed to get a grip on himself and hurried to the cabin door and opened it. He returned to DeMarco's body, and after stuffing the Glock in a jacket pocket, grabbed him under the arms and dragged him across the cabin floor. The door closed behind him with a bang.

Pete looked around, afraid to take deep breaths because of the shooting pain. Angie huddled against the wall as though seeking solace from the logs, partially naked, her body jerking with sobs. Harry's eyes were open, but didn't appear to be focusing. Dried blood from a gash on his forehead streaked his face.

As Pete lay there, he wondered if the nylon stocking man was going to come back. Then he heard an engine start and saw lights flash through the cabin windows. The sound grew louder and then faded.

FIFTY-THREE

"Welcome back," Harry said with an ebullient grin. "How was Philadelphia?"

"Terrific. Julie didn't even make me race up and down the Rocky steps."

Harry's grin got wider. "I bet you were happy about that. Your ribs probably thanked you, too."

"And, get this. She's coming home for good in a week. Until she leaves for college, that is."

"Does that mean her search for Leslie Lehr is over?"

"For the time being, at least. She's referring to it as her 'cold case' these days. It's interesting what a ten-word message from an unknown caller will do to tamp down the enthusiasm of an eighteen-year-old sleuth."

"Do you think it was Leslie?"

Pete shrugged. "I don't know who else it would have been. Julie and her friend, Effie Zepp, have this theory that Leslie has fallen prey to the Patty Hearst syndrome."

"Mmm," Harry murmured. "So she'll be home for Thanksgiving, then."

Pete nodded.

"You know what I think we should do? Get a bunch of us together for turkey, pumpkin pie and the other good stuff, watch a ton of football, just have a great time with family and friends. Besides you and Julie and Rona and me, we could invite Joe Tessler and that gal friend of his. Others, too, if you want. Do you think Angie would have any interest in driving up?"

"I doubt it. I touched base with her yesterday. She doesn't seem like the same person. The experience with Carmen left some pretty deep scars. Steve Johnson, my former law partner, says the same thing."

"Do you think she'll go back to your old law firm?"

Pete shrugged again. "Now that everything is out in the open and people know she's alive and what happened to her, Steve told me the partners got together and voted unanimously to ask her back. Her birthday was two days ago and they sent her forty-seven of her favorite tangerine roses along with the invitation."

"Forty-seven. Wow! Stories like that make you believe this world isn't such a bad place."

Pete didn't say anything.

"You know," Harry continued, "I still wake up at night in a cold sweat thinking about that night at Millie's. You live on the edge a hell of a lot more than I do, but it'll be a long time before I get over that one."

Pete breathed deeply and nodded.

"Why do you think the guy with the stocking mask did what he did?" Harry asked.

"Don't know. All I'm certain of is that but for him, we'd all be dead. I doubt if the guy did it out of concern for us, though."

"Maybe you got through to Zahn."

"Possible, but the timing makes me wonder. Maybe something was going on we don't know about."

"Mmm. And DeMarco and his henchman were able to track you everywhere that day because of the sensor they planted on the undercarriage of your Range Rover."

"Uh huh."

"What's Zahn like?"

"Did you ever see the movie *Lion in Winter* about Henry II? That's kind of what Vinnie reminds me of. He's still on top of the heap and doesn't want to let go, but also wants to live the rest of his life in peace. He talks a lot about his grandfather's vineyard in Sicily and likes to listen to opera tunes sung by Italian tenors."

Harry squinted at him over his half-glasses. "Let's face it, though, what you were asking him to do was a pretty tall order."

"I wasn't asking him to put a hit on his nephew. I was just asking him to control him and suggested some of the bad things that might happen to his organization if he didn't."

"Still, there's the blood thing."

"Not actual blood. Carmen was adopted, remember."

"Maybe it wasn't thick Sicilian blood, but it's blood just the same."

Pete pursed his lips. "Getting back to the stocking mask guy, when Joe Tessler and I called his pal in the Chicago PD who's investigating the bombing and told him what happened, he said it could have been DeMarco's longtime henchman, Joey Lebo."

Harry's eyes widened. "What do you make of that?"

"That's what I was getting at a minute ago when I said something might have been going on inside the mob we don't know about."

"That was part of Angie's story."

Pete forced a laugh. "Ironic, isn't it?"

Harry grew pensive. "I still can't believe she lied to you like that."

"Yeah, well . . ."

Harry snuck a look at him. After a minute he said, "You know who else we could invite for Thanksgiving? Millie Tate. But for her coming along with those breakfast goodies, we might still be laying there on that cabin floor."

"Millie would be good."

Harry was thinking again. "Those people from the local sheriff's department sure as hell weren't much help, were they? They looked at us like we'd been smoking weed or something when we tried to explain everything that had happened."

"Law enforcement deals in facts, Mr. Editor. Or at least they're supposed to. No dead bodies. No sign of weapons. Just three people telling how they were almost done in by mob hoods from Chicago in a rustic cabin on one of the world's great trout streams."

"Mmm. Speaking of trout, do you think it's too late in the season to make our last trip this year?"

"Probably."

"You don't want to change your mind about inviting Angie for Thanksgiving, huh?"

"I was thinking of fixing her up with Jimmy Ray Evans instead."

ABOUT THE AUTHOR

Robert Wangard is a crime-fiction writer who splits his time between Chicago, where he practiced law for many years, and northern Michigan. *Vendetta* is the eighth Pete Thorsen novel. The first seven, *Target, Malice, Deceit, Payback, Stalked, Framed,* and *Victim* have been widely acclaimed by reviewers. *Payback* was also named as a 2014 INDIEFAB Book of the Year Finalist. Besides his novels, Wangard is the author of *Hard Water Blues*, an anthology of crime-fiction short stories. He is a member of Mystery Writers of America, the Short Mystery Fiction Society, and other writers' organizations.

Readers:
• Robert Wangard's books are available in both print and as e-books
in independent bookstores and online at amazon.com and bn.com.

• Did you enjoy *Vendetta* or one of the author's other books?
If so, please post a review on the appropriate book pages
on amazon.com, bn.com and goodreads.com. Thanks.

www.rwangard.com